A stranger
in a strange land . . .

Yesterday Melanie had been thrilled by the running of the bulls. Today she still felt that thrill, yet the mood had turned sinister and ugly. Not only had her sister, Cecily, really been kidnapped, but the price of her freedom was half a million dollars!

Melanie looked up from her coffee cup as Teo began to speak to his uncle. As if struck by the force of an electric bolt, she realized that neither man had been surprised at the news of Cecily's kidnapping. That meant they'd both known . . . and perhaps were even at the root of Cecily's—and her own—terrible dilemma. . . .

ABOUT THE AUTHOR

Lynn Erickson is the pseudonym of the tireless writing team of Carla Peltonen and Molly Swanton. They have written several books for Harlequin Superromance, all of which contain the special blend of romance and intrigue. Now Carla and Molly have added another ingredient—the rich and exciting backdrop of Pamplona, Spain, to *Arena of Fear*, their first novel for Intrigue.

Books by Lynn Erickson

HARLEQUIN SUPERROMANCE

These books may be available at your local bookseller.

Don't miss any of our special offers. Write to us at the following address for information on our newest releases.

Harlequin Reader Service
901 Fuhrmann Blvd., P.O. Box 1397, Buffalo, NY   14240
Canadian address: P.O. Box 2800, Postal Station A,
5170 Yonge St., Willowdale, Ont.   M2N 6J3

ARENA
OF FEAR
LYNN ERICKSON

Harlequin Books

TORONTO • NEW YORK • LONDON
AMSTERDAM • PARIS • SYDNEY • HAMBURG
STOCKHOLM • ATHENS • TOKYO • MILAN

This book is dedicated to the ladies of the
Pitkin County Library, whose endless help
has been much appreciated over the years, and to
Teo Arnáiz, the dark Spaniard who inspired
the hero of *Arena of Fear*.

Harlequin Intrigue edition published May 1986

ISBN 0-373-22042-1

Chapter One

He was there again on Thursday.

Melanie Royce rolled over onto her stomach and felt the hot Spanish sun pounding on her back. She turned her head very slightly, hoping her sunglasses hid the direction of her gaze.

Yes. There was no doubt about it. The man, unobtrusively sunning himself some fifteen yards down the sandy beach of Torremolinos, was watching her.

Or us, Melanie thought. He might be watching her sister, Cecily, too. Yet somehow Melanie didn't think so. She had the curious feeling that his presence there was solely for her benefit but she didn't know why. It seemed as though they were two leading actors on the crowded beach, as though everyone else was merely an extra. She wondered just what role she was supposed to be playing.

Why would some stranger be that interested in her?

"I'm thirsty..." Cecily groaned and rolled over, too, squinting her gold-flecked eyes against the fierce summer sun. "Let's get a Coke."

"Go ahead," Melanie said distractedly.

"You're lazy today." Cecily stood up and stretched luxuriously as she searched the beach in front of the Los Jazmines hotel for a waiter.

She really was lovely, Melanie thought, noticing the many appreciative eyes turned in her sister's direction. Cecily, at nineteen, still possessed that air of unbridled adolescent pride, that smooth-skinned perfection celebrated by a youth-oriented culture. Her long slender limbs were flawlessly tanned, her auburn hair shone richly in the sun, and she had the tilted golden eyes unique to Oscar Royce's two daughters.

Cecily sparkled like a well-cut gem; Melanie, nine years older than her sister, seemed reserved and withdrawn by comparison. At least, that was the impression people often had of her.

"You know, with the kind of money you're spending here," remarked Cecily, as she continued to scan the beach, "you'd think they could have *one* waiter around."

"Never mind." Melanie pushed herself up from the bright towel and adjusted her dark green suit. "I'll go get us both a drink. Watch my camera, though."

Cecily shrugged and immediately resumed her prone position, intent on soaking up every last ray of sun.

The sand was blisteringly hot under Melanie's bare feet as she forged her way between the sunbathers toward the outdoor bar of the swank hotel.

The beach was only moderately crowded that hot afternoon. Everyone else must have been at the turquoise pools that dotted the grounds of the hotels. The tourists were mostly English and Scandinavian, those notorious sun worshipers from their misty northern isles. In the States, Melanie would have expected to hear a hundred radios blaring, but here the noise was subdued, as if the tourists respected one anothers' privacy.

She glanced around at the bodies that gave clear evidence of the lengths of their owners' vacations: fish-belly white to pink to tan. Even the swimsuits were unique to Europeans. The men all wore the tight-fitting stretch bikinis that outlined their private parts. Among the women there were few old-lady cover-ups. Regardless of a woman's age or shape, she wore a colorful, revealing suit. Some even had on bikinis, their stomachs bulging and heavy breasts billowing.

The atmosphere seemed to say, "Anything goes."

And it was hotter and drier on the Spanish coast than the beaches Melanie remembered in Cape Cod and New Jersey, where she had often gone as a child. Torremolinos was a little like California in the summer. The difference was, of course, the scenery. The rolling, green-clad hills of southern Spain swept down nearly to the Mediterranean shore and were specked with modern one-story whitewashed villas and high-rise luxury hotels with pools and palm trees.

Melanie picked up her feet quickly, gasping once or twice from the burning sand, and sought the cooler cement of the pad surrounding Los Jazmines' bar.

Like her sister, she had every male head on the beach swiveling toward her, but she had long since learned to disregard the unwanted attention. That way, they left her alone. Besides, she thought, with her pale skin, she never looked her best in a bathing suit. While Cecily tanned, Melanie merely sprouted more freckles.

It *was* hot. She leaned against the smooth tiled counter and felt the heat of the day close around her. Her dark red hair hung half in and half out of a loosely wound knot, the long strands stuck to her burning back.

"Can I get two Cokes?" she asked.

"*Sí,*" said the bartender with a grin, "for the pretty *americana*."

Melanie turned toward the water again, looking for Cecily. There she was with two beautifully tanned young Europeans standing over her, practically panting like puppy dogs. Melanie could so easily imagine the scenario: one of the men reaching down and snatching her valuable camera while Cecily flirted with the other.

She waited for the Cokes. In Spain, she'd learned, nothing was done with great haste. Automatically, her gaze strayed down the beach to the stranger and she saw that now he was staring directly at her; she hadn't expected to catch him at it. Inexplicably, Melanie felt a shock of adrenaline rush through her body. In the two days that he had been there, not once had she actually caught him looking straight at her.

She turned away quickly, unaccountably confused. Her Cokes were ready and she signed the check, then began heading back toward Cecily. The unforgiving sun was pressing on her shoulders and the sand still scorched her feet. She took great care, even while hurrying, not to spill the drinks, but her mind was on those two Continental types ogling her sister, and she wondered just how to get rid of them.

"Here's yours." She handed Cecily a glass.

"Thanks." Cecily looked pleadingly at Melanie, then rolled her eyes. "I was just telling these nice men that we're expecting friends. Right, Mel . . . ?"

"Oh, yes. We *are* waiting for someone. Do you mind?" She took up the game. One might have thought from their groans and protests that the two men were mortally wounded but they did finally leave, promising in very good English to return the following day.

"That's not like you," Melanie said, settling herself on the towel.

"What isn't?"

"Ditching those guys."

"I'm not interested." Cecily flopped onto her back and shaded her eyes from the sun.

"You've got someone else, I bet."

"Maybe." Cecily's voice was carefully nonchalant.

"Someone from the university?" Melanie probed.

Her sister had been attending the University of Madrid for a year, studying Spanish history and language. Melanie had a sneaking suspicion that Cecily had chosen Madrid rather than London or Edinburgh or the Sorbonne just to spite their parents. In the view of the elder Royces' social circle, Madrid didn't have the same respectability or prestige as the other places.

"Why do you want to know about my private life?" Cecily demanded. "What is this, the third degree?"

"Is he married or something?" Melanie asked cautiously. "I mean, what's the big secret?"

"No, he's not *married* or something," her sister said, pouting a little.

"Sorry, I'm just curious."

Silence from Cecily. This man must be different, Melanie thought. Usually her sister bubbled over with descriptions: neat, gorgeous, a hunk, cool. Those were her favorite words. But this chilly silence was unlike Cecily.

Melanie turned her head to study her sister. Cecily's eyes were closed, the sun gilding the tips of her long lashes. Her expression was sulky, yet her face seemed terribly young and vulnerable. Or was it just that Melanie had become bitter and dried up and spinsterish?

Yet her sister *was* different somehow. Perhaps this was simply the sign of a new maturity, unfamiliar to Melanie. Though there seemed to be a kind of anger in Cecily's sullen responses. Growing pains? Adolescent problems? Shouldn't Cecily be past that sort of thing by now?

"Here we are, lying on a beach. The lap of luxury," Cecily said abruptly, rolling over to face her older sister.

"Nice, isn't it?"

"Well..." Cecily hesitated, as if debating something. "But the whole world is still going on around us. Famines. Disasters. Injustice. Don't you ever feel a little...guilty?"

"I got over it," Melanie said lightly.

"Mel!" Cecily sounded outraged.

"I mean I try not to dwell on it. I can't apologize forever because of my family's good fortune in owning a steel mill. I give to charity. I do the best I can at my work. I keep up on the world's problems. I vote responsibly." She shrugged. "What else can I do?"

"Get involved," Cecily said seriously.

"I'm involved in lots of things."

"You know what I mean."

"Not really. Do you mean I should wear camouflage gear and join some underground group? Or should I stuff envelopes for my favorite senator?"

"I do *not* mean that. I mean...well, find a cause you believe in and *do* something about it."

Melanie shut her eyes for a moment in reflection. "I think what I do is important."

"Photography?"

"Yes. My work lets people see the world. I just finished a layout on Ethiopia, if you'll recall."

"I know, but taking pictures isn't like filling their stomachs or bandaging wounds or educating—"

"No, it isn't. But what it does do, Cecily, is let people really see the conditions others live in. Sure," she said, "they read about it and see a few minutes of film shot for the nightly news, but a layout like the one I just finished really tells the story. Believe me."

"I suppose it's just not my kind of thing. I feel as if I need to get more involved. You know, maybe live in a place like that for a year or two. Really do something." Cecily's brow knitted. "It's more than just famine, Mel. It's politics and warehouses sitting loaded with grain on the docks and dirty old men lounging behind big desks selling guns and planes to kill innocent people."

That was idealistic youth speaking. Who exactly was this new man in Cecily's life? For that was where these ideas came from—Melanie was sure of it.

"I went to Washington once and demonstrated for women's rights."

"You did?" Cecily was wide-eyed.

"I felt slightly foolish but I was glad I'd gone. There was a certain feeling…comradeship, commitment—it's hard to describe." She paused. "Bob walked out on me the next day."

"The bum."

"True," Melanie said wryly.

"Not all men are like Bob."

"Also true."

Cecily turned onto her back again. "I want to do something really important. I refuse just to sit around on my behind and go to school, get married, have kids…you know."

"You can do whatever you like, Cecily. Nothing's stopping you."

"Only Mother and Dad."

"They never stopped you from doing anything," Melanie said with a laugh. "I was always the one who had to do that!"

"Mel…" Cecily's voice was very serious, very young. "I don't want to go home to Cleveland."

"Why not? You'll be back in Madrid in six weeks."

"I just don't want to. I can't face being shut up in the mill all summer, doing some job that doesn't mean anything to me. I'd rather die!"

"You have to go home now. They've planned to be there. They're even cutting short their trip to China, for goodness' sake."

Cecily rolled her eyes. "Wow! Terrible calamity!"

"Come on, Cecily, you know you have to go home."

"Why, damn it? They don't care about me—or you. What they care about is their social life and their cocktail parties and dinners and golf and tennis. They only had kids because it was the expected thing to do and you know it!"

"They care. I know Mother and Dad often seem... distracted, but they're looking forward so much to seeing you. Really. Try to understand."

"I don't want to understand their way of life. It's disgusting. They don't *do* anything. They're useless."

"The world needs people like them. People who can run the economy, manage others. Everyone can't be a crusader."

Cecily made a face. "This world needs lots of crusaders. It's a rotten place and it's going to get worse. Somebody needs to do something."

"Like what?" Melanie pressed.

Cecily didn't answer. A small bubble of alarm swelled in Melanie's chest. But that was ridiculous. She probably wouldn't be worrying if Cecily were going to school in the good ol' U.S. of A. but a Spanish University was a different matter and one about which she knew nothing. Good thing Cecily was going home for a little while.

"Do you ever hear from Bob?" Cecily asked unexpectedly.

"No. Not for many years."

"You know, I had a crush on him. A terrible one. I felt so guilty."

"How old were you? Twelve? Perfectly natural."

"To have a crush on your older sister's husband?"

"Sure. Although what you saw in him..." Melanie shook her head.

"Same thing you did. Handsome and charming—that was Bob."

"Yes."

"Does it still hurt?"

Melanie ducked her head as if to avoid the question. "Sometimes," she finally answered.

"Bob, the two-month wonder. All my friends felt sorry for you. Married two months and he splits."

Melanie grimaced. "Pity from teeny-boppers. Ugh."

"Bob was a gold digger. Big deal. I brush three of them off a day."

"Good for you," Melanie said. "I didn't have the sense to see it then and I wonder if I could spot one today."

"You could, all right, if you weren't so naive." Then suddenly Cecily's face was suffused with shame. "I'm really sorry. What a jerk I can be."

"It's okay."

"No, it isn't. Rubbing salt in the wounds. Forgive me?"

The lines in Melanie's face softened. "Only if you get us two more sodas and *only* if you let me photograph you."

It had been two years since Melanie had last seen her sister. They had both been home in Ohio from time to time over the past years, but somehow always missed each other by days.

Melanie put aside her anxiety over her sister's unsettling new ideals—weren't college kids allowed a little anger at the world?—and began shooting a few pictures of Cecily, trying to catch the fluid grace of her movements. Then she swung the camera toward the water's edge, looking, as always, for that perfect, natural shot.

She took two pictures of a toddler but the light wasn't quite right. Later in the afternoon, everything would be bathed in that soft gilded Mediterranean light, as if the atmosphere were filled with gold dust. If she could capture that light . . .

Click. This one might be okay. Click. An old man and his wife laughing, letting a cold wave break over their sunburned backs. Click, click.

She scanned the blue water through the long telephoto lens. Out past the softly breaking waves was a man... Beautiful. She brought him into focus. Better than beautiful. His black hair was glinting in the bright sun as he swam, and his head turned easily from side to side, as one long arm reached out to pull the water behind him and then the other arm was swinging forward. She saw the arm muscles working, the cords bunching in his shoulders, the body sliding smoothly, lithely through the sea.

Yet... familiar somehow.

Slowly, carefully, as if she might shatter the moment, Melanie moved her camera away from the man, back to the shore and down the beach.

His towel had been vacated.

Swiftly, she swung the camera out to sea again; there he was, still moving gracefully through the water. The stranger.

Then he stopped. He trod water for a prolonged time and he looked across the blue sea and across the expanse of sand and directly into her golden stare behind the lens. She didn't dare breathe. She took a picture and willed her hand to hold the camera steady, for she didn't want to risk losing this unpredictable game.

Only when he tired of treading water and his powerful stroke began to carry him back to shore did she let the camera hang at her neck once again. She took a deep breath.

"Your ice is melting," Cecily suddenly piped up from her place next to Melanie.

"My... ice?" For long minutes now, Melanie had not been conscious of anything else on the beach, had not even noticed Cecily returning.

"In your drink, Mel." Cecily rolled over again and closed her eyes.

He finally emerged from the water like a glistening god, a god of myth, certainly not a mortal man. He was all long limb and lean muscle and tapered waist. Tan from head to foot, except for a thin line around the waistline of his bathing suit when he moved.

His facial expression was impassive but he didn't look at her as he made his way to his towel and stretched out under the sun once more.

She wondered if he was a Spaniard. Could be. But with that distinctive bone structure—the very dark shadowed eyes, the thin nose, the high cheeks and strong jaw—he was definitely not from the southern provinces of Spain. Where, then? Curiosity gnawed at her, making his presence there on the beach even more overwhelming.

Her eyes tried to leave him, then with great reluctance returned to stay. It seemed that she saw each droplet of water on his chest evaporate, saw the rivulets of seawater dry to salt on the long bulge of thigh, saw the thick dark hair stiffen into unruly waves.

He appeared to be relaxed. Melanie told herself that he was just a man on holiday, obviously enjoying the beach in the south of Spain, as well as the sun, the sea, the wine. Of course. Did it matter that he looked at her so often, that she could *feel* his eyes on her? Wasn't it normal? Man stares at woman, she glances over, he looks away.

What's so mysterious about that, she wondered.

And yet he was somehow too alert in his apparent repose. The mere angle and immobility of his handsome head seemed to suggest that he was there for a single purpose: to observe her.

Ridiculous. The whole thing was in her mind. A fantasy. It had been too long since she'd looked at a man in that way; she'd deliberately kept herself from noticing.

When had she first begun to hide from the pain of the real world—or, more accurately, from the painful possibilities of emotional commitment? After Bob, or even before that, when she'd taken up a camera in her sophomore year at college? And now her life had settled into a kind of routine. Plenty of travel, enough assignments to keep her busy, an occasional date with a reporter she met on location.

Oh, they were easy sorts to have dinner with. An assignment, especially in a crisis area, only lasted so long, then everyone flew out to the next site. New places, new faces. She would lift her camera and snap away, seeing the world through the safe barrier of a camera lens.

Sure, she'd had a couple of flings in the past seven years. There had been that absolutely stunningly gorgeous blond Swede she'd met in Stockholm when she'd been covering a marathon. And the dapper Englishman in Nicaragua. But they'd both disappointed her; they'd treated her so casually and coldly and temporarily that she'd withdrawn behind her camera completely. As she thought about her life, she began to feel a little sorry for herself. Drab old Melanie Royce, twenty-eight, unmarried and uninvolved, heading to the ends of the earth. Heading nowhere.

It suddenly occurred to her why this stranger on the beach struck her so forcefully. He seemed almost to know something about her. She had the feeling that he was not only looking at her but through her, as though he saw past the facade of cool competence and recognized the void that was there.

A tiny thread of anxiety continued to coil and uncoil in her belly, annoying but impossible to ignore.

The afternoon waned. Cecily napped comfortably; Melanie dozed off once, then rose and went for a swim. When she returned to her towel he was still at his post, never turning his head in her direction, yet ever aware.

She considered standing up, shoulders set, and marching over to confront him. But what would that prove?

She began to imagine all kinds of things. He was Madrid's James Bond, yes, come to the beach because she'd been mistakenly identified as a Soviet spy. Or Oscar, their father, had sent him to watch over his daughters. No way.

No matter how lovable, Oscar and Muriel Royce were the most unlikely candidates in the world for Parents of the Year. Maybe the strange man liked tall females with wide mouths and freckled skin? And if he *did* simply like her looks, why not approach her? Married? Was he married with ten kids? When did that ever stop a man, especially a Continental type, from at least offering to buy Melanie a glass of wine?

Stop watching me! Melanie's brain cried out. Yet when she looked through the throng on the beach once more, she saw that his eyes were closed. But couldn't she see a muscle ticking in that finely chiseled jawline? Not from fifteen yards away.

Eventually she noticed that the afternoon sun had sunk low in the sky. Everything shimmered as if dusted with gold by the magic Mediterranean light.

She dropped her magazine with a sigh and rested her chin on a fist as she watched the beach empty. The man was still there, lying on his back with one knee up, completely relaxed. She even thought she could see the calm rise and fall of his smooth brown chest. In the splendid light of late afternoon, he had a truly godlike beauty, she thought. And it only enhanced the mystery.

She rolled onto her back and stared at the palm-fringed shoreline and the row of tall white hotels lining the beach. Soft, mellow, burnished gold against gently sloping deep green hills. An exotic setting for her mysterious stranger. Or maybe Melanie was being ridiculously fanciful. Maybe there was nothing more to him than to any other man on the beach. She'd ask her sister what she thought. Cecily would tell her if she was crazy or not.

"Cecily," she said suddenly, "see that man over there?" She turned to point out the stranger.

But he was gone.

IT WAS TO BE their last night in Torremolinos and Cecily wanted to celebrate.

"Let's paint the town red." She dressed in baggy wrinkled cotton slacks and an oversize T-shirt—no bra—then stood looking at herself in the hotel's full-length mirror. "Not bad," she said. "At least I managed to get a decent tan before I have to lock myself up in an office for the rest of the summer."

"Maybe you'll enjoy the work," said Melanie as she stepped from the bathroom into the suite and stopped short, taking in her sister's dinner outfit.

"Not bloody likely, as my last boyfriend used to say."

"English?"

Cecily nodded. "But that's over."

"So you just have this one guy you're dating now?"

Cecily nodded.

"But you still don't want to talk about him." Melanie tossed her bath towel onto the bed and slipped on her panties and bra.

"I don't know if you'd understand him."

"So...am I going to be allowed to meet him back in Madrid?"

"Maybe. But you'll probably run to Mother and Dad and say he's weird or something."

"Why do you say that?"

"Oh, I don't know," she said, shrugging. "No reason, I guess. He's just a little different."

And that was the end of that, thought Melanie.

Cecily began to push aside hangers in Melanie's closet. "Nice dresses, Mel. But terribly American."

"Really? Should I try to dress like a Frenchwoman?"

"Wouldn't hurt. Wow!" she breathed. "Now *this* number is perfect." Cecily pulled out a summer-weight melon-and-rust-colored print that had no back but sported a loose plunging neckline and promised to cling to every contour of

Melanie's lean figure. "This is *you*." Cecily held up the dress expectantly.

"I feel like I'm back in college with a roommate trying to help me choose a dress for some big date." But it was sort of fun—the companionship of a sister all grown up and caring.

"Oh, wear it. We're going to that great seafood place. You promised. And we can eat mountains of lobster and butter and have every man in the place drooling after us."

"Is that the purpose of painting the town?"

"Sure. Food and men."

"What about your boyfriend?"

"He's in Madrid."

"Oh. Then it's not all that serious."

"Of course it is. Now come on, get dressed. I'm totally famished."

Cecily wore her auburn hair down, swinging casually at her shoulders. Melanie twisted her even longer dark red hair into a knot and fastened it with a bamboo catch.

Of course Cecily had a comment. "That's too old-fashioned. You should get a good cut and let it hang. Your hair is much thicker than mine and would look fabulous."

"Maybe I will," Melanie said, "someday."

She did borrow some of Cecily's eye shadow, stroking on three blending shades of blue and green. Melanie had never considered herself a beauty, but she did have great eyes and an acceptable nose, nice and straight even if it was a touch too long. Her mouth was wide, but that was okay, too. At least according to that fortune hunter husband of hers, who had told her men were attracted to women with wide, sensual mouths.

"Think you'll ever remarry?" Cecily asked as they stepped out of the hotel and began to stroll slowly along the promenade.

"Maybe," Melanie admitted. "I've met a couple of guys here and there but they all seem to know about Royce Steel."

"That's just in your head. And even if it isn't, not all men are gold diggers."

"It's hard to weed them out, though. I realize how this sounds, Cecily, but it's easier to travel around by myself and take pictures and play it safe."

"You'll never meet anyone special until you get out from behind that camera."

"You're getting awfully wise in your old age, little sister."

"Aren't I, though?" Cecily agreed smugly.

Melanie made one more casual attempt to find out about Cecily's new boyfriend, then gave up. Why the secret, she wondered. Was he someone that Cecily knew their parents would disapprove of? Someone Melanie herself might find a reason to distrust? After all, she was almost a parent to her sister. Even though they rarely saw each other nowadays, they were in frequent touch with phone calls and letters. And until Cecily had come to Spain and the university, the communication between the two of them had been special.

Melanie guessed that her sister was growing up, and becoming independent at last. That was good. But this somewhat radical talk intimidated Melanie more than a little. It brought to mind what had happened two decades ago in the sixties, when so many of the naively idealistic young had failed to come to grips with reality.

Where had Cecily picked up these ideas? Were they simply the influence of her new boyfriend, as Melanie suspected?

They walked by several fine tourist boutiques and some restaurants with outdoor seating under colorful umbrellas and palm trees. The special atmosphere of southern Spain surrounded them: the combination of medieval tradition and modern resort, liberally sprinkled with signs of the

Moorish past. *El Andalus*, the conquering Moors had named southern Spain, or Andalusia, as it later came to be called. A land of milk and honey with a benign climate and fertile soil and ample rainfall. A land where the sweet scent of orange blossoms filled the air.

The contrast with Madrid's hectic big-city pace was amazing. To the Andalusians, the Madrileños, or natives of Madrid, were hard and brash, and the Castilians of the capital thought the southerners lazy and self-indulgent. A bit like New Englanders and southern plantation-owners in nineteenth-century America, mused Melanie.

The shops were tasteful, offering elegant leather goods from Madrid, silk blouses and dresses and lingerie, gorgeous shoes, paintings by local artists. Picasso had been Spanish, she recalled, even though he'd lived in France. She should have looked in the galleries. Maybe there was a young unknown talent, a new Picasso, languishing around here somewhere.

They passed a poster shop and Cecily stopped to look in the window. "I love that one." She pointed at the picture of a black bull charging a gracefully poised matador. The tableau held a certain amount of tension, Melanie had to admit. Across the top of the poster was announced: *Corrida de Torros. 10 Julio 1980. Pamplona.* Cecily translated automatically: Bullfight. July 10, 1980. Pamplona.

They turned away from the window and continued walking. Their final destination was still farther down the long well-appointed promenade known as the Carihuela to the locals. They were dining on seafood—the best in Torremolinos—at a restaurant called El Cangrejo, which meant "the crab," Cecily had explained.

The evening air was warm and dry. On the hills behind the beaches the villas glowed serenely in the last of the sunlight. Melanie thought it was a pity they couldn't stay longer in Torremolinos but they were heading back to Madrid the

next day, then to New York and Ohio. She supposed she was
fortunate to have been in Africa finishing a magazine assignment at the time that Cecily was due to fly home. They
had at least been able to spend a few days together.

"There's the place," Cecily said, breaking into Melanie's thoughts. "Looks perfect. I can even smell the
shrimp."

They entered the restaurant and Cecily spoke to the maître
d'. Melanie spoke very little Spanish but her sister was
completely fluent now. It came in handy, even though most
of the people in Torremolinos spoke some English. The
maître d' immediately flashed the two sisters a very special,
very appreciative Andalusian smile, more eloquent than an
entire conversation, and bowed them into his domain. Cecily winked at Melanie over his head, then adjusted her
triumphant smile to one of politeness as he straightened up
and, with a flourish, began to lead them toward a table.

As they followed him, Melanie looked around her at the
attractive dining room. There was a small tiled fountain in
the center and myriad shells and pieces of coral adorning the
beams and walls. She noticed the softly candle-lit tables, the
fine shell-pink linen and sparkling silver. The stucco walls
were punctuated by windows, all wide open, and the atmosphere was heavy with the aroma of fresh fish cooking
and salty sea air. Very nice, very appealing. And quite
crowded.

They were nearly at their seats when Cecily stopped
abruptly, gazing across the fountain toward a table against
the opposite wall. "Why...why that looks like..." And she
took Melanie's arm and began to steer her toward the distant table. "I can't believe it! But it is!" She turned to Melanie. "Come on, I want you to meet this really great
guy."

Melanie was behind Cecily and until the women were directly in front of the table, she couldn't see this man her sister was so delighted to have run into.

Then she was standing there and he was smiling at Cecily and getting to his feet, shaking her sister's hand warmly. It was all too dreamlike. That handsome finely chiseled face, the casual white shirt and trousers, the long lean body, the very dark eyes that came slowly and inevitably to rest on Melanie.

Cecily was talking. Melanie forced herself to concentrate on her sister's words. "And we're just here until tomorrow," she was saying pleasantly. Then, "Professor Sanlucar, this is Melanie Royce, my sister."

He reached out his hand and took Melanie's. His grip was firm but gentle; his smile seemed charming and quite genuine. Melanie shook his hand but the words stuck in her throat.

"Your sister mentioned that she was going on holiday with you," he said in practically perfect Oxford English. "It's so nice to meet you, Miss Royce."

And Melanie could only murmur something trite and meaningless in reply while her mind spun away in chaos, crying, *it can't be him, my stranger . . .*

Chapter Two

Cecily seemed to assume, as a matter of course, that they would join Professor Sanlucar for dinner. Melanie wanted to grab her sister's arm and bolt. She wanted to make some excuse to leave his table, but Cecily was chatting away as if it had already been settled that they were having dinner with him. There was nothing, absolutely nothing, Melanie could do.

And inevitably, he asked, "You will join me, won't you?"

"Why, sure, we'd love too," Cecily said gaily. "Wouldn't we, Mel?"

There was a terrible moment of strained silence as the man's dark eyes swung around to her, then Melanie forced herself to smile. "Why, yes, thank you, Professor."

The waiter scurried for chairs and place settings, grinning and nodding at them as if he had personally engineered the fortuitous meeting. Finally they were seated and wine was poured into their glasses. Melanie felt a vortex of intolerable confusion and embarrassment whirling within her. She fought for her equilibrium.

"You must not call me Professor, Miss Royce. My name is Teo." He pronounced it "Tay-oh" in the Spanish style.

She nodded inanely, knowing she would never, never call him Teo. Nor would she offer him her own Christian name.

Up close he looked a little older than she'd imagined, with strong lines on his face and a few gray hairs among the jet-black curls. It seemed to her that the mysterious watchful stranger on the beach had receded. Physically, he now looked more subdued, less imposing than that man whose body had glimmered with energy and danger.

It was all so awkward. Did he know she had seen him observing her on the beach? Did he know she had watched him through her lens, studied him as if he were a specimen under a microscope? Melanie shut her eyes in humiliation.

"Cecily tells me you are a free-lance photojournalist," Teo Sanlucar was saying to her in his smoothly modulated voice. A lovely voice, full of warmth and interest and sincerity. Yet full of secrets, too. Or was that only Melanie's wild imagination again?

"Yes," she answered shortly, sipping her wine.

"And you've just flown here from Africa?" he prompted.

"I was working in Ethiopia at one of the relocation camps."

"It must have been very sad," he said gravely.

Mutely, Melanie nodded. It had been terrible. The proud fine people reduced to dust-covered skeletons. The suffering, the inexcusable dying.

Teo spoke in a low gentle voice. "I must confess that I am fascinated by a woman who can do such things and go to such places and yet remain so beautiful and untouched by it all."

"Really," Melanie murmured, flustered. She twirled her wineglass between her fingers and refused to meet his gaze. "Are all Spanish men so bold?"

"I would not know, not being Spanish, Miss Royce," he replied.

She looked at him in confusion.

Cecily was grinning. "That's a mortal insult, Mel. The professor here is a Basque."

"Yes, Miss Royce. I come from an ancient race that has lived in the Pyrenees mountains since pre-Roman times. We have our own language, our own laws and our own rather different way of looking at life."

"How interesting," Melanie said coolly. "What way is that?"

Teo smiled at her in challenge. "You must visit my part of the country and find out."

"It's kind of you, but Cecily and I are leaving for home in a few days and I doubt we'd have time."

"What a pity. I think you would enjoy our cool green mountains. The opportunities for photography are endless." He smiled at her as if they were old friends and repeated his invitation to visit his family someday. "We Basques are a very warm people. We live passionately, savoring each day, never hiding our emotions, for they are life itself to us."

Then what had he been doing on the beach, watching her through those unreadable dark eyes of his, so secretive?

And yet she saw the smile that curved his chiseled lips now, the frankness in his eyes, the *warmth*. Could this conceivably be the same man who'd behaved so mysteriously on the beach?

"Yes," he was saying, "I feel I should try to persuade you to visit the Basques someday. Truly."

What kind of game was he playing? Did he seriously expect her to take him up on his offer? Or was his manner just another variation on the typical Continental approach? He made her uncomfortable and Melanie felt again, as she had on the beach, that he seemed to see right through her, to know her most private thoughts and emotions. Yet how could he? They had just met.

"How did you learn such excellent English?" Melanie asked, parrying his suggestion.

"I attended Oxford University as an undergraduate and read history there."

"I see."

"I should have gone to the United States and studied, you are thinking, and then I would have learned my English with an American accent," he said lightly.

"Oh, no!" put in Cecily. "I *love* your English accent. It's so elegant."

"Thank you," Teo said, nodding soberly.

It was on the tip of Melanie's tongue to agree, but she wouldn't give him the satisfaction. He did have a wonderfully well-bred Oxford accent, though.

Cecily seized the conversation at that point, asking Teo about a course she had taken from him. Teo and her sister slipped into Spanish and Melanie felt, paradoxically, both relieved and left out.

The menus arrived—large and glossy, with gold tassels. Cecily would have to translate for her.

"Your sister's Spanish has become quite fluent," Teo said to her.

Cecily flushed and thanked him.

"I'm glad to hear that," Melanie replied.

"Her Basque, however," he said, smiling drolly, "is nonexistent."

"Nobody learns Basque," Cecily said, laughing, "unless they were born Basque."

"Alas, all too true," Teo admitted. He reached into his breast pocket and pulled out a pair of horn-rimmed glasses and put them on to read the menu.

Melanie couldn't help staring, studying with fascination the metamorphosis brought about by the glasses. The intense dark eyes became studious, the face lost its mystery and became mild, the sense of sparking energy became dimmed. The change was so stunning and so unexpected that Melanie practically gaped. Her mind kept trying to

mesh the disparate images of Teo Sanlucar: the friendly
dinner partner, the polite, bespectacled history professor
and the enigmatic stranger on the beach.

Cecily jabbered on about Madrid and Torremolinos and
the university, her usual carefree, high-spirited self. Melanie was grateful for her sister's effusiveness as it covered her
own rather distracted silence. She almost squirmed in
her seat, discomfited by Teo's probing, knowledgeable
eyes.

It suddenly struck her. Had this meeting been coinciden-
tal? Had she imagined his vigilance on the beach? But how
could he possibly have known where she and Cecily would
be? And why would he have cared? He *had* mentioned Cecily telling him about the trip they were making to Torremolinos. But what reason could he possibly have for
showing up in the same place?

It was coincidence, of course. The Costa del Sol, the sun
coast, was a very popular resort area. And El Cangrejo, this
posh restaurant, was just as popular, a natural place for a
vacationer to choose.

Pure accident.

"Isn't that so, Miss Royce?" Teo Sanlucar was asking
her.

She jumped, startled, and her hand accidentally brushed
her wineglass, tipping it. A few drops of blood-red wine
stained the linen tablecloth in the split second before Teo's
lean brown hand reached out, cat-quick, to right the glass.

"Oh, I'm sorry," Melanie said, dabbing at the crimson
spot with her napkin, her cheeks burning.

"I asked if you agreed," Teo repeated.

"I'm sorry, I wasn't following the conversation."

"We were talking about the contrasts between the provinces of Spain, Mel," Cecily said patronizingly. "Like how
different it is here from Madrid and Barcelona."

"Well, yes, it is different but I couldn't venture an opinion. I haven't seen enough of Spain," she responded uncertainly.

"Have you seen a bullfight yet?" Teo asked.

"Goodness, no—we haven't had time."

"It's the season. You should try to catch one. Perhaps when you get back to Madrid. You are going back shortly?" he asked, one dark brow quirked.

"Too soon for me," Cecily said. "I'd rather stay here for a while."

"But surely your parents are most anxious to see you. How could you disappoint them?" Teo said gravely, taking off his glasses and putting them in his pocket.

"They don't care," replied Cecily, pouting. "They're in *China!*"

"On their way home by now," Melanie chided gently.

Cecily pursed her lips and rolled her eyes. She was still terribly immature, despite her veneer of sophistication, thought Melanie. Nineteen. A late-life child of Oscar and Muriel Royce. The nine years between the two sisters made quite a difference—practically a generation. The world's at everyone's feet when they're nineteen, Melanie reflected, and they know more than everyone else on any subject that comes up. They're so absolutely sure of right and wrong. Everything was black and white at nineteen. It was only as a person matured that the shades of gray emerged. Melanie knew all about those shades of gray.

She sipped her wine again and met Teo's eyes over her glass. His were sparkling with a kind of humor, as if he were reading her thoughts and agreeing with Melanie's assessment of her younger sister.

They ordered. Or rather, Cecily and Teo ordered for her. The meal was delicious: steaming saffron rice and butter-drenched Mediterranean prawns. Melanie tried to enjoy it but her appetite had fled. Teo Sanlucar's presence seemed to overshadow everything.

Why? she demanded of herself. Why should this stranger, this college professor, fascinate her so much? What was it about him that appeared so ominous to her? Once dinner was over, they'd go their separate ways and never see each other again. And yet she could not erase from her brain the image of him on the beach, watching her—or Cecily—or both of them. Why?

He insisted on paying the bill, covering Melanie's hand when she reached for it to pay her share and Cecily's.

"No, no," he said, "allow me."

"We couldn't..." And she continued to argue—a trait learned from her generous father—but Melanie hadn't the slightest idea of what she was saying. All she knew was that his hand was resting on hers, warm and firm and compelling, and her pulse began to hammer in her neck. It always did when she was unnerved or confused.

In the end she agreed, but only, she told herself, to make him remove his hand, to be free of his unsettling touch.

After the bill was paid they threaded their way through the rows of tables. The maître d' bowed them out with a flourish and said something gracious in Spanish to Teo and Cecily.

Then they were standing on the promenade in front of El Cangrejo and Teo was offering to walk them to their hotel.

"Really, it's not necessary," Melanie protested, wanting desperately to get away from the man. She felt, somehow, that she couldn't take a full breath in his presence. Her chest was constricted, squeezing her heart, making that pulse leap.

"I couldn't let two such lovely ladies walk alone," he persisted, "at night, in a strange town."

"But our hotel is just down the Carihuela."

"So is mine. Good. Then you have no excuse to rid yourself of my company. I shall walk with you."

Why didn't Melanie appreciate his concern for them? Did he truly care? Yes, she thought, he did, but there was another edge to his concern, a tension of some kind. His offer was not quite as casual as it seemed.

What was he after?

He was an attractive man, polite but not stiffly so, dynamic, intelligent, well educated. She should have welcomed his attentions.

The sea breeze that brushed Melanie's face was tangy and warm. It ruffled the fabric of her skirt and lifted Teo's black curls from his forehead. His face was all shadows and dark hollows in the subtropical night.

"You are leaving tomorrow, you say?" he asked then.

"I didn't say," replied Melanie.

"I'm sure Cecily must have mentioned it."

"Yes, we're starting back tomorrow," Cecily sighed. "But I'm going to stretch it out as long as possible. I'm going to show my sister every tourist spot on the way. It may take us days. Granada, Toledo, the works."

"Of course she must see them."

Teo walked between them, tall and lean in the sultry darkness, his white shirt glowing. People passed them, wearing brightly colored resort clothes, talking, laughing, chattering in several different languages. Melanie remained silent. She listened to the night sounds, to the palm fronds overhead that rattled in the offshore breeze and the sea that soughed at the sandy verge beyond the lighted promenade.

They reached their hotel. Strategically placed spotlights illuminated the beautifully arranged foliage; the large plate-glass doors gleamed and winked, reflecting the light, as people pushed through them.

"Thank you for walking us back," Melanie said carefully. She wanted the man gone. Gone from her side, gone from her life. In some way, he frightened her, though she couldn't have said exactly why.

"I'm so glad we met you in the restaurant," Cecily gushed. "Actually it's been quite boring here."

"My pleasure entirely, *Señoritas*," Teo said.

"Well, I'll see you back at the university in the fall," Cecily said.

"Certainly. Let me know when you return." He turned to Melanie. "I am so pleased to have met you, Miss Royce." He bowed slightly, then straightened. His eyes were dark holes in his shadowed face. She had a sudden compulsion to see his expression but he stood with his back to the hotel lights.

She murmured something polite, then realized he was holding out his hand. She had to return the gesture, to clasp his hand in hers. Her heart gave a lurch as she felt his touch. He held her hand a second too long, his lean brown fingers almost caressing her skin.

"*Buenos noches*. Good night," he said. Then, in an undertone, he added something very odd. "Take care of your sister, Miss Royce. She's so very young."

He turned quickly and vanished into the soft Spanish night.

Chapter Three

Cecily angrily threw some underwear into her suitcase. "I still don't see why I have to go back with you. You can make up some kind of excuse for me." She paced around her tiny apartment.

"You have to go back and you know it," Melanie said sharply. "Look, if it's this new guy, well, he'll still be here when you get back to Madrid. Just think of how happy you'll be to see each other."

"Oh, you just don't understand."

"Did he give you a hard time last night or something?" Melanie hoped her sister wouldn't regard her question as prying, but Cecily had turned singularly sullen after they'd arrived in Madrid and she'd gone to see him.

"His name is Carlos," Cecily grumbled, "and he didn't give me a hard time. He's not like that. He's really wonderful. He isn't one of those useless, frivolous *boys* Mother always shoves at me. And he isn't an uptight, cold Castilian. He's a Basque. He's serious. He believes in serious, important things."

What things, Melanie wondered.

"Basque men are so...so complex, so profound. Don't you think that's true?" Cecily was saying.

"I couldn't say. I don't really know any Basque men."

"Yes you do. Professor Sanlucar. He introduced me to Carlos, in fact."

"I hardly know your professor," Melanie said, thrust abruptly back to that evening, to El Cangrejo, to her mysterious and beautiful stranger...

No. She shook her head as if to dispel the wayward fantasy. Nothing mysterious about Professor Teo Sanlucar. He was just a teacher who had been on vacation, too.

"He *is* attractive, isn't he? With those soulful black eyes and that gorgeous hair," she heard Cecily saying. "And he's a supernice man, too. All the girls at the university are crazy about him."

"I can imagine."

"Of course he's not the least bit interested in any of them," Cecily shrugged. "He's too old."

"Old?"

"Thirty-five, at least."

"Oh, yes, that's ancient," Melanie said dryly.

"Well, you know what I mean."

Melanie raised an eyebrow. "I'm not so sure." Then, casually, "I'm certain your professor has a family, anyway."

"No, he doesn't. Carlos told me. He's footloose and fancy-free. Odd."

"Why odd?"

"Well, he's so good-looking and sexy."

"Mmm."

"And an excellent teacher."

Melanie sat on the bed, watching her sister go about her perfunctory packing. Suddenly she remembered the pictures she'd taken in Torremolinos. She'd just been having fun, she had to admit; even when she wasn't on assignment, she couldn't stop herself from shooting roll after roll of film. Was it simply because she no longer felt comfortable without her camera, as Cecily had implied? Or because you never knew when the perfect picture might appear in your viewfinder? Her black-and-white work she usually developed and printed herself, but these she'd just handed over to a local photography lab as soon as she and Cecily had returned to Madrid. She considered them summer holiday snapshots, she told herself, no more and no less. Some of them were dreadful and some quite good, especially a couple of Cecily that their parents would love to have.

She reached into her ever-handy camera bag and pulled them out. "This is a great picture of you, if I do say so myself." She tipped it in Cecily's direction.

"Ugh! Look at my thighs."

"It's my angle. I was sitting when I took it. It's still a good picture, though."

She leafed through the photographs. There he was. Melanie must have taken ten pictures of him—at the time, she hadn't realized it was so many—and the best were the ones in which he was lying on his towel, one arm behind his head, one knee bent. There was nothing left to the imagination in her shots. She'd used a zoom lens to get in all those details: the dark, salt-stiff hair, the chiseled arch of his nose, the smooth-skinned chest with the crisp dark hairs that grew downward in a line to disappear beneath his trunks. The flat belly, even the masculine bulge in his white swimsuit. The thighs, glistening in the sun. Their long muscles suggested that perhaps he'd been a runner at one time. He even had nicely shaped feet.

She sifted through several more photographs. There were two of him swimming—not so good. Her hand must have been shaking a little . . .

"You took a picture of the professor?" Cecily asked from over Melanie's shoulder.

"Well, I didn't know who he was. He was just a subject," she replied, putting the pictures away in her bag, unaccountably embarrassed.

Cecily yanked some wrinkled clothes out of a drawer then stopped, staring at them, unfocused. "I could fly home next week," she finally said, her voice hopeful.

"Cecily, we're going tomorrow morning and that's that." Melanie readied herself for an argument but when she looked at her sister, Cecily's face was wiped clean of her previous irritation. Somehow that worried her; Cecily was not one to hide her feelings. Nor did she give up that easily.

"I'm going back to my hotel to pack now. I'll pick you up at nine. Is that too early for the Spanish dinner hour?"

"A little," Cecily said, "but it's okay. They've learned to forgive tourists."

"Swell of them. Now you finish packing. We have to leave early and turn in the rental car at the airport, remember? I'll see you later, okay?"

"Sure. I've got a great place I want to take you. Real flamenco dancers. I mean, not the tourist stuff, the real thing."

"Sounds great," Melanie said, preoccupied with gathering up her camera equipment and her purse. She wasn't paying much attention to her sister, who moved around the room in a jerky, nervous manner. She did notice that Cecily wouldn't meet her gaze or hug her goodbye. So she was going to sulk, after all, Melanie thought.

She drove back toward the center of Madrid, where her hotel was situated. The traffic was heavy, as usual, but because it was Saturday, she was at least spared the rush-hour hysteria. The day had been hot and Cecily's apartment even hotter. Melanie's thick hair stuck uncomfortably to her neck. But the cool breath of wind coming in the open car window was soothing, even though the Spanish sun hung high and still in the western sky. The quality of the light up here on the central plateau was entirely different from that in southern Spain. It was crystal clear and sharp, not the least bit golden, Melanie noted.

She had her street map laid out on the passenger seat and stopped several times to check it. Without Cecily, she was lost in the sprawling capital, especially when she reached the rabbit-warren of old winding cobblestone streets around the Plaza Mayor. Now if only she could recall exactly where to turn...

She was staying in a small, elegant private hotel in the old part of town, a place Cecily had found for her. Full of atmosphere and real Spanish hospitality. But a little hard to find. As for parking...well, she guessed Madrid was like any other big city.

She was straining to locate and read the street signs when she inadvertently strayed into the wrong lane. There was a sudden screech of brakes from behind. She, too, quickly slammed on her brakes, realizing what she'd done. A middle-aged man pulled his car beside hers, holding up traffic as he leaned across his seat and gave Melanie a good tongue-lashing to the tune of a dozen horns.

Then he did the craziest thing; his eyes widened, as if he'd only just seen her, and his face split in a huge smile. He winked and then he was gone in a symphony of horn blowing.

She really needn't have driven all the way from the campus back into the heart of Madrid, but she'd wanted to give Cecily a couple of hours alone with Carlos. Their last night and all. But now it seemed a really dumb idea. She should have stayed around to meet Carlos. Or, better yet, she should have made Cecily come back with her and stay in her hotel room. Why hadn't she thought of that? Perhaps she'd suggest it tonight.

Twenty minutes later, as she finally entered her room and kicked off her shoes, Melanie hoped Cecily would have stopped sulking by the time they got back to Ohio. Surely her sister wasn't that immature. It wasn't as if she were being

dragged away forever from her life here in Madrid. It was
only for six weeks. . . .

The shower was refreshing; afterward the air conditioning chilled her wet skin. She dressed, then threw a few last
things into her suitcase and checked her purse, a habit she'd
developed since she'd started traveling so much. Passport,
traveler's checks, credit cards, international driver's li-
cense, airplane tickets. All set.

The doorman handed her into the gray car she'd rented,
smiling and nodding as he wished her a good evening.

The sun was setting behind the Guadarrama mountains
as Melanie drove out Calle Princesa to university city. There
was an orange glow behind the rough-edged black hills. The
colors were as clear as the air—brilliant, too perfect to last,
almost tragic in their brief glory.

She pulled to the side of the road and took her camera out
of its case. Then she walked across the street, dodging a car
or two. She carefully chose her angle and composed her
shot, focusing on a small stone church, stark against the
vivid sunset colors. A dramatic picture.

A dramatic city. No wonder her sister had fallen in love
with Madrid. The highest capital in Europe. Its undulating
plateau of sand and clay had once been the site of a Moorish fort, Cecily had told her. Yet for Melanie the city con-
jured up images of medieval Europe; it was in the air, down
a winding alley, across a sun-beaten hill. It caught her senses
and caressed them pleasantly.

The Old World was compelling, Melanie thought once
again. Its ancient cities and timeless villages had a kind of
serenity, a calm beauty that she was able to capture in a series of perfect images.

For a moment she regretted having no one with whom to
share her vision. But she always traveled alone. She was used
to it and had developed automatic defenses against uncomfortable situations. She was quite capable of withdrawing

into herself completely or reading with utter concentration. Still, it could be lonely, she admitted to herself. Safe but lonely.

This evening, however, she would have her sister's companionship. Melanie was looking forward to a pleasant night out, not quite the usual tourist's view of Madrid. And perhaps Cecily would tell her a bit more about this Carlos. Then, the next day, she and Cecily would fly home and her sister would get a good dose of midwestern America. Life would look a little less romantic in Ohio than it did in Spain. A little less romantic and a lot more realistic.

It was a good thing Melanie had come to Madrid.

She pushed open one of the double doors leading into the courtyard of Cecily's building and walked up the wide elaborate staircase. It was all for show—the apartments were tiny and plain. She knocked on Cecily's door once, then opened it and walked in. "Cecily? Ready yet?"

The room was silent and too empty. Melanie knew instantly, instinctively, that it had been vacant for hours.

Her first thought was that Cecily had run away, gone into hiding—with Carlos most likely—to avoid going home. Cecily had always been a willful child who got what she wanted, and she'd made it only too clear that she hadn't wanted to go home to Cleveland.

Anger welled up in Melanie's chest. How could Cecily do this? How could she leave Melanie in the lurch and disappoint their parents? How dared she indulge herself in this childish way?

Melanie stood in the small apartment and looked around. There were two half-empty cups of tea on the kitchen counter and dirty dishes in the sink. Someone had been there with Cecily. Carlos? Had he convinced her to go away with him? Young passion could be powerfully persuasive.

She went into the bedroom and stopped short, her heart flying into her throat. The covers had been pulled off the bed, a chair lay overturned on its side and papers from a small table had fluttered to the floor. It looked as though a struggle had taken place there. What had happened?

Melanie's brain raced with possibilities. Carlos and Cecily had had an argument and Carlos had become violent. Or Cecily herself had flown into a rage of some kind. But then, where *was* Cecily?

Or—the thought struck her sickeningly—with all the violence going on in large cities, and Cecily coming from a wealthy background, could she have been...abducted?

Melanie sucked in a terrified breath. She tried to calm herself, to think. She examined the room, desperately searching for clues, not knowing what she was looking for. The two suitcases Cecily had packed that afternoon sat in the corner. Her sister's purse was gone. Drawers were mostly empty, but she had no way of knowing whether Cecily had taken anything with her or not. A knot of fear twisted in Melanie's stomach.

A lone sandal lay by the bedroom door. One sandal. Had Cecily been dragged out? No, there were neighbors. Wouldn't someone have heard?

Quickly, her heart pounding, Melanie went out into the hall, chose a door and knocked on it. No answer. Another door. An elderly lady opened it but couldn't understand what Melanie was asking.

"Cecily?" the old woman quavered. *"Sí, la americana."* The American.

Eventually Melanie gathered that Cecily had left earlier that evening with a young man. *Un novio.* A boyfriend. His name? The lady didn't know.

Other neighbors knew nothing, hadn't seen Cecily or refused to comprehend Melanie's minimal Spanish.

She went back to Cecily's place and threw herself down in a chair. It had to be Carlos. She had no other leads, not a clue, not a note. Only the awful emptiness of the apartment and one lonely sandal.

Could Cecily be late returning from somewhere? Should she wait? She checked the time: almost ten. And Cecily had expected her at nine. Could her sister have deliberately messed up the bedroom to mislead her? Could she have?

She had to look for Cecily. Carlos was a start but she didn't know his last name. She had to find out.

Quickly she scribbled a note, on the remote chance that Cecily might return to the apartment. All the while, she searched for reasons, possibilities, explanations. Was Cecily pulling some sort of sick stunt? Were she and Carlos conspiring together to make this look like a kidnapping? No, that was too farfetched. Or was it? Cecily had been acting strange lately, talking of causes and crusades. Or was she, perhaps unwittingly, involved in some kind of crime? She had to find out.

What should she do?

The first thing was to find someone Cecily had known, someone who spoke English. Someone who might know something. Carlos's last name, at least.

She rifled every drawer in the apartment and finally found an untidy pile of paper scraps with names and addresses scribbled on them. Most of Cecily's friends and acquaintances had Spanish names and Melanie was afraid they wouldn't speak English. Then she found one: Joan Tattenham, Residencia de Mujeres, 505 Calle Isobel. No phone, but then Cecily's apartment had no phone anyway.

She left the tiny apartment, hurtling down the stairs to her car. It was almost dark by now. She tried to read her map by the car's interior light but the street names were so tiny. Thankfully, the *sereno* came by with his flashlight. The *sereno*, that medieval character, an anachronism somehow carried over into the twentieth century. The man who saw to the safety of the neighborhood after dark, who had on his

ıron ring the key to every courtyard on his beat and unlocked one's door if one clapped loudly in the dark, echoing street to attract his attention.

"*Señorita.*" He nodded politely.

"Could you tell me where Isobel Street is, please? *Por
favor, la Calle Isobel.*" Melanie asked. But his answer was
too rapid for her to understand. Eventually he put his finger on a spot on the map—a dirty finger, with a thick
blackened nail. "*Aquí,*" he rasped, "Here." The street was
not far away. Melanie thanked him profusely, tipped him
and waved goodbye out her window.

Calle Isobel. She found it after a few unsuccessful tries.
The address turned out to be a dormitory. The matron, dis-
gruntled, went up to get Señorita Tattenham for her. Melanie waited, heart pounding, fingers nervously tapping the
arm of her chair. Perhaps Joan Tattenham wouldn't know
anything....

"Hi!" A young, rather stocky girl with a bright smile was
walking across the room. "I'll bet you're Cecily's sister. The
hair..."

"Joan Tattenham?"

"Yes. Not too many of us Tattenhams around here."

"I'm Melanie Royce. I do appreciate your talking to me
so late." She tried to keep the panic from her voice.

"Late? It's early in Madrid. I was bored, anyway. Is there
something wrong? I mean, I wonder why you looked me
up."

"Well, not exactly wrong. I just wondered how well you
knew my sister."

"Pretty well. I mean, we Americans seem to naturally
gravitate together. But lately, Cecily's been hanging out with
a new group. Some guys. For a while there, I thought she'd
forgotten how to speak English."

"What group is this? You see, I'm trying to locate her. A
family crisis," she lied.

"She's not in her apartment?"

"No."

"Well, I hate to give her away. I mean, I don't want her getting in trouble or anything..."

"Oh, she won't, really. This is kind of an emergency."

"She's probably with Carlos, then, Carlos Echeverria."

"But where is this Carlos?"

Joan shrugged. "He's probably gone home for the *feria*. The fiesta. It starts on the sixth. All the Basques go home for that week. It's a big deal."

"Where is his home?"

"Somewhere up in Basque country. Near Pamplona, I think."

"Pamplona? You mean that town where they have the running of the bulls?"

"Yeah. You know, Hemingway and bullfights and lotsa vino. It's this week."

"And you think Carlos and Cecily have gone there?"

"Probably. If Carlos isn't still here, that's where he's gone. But I'll tell you how to find out." She paused a moment. "Professor Sanlucar. He'll know. He's sort of a mentor to Carlos. They come from the same neck of the woods and they're pretty chummy. Those Basques stick together."

Professor Sanlucar! Melanie felt as if someone had punched her in the stomach. So he was involved in this somehow. It wasn't a coincidence, then, that he'd been on the beach in Torremolinos watching them. And that he'd shown up at the same restaurant. The sense of foreboding she'd felt had been accurate enough, after all. He'd been following them! He knew Carlos—it just couldn't be a coincidence. And what had he said that night? "Take care of your sister." She hadn't given it much thought then, but now...

What had Cecily got herself into?

She forced herself to sound calm; her voice quavered only a little when she spoke again.

"How can I find Professor Sanlucar, Joan?"

"Well, I have no idea where he lives but he'll be in his office tomorrow morning, I'm sure. He's generally around on weekends in case a student needs him or anything," she added helpfully.

Melanie left the *residencia* with the directions to Teo Sanlucar's office on a scrap of paper in her pocket. A grim feeling of futility gripped her—and of apprehension. The mysterious professor was the link. She was sure of it. Somehow he tied everything together; somehow he was involved in Cecily's disappearance. But how? And why?

She stopped by her sister's apartment again. There was a light on when she pushed the door open. She burst inside. "Cecily? Cecily!" But the apartment was empty. The light was the one she'd turned on herself and forgotten to click off.

She felt wretchedly near tears. It was too late to do anything that night. She briefly considered calling the police, but that would be a serious mistake if it turned out Cecily was merely having a fling with her lover. The Spanish police—the notorious Guardia Civil—were touchy and unforgiving, especially with foreigners. No, she couldn't go to them, not yet.

Slowly, tiredly, she drove back to her hotel through the heavy dinner-hour traffic. The streets teemed with people—walking, laughing, smoking, gesturing. The restaurants were crowded, the lights bright, the air warm and filled with the smell of olive oil and garlic and old cobblestones and dust.

Melanie went back to her hotel room and sat on the edge of her bed, thinking. She felt that something was terribly wrong, something was out of place. A large piece of the puzzle was missing.

And it was very likely that Professor Sanlucar could give her that missing piece—if he wanted to.

THE NEXT MORNING, Melanie was up early. She had her coffee and roll alone in the hotel dining room. The residents of Madrid rose late and breakfasted even later, about ten, and foreigners usually took on the custom when they visited. She was nervous and edgy, afraid that she wouldn't be able to track down the professor. Perhaps he hadn't even returned from the south of Spain yet.

She sent a telegram to her parents. She and Cecily wouldn't be home that day. Not for a few days. Something vague about Cecily missing an examination... She hated to lie but she couldn't bring herself to tell them the truth. Why should they worry until she was sure there was really something to worry about?

The drive out Calle Princesa to the university was becoming familiar; she didn't even need her map. The hills were illuminated with the morning sunlight but the streets were nearly empty, except for the ubiquitous elderly ladies dressed in black, carrying their string bags full of the day's groceries. The cafés were vacant, too, save for the proud, white-aproned owners standing behind their bars polishing glasses, and the young sweeper boys busy with their brooms.

The university was still asleep this Sunday morning. It was hard to believe she'd find anyone there at all. Melanie chewed her lip—her mission might have to wait. She even stopped by her sister's apartment, not really expecting Cecily to be there, but just in case... Then she carefully followed Joan's directions. She got confused once in a labyrinth of narrow streets but eventually found herself in front of the building that matched the address. It was ordinary and fairly new, one of those generic European buildings devoid of character, constructed of cement blocks, plain and utilitarian in design.

She parked the rental car and stared up at the windows. It was an uncivilized hour for the Spanish—not even nine o'clock. She wondered whether anyone would be at work in these offices so early in the morning. But the glass panes only reflected the morning sunlight, telling her nothing.

Taking a deep breath, Melanie pushed tentatively at the front door. It opened. So someone, a janitor perhaps, had already arrived. The musty, familiar smell of classrooms and chalk and paper assailed her as she stood in the dim corridor, listening. There was no sound. She checked the professor's office number on a directory board—twenty-one. Upstairs? She'd wait forever if she had to. Her footsteps echoed as she walked down the hallway and climbed the stairs. She tried to soften her steps. Ridiculous. There was obviously no one around to notice. No one at all.

Number twenty-one. A blank brown door. Timidly, Melanie knocked. The sound was shockingly loud in the hollow silence. She reminded herself that there was no one to hear her knock and she rapped at the smooth brown wood again, gathering courage. She'd just have to wait, then. Perhaps there was a café nearby.

The door swung inward as if in defiance of her very thought. She stood there, stupefied for a moment while her heart gave a great lurch.

"*Sí?*" a voice asked, a voice she remembered well. A deep mellow voice, now edged with a hint of annoyance.

Then he was standing before her, his expression quizzical behind his glasses. "Ah, Miss Royce, excuse me for sounding a bit put out. I try to work early, when the rest of Spain is still abed or in church. Do come in."

There was no surprise in his voice, Melanie observed. It almost seemed as though he'd expected her.

"I'm sorry to disturb you, but I'm having a bit of trouble locating Cecily." She knew she must have sounded ridiculously juvenile, and alarmist, to boot.

"Cecily? Ah." He gestured to a chair, then sat behind his desk, leaning forward in his seat and clasping his hands together in front of him, elbows resting on the desk. He wore a short-sleeved shirt, white against his tan. Melanie could see the muscles in his forearms tighten under the brown skin.

"Actually, she disappeared last night. She didn't leave any kind of note or message. We were to have flown home this morning. Naturally I'm worried."

His dark eyes met hers impassively over the folded hands. "What exactly do you mean, 'disappeared'?"

"I mean just that—disappeared," Melanie said curtly.

"Why do you come to me, Miss Royce? I haven't seen Cecily since Torremolinos."

"One of my sister's friends told me you know Carlos." She met his eyes levelly and was surprisingly upset by the frown that creased his brow.

"Carlos?"

"Carlos Echeverria, her boyfriend. You *do* know him?"

"Yes," Teo said slowly, "I know him."

She waited but nothing more was forthcoming. What was going on here? Teo Sanlucar didn't even seem very surprised by her visit. She had a sudden horrible feeling that he knew precisely what had happened to Cecily.

"Well, do you know where my sister is?" Her voice rang shrilly in her own ears.

The man looked at her carefully, his eyes narrowed in deliberation. "No," he said after a long moment, "or I would tell you."

He was lying, she thought instantly, irrationally. She felt stifled by the miasma of confusion and deceit that seemed to fill the small room. Why wasn't he telling the truth? She tried to calm herself, to think logically, but her mind raged with questions.

"Well," he said finally, "I would hazard a guess that your sister ran off with Carlos Echeverria. But I'm sure there's nothing to worry about."

"Nothing to worry about? When we're supposed to be on a plane right now? When she's disappeared without leaving word and there are signs of a struggle in her apartment? If it were your sister, wouldn't you be worried, Professor Sanlucar?" Melanie stopped abruptly, fighting panic, then cleared her throat. "I'm really terribly upset. If you don't know where she is, do you think I should go to the police?"

His dark eyebrows drew together and Melanie thought she saw his hands tighten. "The *policía*? No, Miss Royce. This is merely a summer fling."

"I don't think so, begging your pardon, Professor Sanlucar. There *is* something going on here. Something concerning Carlos."

"You have not met Carlos?" he asked.

"No, but Cecily told me a little about him."

"A handsome young man. Very bright. A touch wild perhaps. Like your sister."

He was telling her nothing, evading the issue entirely. Did he think this was some kind of joke? "Where are they?" Melanie demanded. "You know where they've gone, don't you? I have to talk to Cecily."

"I think perhaps you'd best leave them alone. Your sister will hardly thank you for chasing her down. You are not, after all, her mother. Why don't you go home, Miss Royce, as you planned?"

"I'm not going anywhere without at least talking to her!" Melanie got up and leaned over the professor's desk.

"Please, don't upset yourself so. They've probably gone to Pamplona, to the *feria*. Everyone goes there this week. It's a grand event. The young people adore it." He met her gaze openly, his dark eyes probing hers deeply. Then he shrugged in a very Spanish gesture. "Carlos is a Basque. He could not miss the *feria*."

"Then I'll go to Pamplona and find her!"

"An impossible task. The city is so full of people this week that without help, it is simply not possible to find someone among all the crowds. Especially for a stranger like yourself. Truly, you should go home and your sister will call you. Then think how foolish you'll feel that you went to all this trouble."

He rose and walked around his desk to stand over her. "Trust me, Miss Royce. I know these young people. They are thoughtless, but they mean no harm. Go home, Miss Royce," he said in a concerned voice.

Melanie stood up and straightened her shoulders. His nearness made her uncomfortable, but she forced herself to look him squarely in the eye. "I guess I'll just have to go to this Basque country of yours by myself. Without anyone's help. I'll find her. Believe me, I'll find her." She swung the strap of her purse firmly onto her shoulder. "And I think, *Professor*, that you are not telling me as much as you know. There's something strange here, I know there is, and I'm going to find out exactly what's going on!"

"I'm terribly sorry you would think such a thing of me. What could I possibly have to hide?" He spoke softly, spreading his hands in a gesture of innocence.

"I have no idea. But I'll find out. Thank you *so* much for your help," she said sarcastically. She turned to leave, then impulsively whirled around to face him again. "By the way, why were you watching us on the beach at Torremolinos?"

He removed his glasses; instantly Melanie sensed the uncanny energy, the power he discharged. She instinctively backed off a step.

He watched her closely for a moment, then said, "Why, protecting you, Miss Royce. What else?"

Chapter Four

Melanie drove north out of Madrid very early the next morning. She'd had to hire the car for an indefinite length of time and locate a map—a good one, as she was traveling alone and couldn't afford to get lost in the vast central region of Spain.

The Feria de Pamplona. A week-long festival—a fete—honoring San Fermín. Melanie had already learned from a travel agency in Madrid that there were no rooms to be had anywhere in the Pamplona area, just as Teo Sanlucar had warned her.

First it had taken her most of the previous afternoon to even find a travel agent working on Sunday. Then he'd had no success at reserving accommodation for her. "Lock your car and sleep in it," had been his final suggestion. *Swell.*

The sere rounded hills of the interior Iberian Peninsula fell away behind her as she drove. It was harsh unforgiving country. Every so often she passed through a small village nestled on a hillside, but the populated areas of the plateau were few and sparse.

To the north and east, the landscape began to alter subtly. There were more villages and the rolling hills grew greener; they were dotted with brush now. When she stopped for fuel and lunch at Soria, she could see the mountainous terrain in the distance, misted to a bluish hue.

She took several pictures and delighted her hosts at the restaurant by including them in her photographs.

Very gradually the road began to rise after Soria. The hills gave way to green, steep-sided mountains covered with deciduous trees. Melanie drove through ancient villages of small stone houses whose walls were smooth and worn with age. She felt as though she were suspended in timelessness; these places, she thought, looked much the same as they had for the past hundred years. Old stone wells still sat in the village squares although they were no longer used. The faces of the women were seamed and their black, proud eyes followed Melanie as she drove slowly through their towns, making her feel an oddity among them: a woman traveling alone to some faceless destiny.

These Spanish women rarely traveled. Even in this day and age they were tied to their villages, their homes, their church. And Melanie felt their scornful black eyes on her as she drove into their vision, then past, then beyond.

She saw her first sign for Pamplona and sighed in relief. Her back ached and she was hungry again. She already knew about the lodging; would it be difficult to find a restaurant, as well?

From far off she could see the plateau of Pamplona. The great dark cathedral was outlined against the mountains that rose behind the city, each successive layer of hills mistier than the one before.

Pamplona. The capital city of Navarre, made famous by Hemingway's novel *The Sun Also Rises*. Melanie had read the book in high school but couldn't remember it very clearly. Something about bulls and wine—lots of wine—and Jake Barnes's hopeless love affair.

The moment she hit the outskirts of the city, she could feel the excitement, an explosion of emotion that swept everything before it even though the *feria* didn't actually begin until the next day. Yet the people were already gathering from everywhere. It was impossible to drive farther than the outlying streets, for the roads were thronged. Melanie finally found a place to park near the soccer stadium and locked her car, taking her camera and her heavy purse.

She began to walk toward the old city, jostled all the way by the *feria*-goers who were gearing up for the first day of the fiesta. The houses here were nestled close together. Above her, she saw flags of red, white and green—the Basque flag—draped from narrow windows. Anticipation hung in the air, as palpable as the heat.

And it was hot in Pamplona, all right. Perhaps the crowds made it seem hotter than it was, but even in the late afternoon, Melanie was covered in a fine sheen of perspiration.

She almost forgot why she had come. The folk dancing in the streets, the singing and the haunting rhythms of the hollow drums and the Basque flute were hypnotic enticements to let herself go. She felt a kindred thrill in spite of herself.

Hemingway. She was beginning to understand his zeal for this untamed place, for these proud, independent people. On the sides of buildings were posters of the bullfights: the handsomely clad matadors, the snorting wild-eyed beasts. There was one just like the poster they'd seen in the shop window in Torremolinos. It struck her that, in a strange way, she had come full circle. She remembered standing on the Carihuela, studying the poster, and it almost seemed that if she turned, Cecily would be there beside her saying, "I love that one." But she was a world away; Cecily was missing and now Melanie stood alone on a street in Pamplona, blasted by sound and heat and people. She recalled the utter dissipation of Hemingway's Jake Barnes as she watched the crowds dancing and drinking and shouting with hysterical fervor. Despite her anxiety, her heart beat with the rhythm of the hollow drums.

"Vino! Señorita?" A bota bag was raised above her head and she drank, the warm red wine hissing into the back of her throat, dribbling down her chin and staining her white blouse. Melanie laughed, caught hopelessly in the lusty moment. The fiesta was truly a time apart, with no past and no future.

Occasionally a strange language caught her ear. Once she stopped and asked an English-speaking tourist what it was.

"Euskara," the young woman told her. "It's the Basques' word for their own language."

"I don't recognize a word of it," Melanie said.

"No one does, except them," the woman said simply. "As far as anyone knows, the language has no relation to any other. It's a real mystery."

"Someone should solve it," Melanie mused.

The central plaza, which was surrounded by dozens of hotels and cafés, was so crowded that she was forced to let the throng carry her in its flow. She could see a bandstand in the center of the plaza where men in white shirts and loose white trousers were playing a frenzied tune on guitars, to the overpowering encouragement of the people. She tried to take a picture but it was impossible, for she was wedged in the crowd, shoulder to shoulder, trapped. Finally she managed to break free and, spun off to one side, wound up nearly in the laps of some people sitting around a table at an outdoor restaurant.

"Excuse me!" Melanie gasped, but they only laughed and offered her a glass of wine. Eventually she disengaged herself and sought a safe—if still crammed—hotel lobby.

There were definitely no rooms to be had. *"Nada, señorita.* Nothing."

"A telephone?" Melanie inquired.

He pointed to a quieter corner of the narrow lobby. *"Teléfono."*

Of course she had to wait even to use the telephone book, and then when she finally had it in her hands she was crushed to see the list of Echeverrias in the book. There were hundreds of them. It was like looking up a Smith in the New York directory without knowing a first name or an address.

Apprehension gnawed at her, but Melanie pushed her fears to the back of her mind. Cecily was out there somewhere. She knew it. And if she waited, if she sat in one of the cafés long enough, surely Cecily would eventually come by.

She began to look for an empty seat. Finding a table by herself was out. There obviously were no private tables to be had, but a group of Australian students who saw her casting about graciously asked her to join them.

"It's great, isn't it?" asked one girl whose features were distinctive and generous, her smile bubbling with life.

"It's breathtaking," Melanie agreed.

She bought the group a carafe of wine and ordered some food: cheeses and fruits and lamb tidbits in oil and garlic. The students were grateful and eyed her traveler's checks longingly.

"*You* must have a room here," one of the young men said.

Melanie shook her head. "All the money in the world couldn't buy a room this week."

"So sleep in the soccer field," he suggested. "We're going to."

It was a grim prospect, but Melanie was starting to think she might not have any choice.

"You all alone?" the girl asked.

"Sort of. My sister is here but I've lost her."

"No wonder," threw in a handsome towhead.

Melanie sat there for what seemed like hours. Dusk began to settle over the plateau of Pamplona, moving in from the mountains and resting lightly on the festive city.

Young boys, dressed in the ubiquitous white, stood on brawnier shoulders and lit the street lamps.

"At least it's cooling off," Melanie observed. "It's much more humid here than in Madrid."

Her eyes began to ache from scanning the ever-moving throng in the plaza for a possible sight of Cecily. The din grew louder—impossible, but it did—and the drinking more ferocious. In spite of the meal, Melanie was definitely feeling lightheaded from the strong wine. Finally she couldn't stomach another drop and managed to get herself a soda and lime. It didn't help the throbbing in her temples in the least.

No wonder Hemingway had such an earthy reputation, she thought, and no wonder he wrote so convincingly about physical excess. He used to do this for an entire week!

"You know," said the towhead, "you'll never find your sister in this. Not unless she's looking for you."

"Well..." Melanie said, disheartened, "I just have to keep trying, don't I?"

The music from the bandstand was almost obscured now by the ever-increasing clamor from the hordes of milling revelers. Melanie's head was pounding. It seemed to her as if some invisible hand had pushed everyone's self-destruct button. Wild!

Her sister was out there somewhere in that crazed throng, perhaps only a few feet away. But it was becoming painfully clear to Melanie that her chances of finding Cecily in this madness were scant.

She was never sure, afterward, exactly what it was that caught her eye, that prompted recognition. The familiar outline of cheek and hair? Or perhaps it was the carriage, relaxed yet ever aware. In any case, he was there, moving along with the flow, passing in front of the café, his head appearing once, then again, among the masses.

She knew only one thing: there was the man who was her link to Cecily.

Melanie jumped to her feet, ignoring the surprised faces of her young companions. "Bye," she cried, snatching up her purse and her camera. She looked frantically through the throng, standing on tiptoe. Where was he? She pushed into the eddying crowd. "Pardon me. *Perdóname*," she kept saying, shoving through the tightly packed bodies, tapping the shoulders of a dozen men until they turned and looked at her quizzically or expectantly. It was always the wrong man. Oh, no! She'd lost him.

Melanie moved on, pushing by the slow-moving, sated carousers, edging around the groups that were standing still, forcing her way past the lines of dancers and drinkers. On and on.

It was like a dream in which she was rushing and everything else was in slow motion.

Where had he gone?

"Vino!" came a booming voice in her ear, *"Trinken! Beber*. Drink!"

Melanie felt a hand on her arm and turned, startled. "Let go of me!" she cried. "Please!"

He only threw back his big head and laughed lustily, drunkenly clutching her sleeve.

An inexplicable, claustrophobic panic engulfed her. And then suddenly there was a hand on her other arm and she pulled away desperately. Music crashed in her ears; the odor of wine and sweaty bodies assailed her sickeningly.

"Let *go* of me!" She managed to yank herself free from one of her captors.

"Melanie..."

She spun around to gape at the man still gripping her other arm. "It's *you*," she gasped.

"Come on," he said tugging gently at her wrist, "let's get out of this crowd."

As he led her from the central plaza, she felt fresh moist air caressing her skin. She began to breathe normally again, no longer so intimidated by the crush.

She finally stopped and disengaged her arm from his hand. It felt, strangely, as if she'd severed herself from a lifeline.

"Professor Sanlucar," she said, "why are you here? How did you find me?"

"It's Teo," he stated evenly. "So many questions, Melanie."

"But why?" she pressed, searching his face.

Teo Sanlucar shrugged eloquently. "There is nothing mysterious. I always come to the Feria de Pamplona."

"Okay. Fine," she breathed, "let's say I believe you . . ." He regarded her closely. "Then do you mind explaining how you just happened to walk directly in front of me like that?"

His finely sculpted lips parted in a wide, amused smile. "Mere coincidence."

There was no doubt in her mind that he was lying. She looked at him keenly, noting the way he stood there, the easy relaxed set of his shoulders, the self-assurance of his bearing. He was a man totally in control, a man who could look her directly in the eye and lie through his teeth.

She backed away from him slightly. "You were following me."

He laughed and the deep masculine timbre sent shock waves through her limbs. "We Basques are always looking for a lovely woman, Melanie. I am only too human."

She felt hot waves of embarrassment washing up her neck. What was he doing to her? What kind of game was he playing? "That's . . . a lie," she shot back. "That has nothing to do with why you followed me."

The laughter left his dark eyes abruptly. "Think what you will. But might I be so bold as to suggest that you should appreciate a sincere compliment for what it is?"

European men certainly had a way of jumping right in. Their unsubtle flattery and straightforward propositions discomfited Melanie right down to her toes.

"I have said too much." Teo cocked his head slightly to one side. "You must forgive me. I will let you go on your way now. I have detained you long enough." He bowed, a mere nod of his head, but did not turn away to leave.

Sudden panic seized Melanie. "Wait," she whispered uncertainly. "Please, wait..."

She could see his dark raised brow and the thin, uncompromising set of his lips. It was all so ironic. She *couldn't* let him go. He was her link to Cecily and Carlos.

"Yes, Melanie?"

"I...well, couldn't I buy you a drink or something?"

"A drink, Melanie?"

Her reluctance to let him leave was painfully obvious. Humiliating. He probably figured she was trying to pick him up—the brazen *americana*. This was so awkward. Oh, why couldn't he make it easier for her? But then, Melanie suspected that he'd never intended to simply walk away.

"I really couldn't stand another drink," she admitted, breaking the silence. "Perhaps you would walk with me for a while?"

"Of course."

He took her arm gently—but possessively, she thought—and they walked the narrow, cobbled streets of Pamplona.

"What do you think of the Basque country?" Teo asked her.

"I haven't seen much. Just this...this..."

"Insanity?" he asked and she could hear the laughter in his voice. "The Basques play as hard as they work. We have a saying: 'To know how to live is to know enough.' Do you not think that is the best way?"

Melanie looked at him to see if he were teasing. "No, actually I prefer the golden mean prescribed by the ancient Greeks."

"A woman of her own mind."

"I hope so," she replied coolly.

"It has been said of us Basques that we are crusty individualists, hard and independent. But the truth is we only seek the leisure to enjoy ourselves," Teo said.

"Are you speaking for yourself?"

"Not entirely. You see, I am educated and my crust has worn smooth. My father tells me I have grown soft."

"Soft," Melanie repeated, recalling his lean brown body on the beach.

"He also says I must prove my manhood by having sons." And Teo smiled deliberately, tauntingly.

"Well, what's stopping you?" Melanie asked.

He shrugged, adroitly sidestepping a young man, who staggered into their path. "The small question of morality. I have no wife."

"That should be easy enough to remedy."

"Not as easy as you might imagine, Melanie." His voice was low and he bent his head so that she could hear him above the din. She wondered why he was saying these things to her. And all the while, as they walked through the crowded streets, she searched for a glimpse of Cecily.

He finally asked the question which had formed, unspoken, between them. "Where are you staying?"

She stopped and looked up into his eyes. "Well, I've got a purse full of traveler's checks but no one seems to want my money."

"I thought as much."

"Any suggestions?"

"Several. You could, naturally, sleep in your car."

"So I've been told."

"Thousands sleep in the soccer field."

She nodded wearily.

"Then there is a place . . . No. I would offend you by suggesting it."

"Try me, Teo."

"My uncle, Esteban, has a lovely home some ten kilometers from the city."

"I couldn't."

"You most certainly could. In fact, if I were to tell him I left an *amiga*, a lady, on the streets at night and alone . . ." He spread his hands in mock shame.

"I really . . ."

"Allow me to persuade you, Melanie."

"I simply can't impose on your uncle. Imagine how mortified I would feel if I let you take me there and dump me on his doorstep. . . ."

"I would be alongside you, Melanie. And my uncle is a very hospitable gentleman."

"And you?" she asked curiously. "Where will you stay?"

"At Esteban's, also. You see, my parents reside in Bilbao, close to the family business, and my sister lives with her husband up on the coast. And I myself, naturally, reside primarily in Madrid."

"You usually stay at your uncle's, then?"

"Always, when I am in the area." He studied her quietly for a moment. "You would, of course, have a room to yourself."

"Of course." Melanie looked away hastily.

"Then it is settled."

She suspected then that he had planned the whole thing—probably when she'd left his office in Madrid—but right now it didn't matter. He was absolutely correct. She'd be foolhardy to remain on the streets at night alone.

He'd said quite pointedly, a room of her own. Still, she hardly knew him . . .

Melanie searched his expressionless face for a moment. She decided that she could trust him not to lure her to this Esteban's house and then turn his hospitable offer into a sick little proposition. He considered himself too much of a gentleman, and he took his honor too seriously.

"Where is your car?" he asked.

"Out somewhere near the soccer field."

He smiled charmingly, "So you *had* thought of sleeping quarters."

"Sort of," Melanie admitted.

"We shall go get mine, then," he said, "and I'll drive you to yours and you can follow."

She was so exhausted that it sounded fine; at this point, she'd have settled for almost anything. And the next day she would be rested and could start the search for her sister all over again.

Teo Sanlucar. She ran his name through her mind. An enigmatic man. The link, Melanie still believed, to Cecily and her curious disappearance.

Melanie had been wondering whether to press him on the subject as they threaded their way toward the outlying streets. He had answers; she was sure of it. And yet he remained so politely closed, replying to whatever she said with very correct, one-line answers. "It is always hot during the *feria*." "Yes, the tourists come from many parts of Europe." And when she carefully, obliquely, mentioned her sister, he said only, "No, I have not had the pleasure of running into Cecily."

So smooth, so casual. Even the way he walked beside her, always allowing her to go first, his long-fingered hand at her back, on her elbow, was so—she searched her mind for the word—so intimate.

There was something nightmarish and yet alluring about the whole situation. This man inspired strangely contradictory emotions in her: she feared him, yet she was unac-

countably attracted to him. How could she feel unnerved by
his presence at the same moment as she felt warmed by the
touch of his hand?

Melanie followed the lights of Teo's car away from the
city. As they drove, fewer and fewer vehicles passed them.
It was pitch-black, and patches of fog hung in the gullies
and ravines along the winding road.

She had an impression of lush mountains on either side of
the roadway—old mountains that were softly contoured by
centuries of rain and wind. There were trees, gloomy, indistinct shapes, by the roadside. The unfamiliar landscape was
eerie in the darkness and Melanie was thankful to see Teo's
lights ahead of her. Strange, she reflected, going so quickly
from the crush of Pamplona to the dark, deserted mountains.

Who was this uncle, Esteban Sanlucar? Where exactly
was this lovely house of his? Was he acquainted with Carlos, too? Were they all somehow involved in Cecily's disappearance?

It was bewildering. Yet the facts stood clearly in Melanie's mind. Teo *had* been watching them on the beach, he
knew this Carlos and he had "coincidentally" run into
Melanie in Pamplona. He was watching her, all right, and
he was somehow linked to Cecily's peculiar behavior. But
was he merely Melanie's acquaintance and would-be protector, as he seemed to want her to believe, or was he there
to keep her from uncovering a secret?

He would say, "So many questions, Melanie," then smile
that infuriatingly charming smile of his.

Esteban's home turned out to be a large stone-and-stucco
structure roofed with red tile and built against a magnifi-
cent hillside. It was impressive looking even at night, with
its long, steep cobblestone drive ending at a circular lawn.
There were granite steps leading up to a small veranda and
the front door, which was guarded by a pair of stone lions.

Teo rapped on the door, then said to Melanie, "You will enjoy Esteban. He is very informal and well educated. His English is not quite as good as mine, but it is passable. He'll expect you not to stand on ceremony with him. Feel free to speak your mind."

"Oh, I will, I'm sure," she said.

Uncle Esteban was hardly the avuncular type. Only a few years Teo's senior—a late-life child, Melanie supposed—he epitomized European dignity and manners.

His silvering hair and finely chiseled features gave him a distinguished appearance. He stood an inch or so taller than Teo's six-foot height and was dressed in a studiously casual manner: a pale blue dress shirt rolled twice at the cuffs, loose-fitting gray summer slacks wrinkled in just the right way, expensive Italian sandals.

When he shook Melanie's hand she saw first the manicure, then the family gold-seal ring. *Impeccable* described Esteban, from his personal grooming to his tasteful, gracious home.

"Allow a *dama* to wander the streets at night?" he gasped at Teo's explanation, "*señorita*, chivalry is not yet dead."

"I'm sure this is a terrible imposition..." Melanie began.

"Nonsense. Come in, come in." He turned to Teo. "Lucia is in Pamplona, so be a good boy and carry the *señorita*'s belongings to the south room." Then he said to Melanie, "I call him my little nephew, but he is not so little, is he? You follow him upstairs and have a nice, long bath. A nap, if you wish. Then we shall have supper—" He stopped himself. "I am so sorry. I have, how do you say it? a mental block. I always forget that the *americanos* dine early and retire early. If you prefer," he added courteously, "you may retire for the night."

"Oh, no," Melanie said, "a bath would be perfect. But I'll certainly be down again. Supper sounds like a wonderful idea."

"*Muy bien*—very good. Now go along and do relax. The *feria* is most exhausting."

Teo ushered Melanie into her room and opened the French doors to the balcony, letting in the cool and refreshing night air. "If you have need of anything, there is a rope over there—" he nodded to the corner of the spacious guest room "—just pull it and a bell will ring in the kitchen."

"Thank you," Melanie said, but somehow she couldn't envision Teo or his gracious uncle rushing up the stairs with buckets of hot water or silver trays of food.

"I shall see you below, then." He left the room and disappeared down the long, dim hall.

I'm impressed, Melanie thought. Sure, her parents had money—new money—but Esteban exuded that special Old World wealth. And it was more than just money. The house itself was hundreds of years old and so were the elegant furnishings. As for his demeanor, it took centuries of breeding and tradition to produce a man like Esteban Sanlucar. Teo, too. Although Teo, she decided, lived in the twentieth century. Esteban, she suspected, was more traditional.

What had he said? "Chivalry is not dead."

She lazed in the blue-tiled bath adjoining her room for what seemed an indecent length of time but kept reassuring herself that here, things were done at a slower pace. Her hosts expected her to have a leisurely bath, so it would have been inappropriate to shower quickly and rush down the stairs.

She swept her hair into a neat chignon and fastened it with a silver clasp that had belonged to her grandmother. She wore the dress Cecily had so liked, the dress she'd worn to the restaurant that last evening in Torremolinos, the melon and rust crepe that displayed her back.

She wandered out onto the balcony off her bedroom and breathed the sweet scent of the misty night. Her headache was gone and she felt oddly relaxed. Reluctantly she walked back in and checked her camera—habit—put her purse in a bottom dresser drawer—also habit—then closed the bedroom door behind her.

Both men rose to greet her as Melanie entered the large living room that was decorated with tiles and rugs in muted earth tones. The furniture was modern and comfortable, blending well with the carefully chosen antiques scattered among sofas and chairs and polished tables.

"This is a beautiful room," Melanie said, glancing around her.

"Thank you," Esteban replied, taking her arm and showing her to an elegant couch, "I arranged it myself."

Melanie raised a brow. "You obviously have a flair for this kind of thing."

"Ah, yes. I enjoy it enormously. But sadly, I lack the time to refurbish the entire house. Always I am too busy."

"It's lovely like this," Melanie said with an honest smile.

"Can I get you a wine or a brandy?" Teo asked.

"A brandy, please."

Esteban seated himself beside her on the couch. "I very rarely go into town during the week of the *feria* any longer," he explained. "I find that it's an experience best savored by the young and, of course," he added with a light laugh, "your marvelous Hemingway."

"I was thinking that myself today."

"Ah, but you're still young enough..."

Teo brought the snifter and placed it on the table before Melanie. She could see that he had just showered, because his hair was damp and curling slightly above the collar of his fresh white shirt. He had shaved, too, she noticed, as she allowed the aroma of his shaving cream to drift into her senses.

"I'm terribly sorry to have to ask, Señor Sanlucar," Melanie said to Teo's uncle, "but I really must call my parents. They'll be worried. Of course, I'll charge the call to my credit card."

"You are welcome to use the telephone in my library. Teo, show her, please."

The library was small and cozy, obviously well used. A pile of papers sat on the desk next to an old-fashioned telephone. "Here you are. Take your time, Melanie," Teo said, "and here is your brandy. You forgot it." Then, discreetly, he left her there alone with the snifter in her hand. She could feel the satiny warmth of the glass where he had held it.

For a few moments she sat in the dim light, breathing deeply and trying to relax before she called her parents. Teo's and Esteban's voices drifted lazily toward her from the other room. Very distinguished, very male. Melanie again had the sensation she'd felt on the beach: that she'd become an actress in a drama she didn't understand. The lines were already written for her, but she didn't know how the story ended.

What had Teo told her in Madrid? He was her protector. She felt suddenly helpless, as if she'd lost control of the situation and was being led down blind alleys, one after the other.

The voices continued to float into the library, sometimes in simple conversation, sometimes lowered and hushed. Always in Basque. What were they saying?

Then, in her mind's eye, Melanie envisioned Teo, his finely chiseled face, those eyes, often warm and friendly, alluring yet sometimes unfathomable. What did Teo want of her; why had he invited her to his uncle's house? What was there about this man that attracted her yet at the same moment caused fear to lurch from the corners of her mind?

She shook off her uneasiness and looked at her watch. Eleven o'clock local time. That meant it would be late afternoon in Ohio. A good time to catch someone at home. While she waited for the call to go through, she sipped her brandy, grateful that Teo had remembered to bring it, and tried to translate the titles of the books on Esteban's shelves.

When the phone finally rang in her parents' home, it was Denise who answered—her mother's maid. "Denise? Is Mother or Dad there? What? Can you hear me now? Yes, I'm in Spain. Yes, still in Spain. No, I don't know. Denise, can you put Dad on? Thanks."

"Mel, what the hell is going on?"

"Dad, oh, it's good to hear you. Everyone okay?" She had to fight the impulse to blurt out the whole story. She had to bite her lip to hold it back.

"Sure, honey. Now your mother had a nice dinner planned, a few old friends, and you two didn't show up. And after the long flight back from Hong Kong, that wire almost prostrated her. What's up?"

"Dad, it's hard to explain. Cecily has this new boyfriend and he wanted her to see this special festival in Pamplona—that's where I am. And, well, it was all very sudden. You know Cecily."

"Where is that girl? I want to talk to her!"

"She's staying with a...a friend. She's not here right now."

"Where are you?"

"I'm with a...another friend of her boyfriend. Esteban Sanlucar. Spell it?" She spelled the name, gave the phone number. "That's where I'll be for a few days. He speaks English. No, Dad, I'm not sure—I'll call. Tell Mother not to plan any of her 'little' parties, okay?"

She hung up and swallowed hard. Then she downed a good stiff shot of the brandy. Lies, lies. She wondered abruptly if Teo had been listening. If he had, he must have been a bit surprised by her end of the conversation.

Returning to the living room was like entering a different world. From Cleveland to the Basque country, from her father's gruff, familiar Midwest twang to the cultured British English of Teo and Esteban.

"You reached them?" Teo asked.

"Yes, thank you."

"Good, good," Esteban said, beaming.

After that, they talked of everyday things—the role of King Carlos in Spain, worldwide inflation, finally her career as a free-lance photographer. Esteban spoke knowledgeably about photography and called it a form of artistry, which delighted Melanie. He made her promise to send him the layout of Ethiopia that she'd sold to *Life*.

Then they strolled into the dining room. Melanie was embarrassed to realize that Esteban had prepared a light supper for them while they'd bathed. He'd even set a handsome table, lit candles and turned on some soft classical music in the background.

"You've gone to so much trouble," Melanie said. "It's very kind of you."

"Ah," said Esteban as he helped Melanie into her chair, "I delight in playing the host. I enjoy cooking and, sadly, there are too few visitors with whom to share my meals."

Between the gazpacho and the salad, Teo caught Melanie's eye. "Would it be rude to explain your sudden visit to Pamplona to Esteban?"

Melanie shook her head but she suspected that Teo's uncle already knew.

"Melanie and her sister were scheduled to fly to the United States yesterday morning but Cecily—who was one of my students, Esteban—decided to change the plans—"

"What Teo means," Melanie broke in, "is that my sister has run off with a young Basque named Carlos Echeverria. And I'm afraid this Carlos is some sort of a crusader..."

"A crusader?" mused Esteban.

"Yes," Melanie clarified, "meaning that he's filled my sister's head full of horror stories—injustice, starving people, all the burdens of the world, Esteban. She kept talking about doing something worthwhile."

"It is merely youth speaking. Growing pains, my dear Melanie. Did we not have our own such worries in our early years?" He waved a hand in the air as if dismissing Melanie's fears.

"It was more than talk, Esteban," she added. "I'm certain Cecily has run off with this Carlos to plan something—"

"Plan something?" Teo interrupted.

"I don't know," Melanie admitted, almost saying *but I'll bet you do...*

"I think you should enjoy the *feria*," Teo said, "then, as I suggested in Madrid, fly home. Your sister will call you and all will be well."

Melanie sighed deeply. "I can't believe that everything is all right. I know my sister. I just wish I knew Carlos." She looked directly at Esteban. "Do you know Carlos Echeverria?"

Esteban's dark brows knitted together. It seemed to Melanie that he took too long to answer. "Perhaps. I cannot recall. There are so many Echeverrias in the Basque country."

"But Teo knows him," Melanie said, pinning Teo with a hard gaze. "Don't you?"

"You know that I do, Melanie."

"And are you acquainted with his family?"

For only an instant—or did she imagine it?—Teo's eyes met his uncle's in a meaningful glance. "I do not believe I know his family, Melanie."

They ate thinly sliced cold beef with béarnaise sauce and sautéed baby carrots, then for dessert, chilled raspberries. Melanie didn't mention the subject of Cecily's whereabouts again, as it was only too obvious that neither man was going to help her.

Why? she kept wondering. What did they know that was too secret or too dangerous to tell her? Or were the Sanlucars involved in Cecily's peculiar disappearance?

Somewhere a clock struck midnight. The candles burned low, and the dimming light veiled Esteban's and Teo's faces in flickering shadows. Outside the open French doors a fog rolled in, low to the earth, obscuring the mountainside. The room seemed moist and close. But as Melanie looked from one shadowed face to the other, she felt a singular chill.

Teo's eyes found hers and held them for a prolonged moment. She had the disquieting impression that he was reaching into her very soul, probing, willing her into submission. And yet he merely sat there, across the well-appointed table, the dim light dancing in those dark, worldly eyes.

She looked down at her hands but she could still feel his gaze on her, more poignant than a touch. Her heart pounded heavily and she tried in desperation to focus this strange, shadowed fear.

What were they hiding from her, these handsome distinguished men, these mysterious Basques?

Chapter Five

Melanie lay in the big, carved Spanish bed and felt sleep drain slowly and reluctantly from her body. Somewhere in the house a door opened and then closed. She rolled over and looked at her watch: six-thirty. Still early. Too early to do anything about Cecily.

Anxiety gnawed at her once more. Where was Cecily? How thoughtless and cruel of her to do this to her family! Or had she been taken somewhere against her will? Melanie rose and stretched, then padded across the big room to the French doors and opened them. Mist curled around the stone balustrade of the balcony. Low on the horizon, diffused sunlight attempted to penetrate the morning fog. As she watched, a bright spot of blue appeared and then widened into a patch of sunlit sky.

The humidity caressed her, causing her dark red hair to spring into curls. She stood there in her sheer nightgown and felt the cool moisture and watched the brilliant green hills emerge damply from the mist. It was the kind of place where fairy tales were born, where princesses were hidden and heroes came forth from fog-shrouded mountain paths, where dragons had their lairs and elves dug caves. Lovely and verdant and a little bit mysterious...

The sun was just striking her balcony, slanting through the treetops, touching the greenery with brightness. Melanie got her camera and checked the light meter. The haze would be hard to capture, but exquisite if she could manage it. She quickly took several pictures, aware that the light was already beginning to change and the enchantment would soon be lost. The blue hole in the sky was steadily enlarging. Then, suddenly, the mist was completely gone; day had arrived. The scene was no longer mythical, merely beautiful. Melanie turned back to her room.

Shaking off her whimsy, she began to get dressed. Something practical: white slacks, a cool cotton blouse in pale green. Today she would have to take some positive steps in the search for her sister. Teo seemed to want her to leave the whole problem of Cecily's disappearance alone. Why? Did he have something to hide? And why wouldn't he tell her everything he knew? Did he have some personal stake in this drama? Or was it merely his reticence that she misunderstood, mistrusted?

She pulled her hair into a ponytail and tied a green scarf around it, placed her camera in its case, hefted her big shoulder bag and stepped out into the hallway. It was very quiet; she suddenly felt a little uncertain. Like an intruder. She barely knew Teo. As for Esteban, he was a total stranger. Another dark-eyed Basque with the unmistakable stamp of the Sanlucar family on him. He and Teo could have been brothers.

The dining room was empty, but there was soft singing coming from the kitchen, an odd, plaintive song in a language that sounded totally alien to Melanie. Basque. She tentatively entered the enormous kitchen. At the far end, in front of the sink, was a woman, the singer. She was busy washing dishes, her song filling the room with a deep, mellow contralto.

"Perdóname," began Melanie. "Pardon me."

The woman turned. She smiled at Melanie. *"Buenos días, señorita."* Then there was a string of Spanish that Melanie could not follow. Eventually she learned that the woman's name was Lucia, the Señores Sanlucar were *afuera*—outside—and that *café* was ready if she wanted any.

She walked out onto the lawn and saw a patio off the dining room, to one side of the house. There it was quiet and secluded, shaded by locust trees so that dappled fairy light fell over the table and over the two dark-headed men who sat in deep conversation, their heads close together. As Melanie walked across the flagstoned patio, she heard them speaking the same odd language as Lucia's song. The same language she'd heard spoken, from time to time, at the *feria*. Basque. To her, it sounded like a series of clicks and *s*'s and *x*'s, as if the user were tapping his tongue on the roof of his mouth.

"Good morning," she said. They both looked up and glanced at each other in what seemed to her a private manner. Then Esteban Sanlucar's face split into a wide smile. He rose quickly and came to her.

"You have found us," he said. "Come, sit down. A lovely morning, is it not?"

"Yes, lovely." Melanie sat in the chair that Esteban held out for her.

"*Buenos días*, Melanie," Teo said softly. "Did you sleep well?"

"Yes, thank you," she replied.

"I wondered . . . I happened to step out onto my balcony this morning and saw you."

She looked down at the flagstones, placing her purse and her camera bag at her feet. "I was taking pictures." But she should have put on her robe first, she thought.

"It escapes me," he said, "the word for such a morning as this."

"Evocative," she said aloud.

"Perhaps. Or perhaps merely lovely."

Lucia came out of the kitchen then, coffeepot in hand. Esteban spoke to his maid in that same strange tongue.

"Teo, that's Basque, isn't it?" Melanie could not resist asking.

"Yes, my dear Melanie, that is our native language. An ancient tongue, unrelated to any other known language. It has baffled language buffs for hundreds of years, being like Hebrew in its pronouns and like some American Indian languages in its verbs."

"How odd."

"Yes, sometimes I think the archetypal Basque individualist concocted it thousands of years ago just to frustrate the modern philologists."

Esteban chuckled. "Is that what you teach your students?" he chided.

"Ah, no. I teach them that Basques are the core of the Iberian character, and that they are the best administrators in Spain and the most vigorous among Spaniards."

"Without prejudice," Melanie said, straight-faced despite her amusement.

"But of course," Teo said, his eyebrows raised mockingly.

He was charming when he wanted to be, Melanie thought. And so handsome in the golden morning light. The planes of his cheeks glistened a little from his morning shave. His eyes were so dark—almost black—that they reflected tiny points of light. Reflected much more than they revealed.

His smile was sincere, yet it held a certain tension. What was Teo Sanlucar hiding? And why, she asked herself, why? Why had he been in Torremolinos? Had he really been there to "protect" her, as he'd stated so enigmatically? And protect her from what?

But, somehow, she knew she'd get no answer if she asked.

Lucia was pouring hot, fragrant coffee into Melanie's cup, all the while chattering away in Basque.

"What would you like to eat, Lucia wishes to know," Esteban broke in. "She speaks Spanish, of course, but since you did not seem to understand her..." He shrugged.

"I'm terribly sorry. My French is better," Melanie said. "But please," she continued, smiling at Lucia, "tell her something simple—a roll, toast. I never eat much in the morning."

Lucia seemed to disapprove very strongly of light breakfasts. Even Melanie could translate her frown and admonishing finger.

"She repeats an old Basque saying: if the belly does not eat, the belly itself will fail," Teo explained. "And she goes on to tell us that you are much too skinny and therefore you will never have healthy babies." His expression was completely serious, though Melanie could have sworn there was a teasing hint of irony in his voice. "But never mind—Lucia has many old-fashioned ideas. I myself am a modern man. I expect you are eminently capable of bearing a dozen fine children. If you should want to." Then he did smile, an open, boyish grin that lit up his face.

Esteban rattled off something in Basque and they both chuckled. "How rude of us," Teo said, "not including you in on our private jokes. But, you realize, Basque is an odd language, impossible to translate. Its meanings are inherent in innuendo and oblique references. What my uncle just said was, literally, 'a fine wine can come in a dusty bottle' but I assure you we do not equate you with a dusty bottle."

"I would prefer to discuss my sister, if you don't mind," Melanie said brusquely. "I really do appreciate your hospitality, but I'm terribly worried. I'd like to go into Pamplona this morning for the running of the bulls. I understand it's an important event and I thought... Well, if, as you said, Carlos is such an avid fan of the *feria*, perhaps they'll be there."

Teo was silent for a moment. "It *is* quite a spectacle, but the crowds are terrible, worse than yesterday. I doubt you'd ever be able to find your sister."

"I must try. I have to do something. At least it's a starting point." She was aware, again, of the two men exchanging glances. "If you'll just give me directions back to Pamplona. It was dark last night—"

"I couldn't possibly allow you to go alone," Teo said curtly.

"I don't need a baby-sitter, Teo. I'm sure I can manage on my own."

Esteban asked something in Basque. Teo answered quickly. Esteban laughed. "Baby-sitter," he repeated. "I was not familiar with the word. But, Teo, you must accompany Señorita Royce. I could not permit her to wander around with those *locos*, those crazies, all by herself. The Fiesta de San Fermín is, how shall I say, *feroz*, wild."

"I lived through a bombing in Beirut and famine in Ethiopia, Señor Sanlucar. I doubt if Pamplona can touch me," Melanie said quietly.

"Nevertheless, I offer my services," said Teo, raising a hand to forestall her objections. "I insist. Although I pray that we run into nothing more than a few drunken revelers," he said with a thin smile. "I am too much the coward to face war and famine. I admire your courage greatly, Melanie."

He was deliberately baiting her. She was sure of it. Not to mention the fact that he was being patronizing. And thoroughly aggravating. Melanie closed her mouth tightly and felt the hot color rise to her cheeks. She finished her coffee and nibbled on the roll Lucia had brought her. Esteban excused himself. Teo remained seated, elbows on the arms of his chair, hands folded, his dark eyes fixed on her. Eventually he said, "I apologize. That was unnecessary. But you had just insulted my role as your host. Basque men are notoriously touchy, you know.''

''I didn't know.''

''Come, let us not quarrel. You are worried about your sister. I am worried about you. We have something in common.''

''You're worried about me? That's ridiculous. Look, you wouldn't be my host if I hadn't practically thrown myself on you. I mean, you were forced to take me in. So there's no reason for you to worry about me and my problems, is there?''

''One is never forced to offer hospitality to a damsel in distress. It comes naturally.'' He was teasing again.

Melanie stood. ''I'm going to Pamplona now. I appreciate your kindness. I'll try to find a hotel room today.''

He still sat there, his chin resting on his clasped hands. ''You'll find no room in Pamplona this week, Melanie. And I *am* going with you.''

Melanie did not like this feeling that Teo was manipulating her. She stood there weighing his offer—no, she thought, he'd issued a directive. On the one hand, her emotional response was to walk out on him, away from this lovely hidden home, to strike out once again on her own. On the other hand, she could view her predicament as an opportunity in several ways. He was providing lodging where there was none. He *did* know this Basque country, whereas she was a stranger. And he was somehow linked to Cecily's disappearance; Melanie would wager plenty on that.

She made an effort to give in gracefully. ''I would be a fool to say no to such a kind offer,'' she said smoothly. ''Shall we go?''

He nodded; one dark brow was raised very slightly.

Teo drove them in his white Mercedes convertible. He skillfully negotiated the winding, twisting roads through the hills to Pamplona, and Melanie found herself relaxing, asking a dozen questions out of sheer curiosity.

"Your uncle. Is he married?"

"No," Teo said, laughing. "He is far too fond of his life of luxury. Women adore him. He is a lawyer, you know, the legal counsel for my family's business in Bilbao. He travels between my parents' apartment there and his country home."

"What is your family's business?"

"Parts for ships. Heavy machinery. I am the black sheep of the family, scorning the exciting world of business for the ivory tower of academe."

"The Basques. Haven't I read about problems here? Unrest. I'm not sure . . ."

"Ah, yes, the eternal problem. The first thing you must know is that a Basque does not see himself as a Spaniard. We are a different race, if you will. Other Basques live across the border in the French Pyrenees. We consider it an insult to lump us in with the Spanish." He glanced at Melanie, noticing her intent expression. "The Basques are a stiff-necked and stubborn people. They want autonomy from the government in Madrid. Frankly, I try to stay out of politics. From time to time, however, there is violence. It all stems from the Civil War back in '36 when the Basques fought against Franco. They lost and were punished. It is said a Basque never forgets and perhaps that is correct. But things are improving these days. Shall we not speak of something more interesting?"

"The running of the bulls. Tell me about it."

"An ancient custom dating from 1591. The fiesta is actually a religious festival honoring San Fermín, the patron saint of Pamplona, who was a martyr. Nowhere in the world will you see quite the same spectacle. One main street is barricaded off down its entire length, from pens at the edge of town to the bullring. The six bulls who will fight in the

afternoon's *corrida* are run from their corrals to the bullring, accompanied by steers to keep them calm. The men
who wish to run in front of them must arrive on the scene
very early—"

"Have you ever done it?" Melanie interrupted.

"When I was young. Many times. Now there are so many
tourists that come for the thrill—one hundred thousand,
they say—that very few Spanish, I think, are included in the
running anymore. The men run in front of the bulls along
the street. When they reach the bullring, the *toros* are put
into pens, but then the fun begins. Young heifers that are
brought into the arena at night are set loose in the ring. They
are not so terribly dangerous because their horns are padded, but they are in a fine panic with the noise and the
crowds."

"I don't really understand why anyone would do it,"
Melanie said pensively. "It's dangerous, isn't it?"

He shrugged eloquently, his eyes never leaving the unpredictable curves. "Sometimes. The bull will only attack
you if he is forced to. He is frightened himself. You see that
scar?" He held up his forearm, and Melanie saw the ropy
white line running from elbow to wrist.

"A bull did that?" she breathed.

"Yes. I was careless once. But it was merely a scratch. I
was lucky."

"Lucky."

"Last year some were killed, many were hurt. Bruises and
broken bones and so on. It only makes more come the following year. To test themselves."

"Crazy."

"Yes, I agree. But there is an attraction that has *fuerza*,
force. You will see."

Just then, as they rounded a curve, they came upon a
shepherd with his flock of sheep milling right in the middle

of the road. Teo jammed on his brakes, automatically putting out an arm to keep Melanie from lurching forward.

"Good Lord!" Melanie gasped.

"Sorry," Teo said. "A frequent hazard on these back roads."

He withdrew his arm, but she could still feel its phantom touch across her chest.

She glanced at his profile as he drove. A strong nose, the beautifully modeled curve of his lips, a firm jawline. And those lovely slim brown hands on the steering wheel. Hands that could belong to an artist, a lover... She stopped her thoughts abruptly and snapped her attention back to the winding road.

It was becoming hot as Teo drove through the outskirts of Pamplona, a depressing area of ugly factories and dirty smoke stacks. It seemed hard to believe that a valiant and exciting tradition took place in such a grimy, nondescript town. Then suddenly they were in the old city, among the narrow cobbled streets, overhanging balconies and dim, smoky cafés she remembered from the day before.

Teo certainly knew his way around. The previous afternoon, Melanie had not had any choice but to leave her car on the outskirts of Pamplona. Now she watched amazed as Teo simply darted down an alley close to the central plaza, pulled his Mercedes into a tiny opening between some trash cans and turned off the key.

"Will your car be safe here?" she couldn't help asking.

"Safer here than on a street."

They walked down the dank alley and out onto a street. Someone immediately bumped into her.

"*Vino?*" slurred a freckle-faced, obviously American young man.

"A little early, isn't it?" Melanie said dryly.

"Hey, an American! Hey, honey, come on, let's go watch the bulls! Hey, wait up, Johnny!" And he ran off, following his friend.

"You see?" Teo came to her side. "They've all got their noses bent with wine, as the Basques would say. You *do* need my protection."

"From the likes of him?" Melanie smiled. "He was ready to pass out. He only needed a little push."

"Come, then—it will start soon. We must find a place to watch. Luckily I know someone who has a balcony right over the street where the bulls run."

They pushed their way through the crowds, Melanie clutching her camera while Teo ran interference. Actually she was glad of his presence. She'd thought it crowded the day before, but as Teo had warned, it didn't compare to this, the first official day of the *feria* and the running of the bulls. All the shoving, cheering, howling young people were crammed in one area, everyone vying for a spot from which to view the spectacle. Young people from every nation on earth had gathered here, all with their bota bags and rucksacks, all looking for adventure, excitement, memories. And Melanie automatically searched every sunburned, sweating face, in case it was Cecily's.

The noise was mindless, the heat and press of the crowd relentless. Melanie wanted to take some pictures, but like the day before in the plaza, she couldn't even raise her arms.

"Are you all right?" Teo shouted once. She could only smile and nod, holding on to his hand for dear life, trudging along behind him. Finally he pulled her into a doorway and the crowd surged by them in all its elemental energy, like a river in flood leaving behind a couple of sticks.

"Wow!" Melanie said.

"Do you see what Esteban and I meant?"

"Do I ever! Yesterday was calm compared to this."

"Come, you must meet Jaime, then we will go up to his balcony."

They were in a long narrow bar. One wall was lined with bottles; a few empty tables were scattered along the other. Jaime came out of the dimness and greeted Teo effusively, in Basque. They spoke for a time, then he turned to Melanie. "*Señorita, bienvenido*, welcome." He shook her hand, grinning, the sweat oily on his dark face. "You unnerstan'?"

"Yes, *sí, gracias.*" She nodded and smiled. "Thank you."

"*Que bonita,*" Jaime said in an aside to Teo.

She understood that much. "Pretty," he'd called her. Did all Spanish—or Basque—men need to comment on a woman's looks?

Teo led her to the back of the long room, to a flight of rickety steps. She looked at him questioningly. He nodded. Upstairs was obviously Jaime's living room, very neat and formal, with doilies on every chair and a crucifix on one wall. The room was heavily curtained, dim and cool. A muted roar filled the air—the crowd outside—then came a cannon blast.

"Quick, they're starting." The bellow rose, reaching a crescendo, a communal howling, a fever pitch of joy and excitement. Teo pushed aside the curtains and opened the doors onto a narrow balcony.

The hot air hit Melanie's face like a blow. The noise pounded in her ears. The crowd clustered along the high wooden barricades that lined the street below. People spilled off balconies and rooftops, hung onto signs, crouched on posts, clung by fingers to walls. Everywhere there were bodies wedged together, screaming, mouths open, faces alight, tense with expectation.

Her camera! Quickly Melanie pulled it out, checked the light meter, focused. There! That dark, slim man with his mouth open. Over there! A threesome, perched like birds on the top of the barricade, handing their bota bag around, their faces red with sunburn, their throats working to swallow the stream of wine.

Then the roar escalated. It didn't seem possible, but still the clamor swelled and throbbed and beat at the air. Faces turned. Melanie thought she felt the floor tremble, vibrate. Then, from the head of the long street they came—the men, the runners, all of them dressed in white with red sashes and red kerchiefs. They ran, jammed together in the narrow, walled-off street, panting, sweating. Hundreds of them, looking over their shoulders to see how close the bulls were.

They ran as the crowd shrieked its pleasure, its fear, its adoration. They fled their deadly enemy, their lover, their best friend, the bull. They ran because they had to feel it, once in their lives at least, to face real, pulsating, snorting physical danger, to prove themselves. And they ran because there were a hundred men—five hundred—behind them, panting, grunting, scrambling, shot through with the same terror and frenzy and thrill.

They were past in a rush of white and red and flying feet. Then the bulls: huge black and brown backs, heaving, shining with sweat, flashing slim legs and ugly hooked horns with tips honed to wicked points. Thrusting, tossing heads on thick muscular necks, the staccato of galloping feet, the smell of animal flesh and hot angry bull breath, the glint of a wicked red eye.

They were gone in a whirlwind of dust and sweat smell and the receding thunder of their passing. Melanie found herself taking a deep breath; she was sure she had not breathed while they were below her. But she had taken pictures, dozens of pictures. She let her camera hang on its strap and felt her hands tremble in reaction.

Now she knew what they were talking about. Now she knew why men came from all over for this insanity, why they gathered and drank and danced and caroused and donned their pure white and their crimson sashes, why they ran before the bulls.

"You see?" Teo was whispering in her ear and the touch of his warm breath on her hair made her shudder with a thrill of exquisite delight. Something about the raw force of the spectacle she'd just seen made Melanie acutely sensitive to sensation. Her belly flip-flopped and the hairs on her neck rose at Teo's closeness. She was suddenly aware that his hand rested lightly on her waist, and she moved uneasily away, trying to put some distance between them.

"Now we must go to the bullring and watch the fun," Teo was saying, his voice intimate and disturbing in her ear, "for there must be a release after all that intensity."

Everyone was going to the bullring. Teo and Melanie were swept along with the crowd, more and more tightly packed together, until they burst through the entranceway and found seats in the huge circular amphitheater. The sun was higher, burning in a pellucid Spanish sky, reflecting off the bright red barrier wall that encircled the floor of the arena. Red, Melanie wondered, to distract the bull? But the bulls were gone now, replaced by several small heifers with padded horns. The men were there, dirtier and sweatier now, grinning broadly. They ran and dodged the cows and jumped out of the way while the crowd screamed its approval.

"What are they doing that for?" Melanie asked.

"To let everyone get a chance at the game, I suppose. An opportunity to prove one's valor without the danger of serious harm. Comic relief, I guess one might say."

"They're not the same as the steers that ran with the bulls, are they?"

"No, these are young cows, *novillas*. Actually they're more excitable than steers."

"And where did they come from?" Melanie asked.

"They keep them in a pen at night. See, over there?" He pointed to a slatted gate across the arena. "They are removed in the afternoon, of course, before the bullfight. It would make them too nervous, you see."

Melanie scanned the crowd through her lens, taking pictures. And looking for Cecily's face. There were so many young girls—thousands, tens of thousands. It seemed hopeless, but still she searched.

"Enough?" asked Teo finally.

"Yes," Melanie said with a laugh, "I've had enough. And you say this goes on every day?"

"Every day this week."

"I'm not sure I could handle it again." She rose and followed him from the stands.

They walked back through the emptied streets, shaded by the graceful old buildings.

"If you are really determined to experience local color you must stay for the *corrida* this afternoon."

"The bullfight?"

"Yes, I believe there are some good men today."

"I couldn't presume upon you . . ."

"But Esteban made me promise, you recall. You are my guest."

"I would love to see one. Is it terribly gory?" She shuddered a little.

"I will not lie. Yes, gory and brave and wonderful and sad."

"I suppose I should. And perhaps Cecily . . ."

"Perhaps . . ."

She had run out of film by the time they stopped for a cool drink in one of the cafés on the central plaza. The place was called the Iruña, Teo told her. The same café where Hemingway had sat and drunk absinthe. As she expected, every seat was filled and they shared a table with a young

German couple who sat entwined, totally immersed in each other. They made Melanie unaccountably nervous.

Teo was attentive, a perfect gentleman. She wondered if she were wrong to distrust him so intensely; she even admitted to herself that she'd needed him to get around this crazy, crowded carnival. And yet...there remained that tension about him, something beneath the surface, secretive and shadowed. His eyes were always on her, studying, watching. She felt the power of his maleness, the attraction of his self-containment, the lure of his dark beauty.

And then her worry would surface again, and she would see him only as a means of searching for Cecily.

"We'll get some film after we relax a minute. You Americans..." He smiled and took her hand in his. "You must learn to relax."

Relax! Every muscle in her body snapped taut, every nerve tingled. She wanted to snatch her hand away but couldn't.

"Let's go get my film," she suggested quickly, "before I forget."

"If you insist," he said.

It was better to be moving, to be doing something. She took an inordinately long time to choose her film, even though she knew exactly what she wanted. Then she looked over the souvenirs and chose some postcards. Teo stood by patiently, his arms folded, his expression blank. She wondered if he were bored but she didn't care—he'd asked for guard duty, hadn't he?

Later in the afternoon Teo took her to Los Tres Reyes for a meal. It was an elegant place specializing in Basque seafood dishes—fish and shellfish cooked in garlic and spices and oil. Strong, heady fare accompanied by harsh red wine and fresh crusty bread. Hungry and exhausted, she ate ravenously.

Teo watched her, apparently enjoying her pleasure. "Lucia would be proud of you."

"So would my mother. Oh, I do feel better, though." It was cool in the restaurant; the service was excellent and unobtrusive. "And please, let me pay for this meal. I'm accepting your hospitality, after all; please let me do this in return."

He waved a hand in dismissal. "There will be no bill. A cousin of mine owns this restaurant. Otherwise, believe me, I would allow you to." He grinned, an eyebrow tilting rakishly. "It costs a small fortune."

MELANIE'S FIRST LOOK at a matador in all his gilded glory dashed her false notions of a bloodthirsty, arrogant Spaniard who fought only for the notoriety.

He stood in the center of the ring, proud and composed, bowing to the crowd. He was dressed in his *traje de luces*, the traditional "suit of lights." She focused her lens on him and saw his dark eyes and was amazed at the sad tranquillity emanating from them.

"Is he afraid?" she asked Teo.

"Of course, but his fear is mingled with compassion. For the bull, as huge and terrifying as he seems, is also afraid. The matador has great love and respect for his adversary."

"Beauty and the beast," Melanie murmured to herself.

The actual bullfight was a carefully orchestrated dance. An undeniable power and excitement clung to every movement of matador and bull. The sadness was there—and the splendor. The mass of humanity jammed in the bullring cheered, roaring their pleasure and their love for the man and the bull, glorying in the courage and the death.

It was cruel, yes, Melanie thought, but there was also something splendid about it, appealing to some primitive human need to sacrifice the most beautiful and the best.

There were three bulls, Teo told her, one to each magnificently arrayed matador; this was followed by a break, then three more bulls. Melanie was surprised; she'd always thought a bullfight consisted of one man and one bull.

Teo pointed out the matador's moves; the crowd sighed and groaned and shouted "Olé" with each close sweep of the deadly horns, so she knew how often the bright, graceful figure was in danger.

"Are you enjoying yourself?" he asked her after the first bull, bending close so that she could hear him.

She turned toward him and saw his eyes fastened on her face. Just then the crowd roared its bold praise; the sound held Melanie breathless and rocked her. Deep in Teo's dark, sober gaze she sensed a question, a question that lured her, enthralled her. The hot Spanish sun beat on her head as she swayed in the fathomless ocean of sound. His eyes, his deep compelling voice. The scent of dust and red wine and sweat.

Answer. She must answer. Tearing her eyes from his, she said, inanely, "Oh, yes. Exciting, isn't it?" and felt her heart begin to beat again, heavy and turgid in her breast.

The second bull thundered into the ring, leaving his hoofprints in the pale sand. He stood there, full of power, his big head swinging around, searching. Again Melanie thought: how could a puny man face *that*?

Teo told her about watching the bull, not the horse, when the bull charged the picador. He told her what to watch for as the picador thrust his lance, placing it with accuracy and precision. She began to understand the ritualized actions. He explained it all to her so that the thing became less a show with random, incomprehensible horrors and more a planned series of events leading to a definite end.

She began to see how a good matador controlled the bull smoothly, effortlessly, and how the bulls differed in temperament, some difficult, some easy. She realized that there was a purity of line to the good matadors' movements, with no wasted motion, no needless gesture.

The fourth bull was the best. He was fierce and ugly, a piebald color, mottled black and white. He had courage and pride and Melanie could see that the matador loved him, even spoke to him quietly, intimately, like a lover.

The bull charged and crooked his horns again and again, never tiring. He was a noble creature. Every move he made was perfect. The crowd screamed its appreciation, adoring the man, the bull, the pair of them.

"Ah," Teo said, "this one is special. A Murcia bull. The best."

The matador's short cape swirled, drawing the piebald bull into its power. The crowd screamed at a particularly close miss. The matador deliberately turned his back on the bull and strutted away, but the bull merely waited, like a gentleman, for his opponent to turn once more.

The duel began anew.

The time for the killing came. The matador had his sword hidden in his cape, ready to plunge it deep into the animal's thick neck. The bull pawed the ground, undaunted. The crowd shrieked as one voice, splitting the air, torn between their reverence for the bull and their admiration for the man. Melanie had never heard anything like it.

The matador walked to the center of the ring and raised his sword, asking the crowd. They screamed in answer, the stands vibrating to the volume. "I don't believe it," Teo breathed. "They will save this bull. He is too noble to die. I have not seen this—ever."

"You mean the matador won't kill this bull?"

"The crowd requires his life," Teo said, shaking his head in amazement.

And this time, instead of being dragged out a carcass, the bull trotted out proudly, his head high, his ropelike tail flicking.

Melanie was utterly drained as they left the *corrida*, carried along by the thousands who poured out of the bullring as water drains when a plug is pulled.

Still she scanned the faces, always watching for Cecily. She wanted to ask Teo, to demand the truth that she was positive he knew, but she was somehow afraid. They rounded the corner into the central plaza. People were taking up their café seats again, to sip a late-afternoon aperitif, to discuss their astonishment at the unexpected outcome of the *corrida*, and to watch the teeming hordes of humanity, a show in itself. Then, much later, they would dine in the warm darkness, drink too much wine, begin the party all over again. And in the morning there was the running of the bulls once more.... An endless cycle of pleasure and thrill and the primitive purging of emotion.

Melanie's head snapped up. Her hand instinctively touched Teo's arm; immediately he halted. "There!" she cried. "Do you see her?" She strained to see through the crowd. Yes! It was Cecily's dark red hair.

"What is it?" Teo asked.

"Cecily!" And she left him, running, pushing past people, her camera bag and purse flapping and banging against her side.

"Cecily!" she cried, following the apparition, but it was like moving underwater, slowed down and horribly frustrating. She thought the auburn head turned once; there was a flash of her sister's profile. But then it was gone, swallowed up in the enormous maw of the crowd.

She stopped finally, panting and drenched in sweat. A group of young people, arms linked, singing and dancing some silly dance of their own, jostled her as they came by.

She felt foolish, bereft, near tears. A sense of futility washed over her.

And then Teo was at her side, his hand on her arm.

"Oh, Teo, it was Cecily! But I lost her. How am I ever going to find her? What's going on?" Her voice was strained and desperate.

He said nothing but gently pushed her loosened hair back from her face. After a while, he spoke, his voice low and soft. "Come, Melanie, you need to rest a bit. This whole thing has been too much for you."

He led her to a café. Miraculously, there was a table and instantly a glass was set before her.

"Try some. It's Izarra, a Basque drink," he said. "Made from mountain flowers."

She wanted to put her head down on the table and cry, but her pride stopped her. Instead she swallowed some of the Izarra; it tasted strong, not at all like flowers, but it slid easily down her throat. Soon a warm glow tingled in her stomach.

"I'll take you home," Teo said.

"Then you won't help me find my sister."

"I can't, Melanie. Truly I can't. I don't know where she is."

"Do you believe I saw her just now?"

He shrugged. "Perhaps you did."

"Why would she run off like that? She knows I'd worry."

"Love—or passion—sometimes twists a person's mind," he suggested.

"You mean Carlos? But still, she could have told me. There's something terribly wrong, I know it."

"There's no more you can do tonight, Melanie. Perhaps tomorrow..."

"I'm going to keep looking," she said fiercely. "Everyone seems to want me to leave it alone, but I won't! I'll find her!"

Teo said nothing, but gave her an odd, worried look. Did he think she was insane to be so stubborn? Maybe she was. Maybe Cecily was only enjoying herself, stealing a moment of pleasure in the turbulent thrill of the *feria*.

The evening shadows grew weak and thin across the plaza. Lights winked on. Once again, young boys stood on the toughened shoulders of older men and lighted the street lamps. People staggered by, arm in arm, laughing, dancing. And always, everywhere, bota bags were upraised, squirting the warm red wine down a thousand parched throats. Somewhere a flute played, a winsome trilling from the shadows.

"*Hola*, Teo," she heard a man say.

"Sevé." Teo nodded at a short, burly man who stood by the table. He wore the white and red of the bull runners, a black beret on his head.

She expected Teo to introduce her, but he didn't; she might not have been there at all. The men spoke Basque. There was a kind of intensity about the narrow-eyed stranger that made Melanie sit up straight. He spoke quickly, quietly, with an urgency that seemed out of keeping with the festivities surrounding them.

Teo answered coolly, his eyes hard and brilliant, and the man seemed to become argumentative. Once, Melanie was sure she heard the name Carlos.

The barrel-chested man—this Sevé—said something staccato and final—a curse?—and disappeared back into the mob as suddenly as he'd appeared.

"Who was that?" Melanie asked.

"An acquaintance."

"He knows something about my sister," she said quietly.

Teo looked at her sharply. "Why would you say that?"

"I heard the name Carlos. Look, Teo, I'm not stupid. There's something dangerous going on—I can *feel* it—and I'm afraid. Where's my sister?"

His inscrutable gaze held hers for a tense moment, then fell away. A muscle ticked in his smooth-shaven cheek. "As God is my witness, Melanie, I would tell you if I could."

Chapter Six

Wednesday, July 7

Melanie drifted slowly out of a deep sleep to the insistent noise of someone knocking at her door.

"Just a minute," she called groggily.

It was barely dawn and the room was still dark as she pulled on a loose kimono and went to the door.

"Excuse the intrusion, Melanie," said Estaban, who was also clad in a robe. "There is an overseas telephone call for you. Your father."

He'd switched on the hall lights and she could see his sleep-tousled hair and his eyes, heavy lidded and solemn looking.

"My father?" she repeated, following him down the long corridor.

"I took the call in my bedroom," he explained, "but you may use the telephone in the library."

She hastened down the long staircase, her bare feet sticky on the cold, polished floor.

Why would her father be calling? He knew it was early morning in Spain. A terrible apprehension gripped her.

She located the telephone and picked up the receiver. "Dad? It's Melanie."

The line crackled. "Melanie—" his voice emerged as if from a tunnel "—something dreadful has happened. I hope this is a joke..."

The apprehension bloomed into full-blown fear and she sank weakly onto the leather couch. "What's happened? Is it Mother?"

"No, it's about a call I had from Spain a few minutes ago. It was a man and he said... Hell, Melanie, he said your sister is being held... He wants me to wire half a million dollars to Pamplona!"

"Oh, my Lord," Melanie breathed. "Oh, no!"

"Is this some sort of sick joke?"

She tried desperately to collect her thoughts. "A joke? No. I don't... think so, Dad."

"How in hell... I can't..."

"Let me think, please, Dad." She was faintly aware of Esteban and Teo entering the room, switching on lamps. And then Teo walked over and sat on the edge of the couch, close beside her. "Dad," she managed, "what else did this man say?"

"He had me write down instructions and told me if I called the police, Cecily... Dear God in Heaven, he threatened to kill her!"

A great sob welled up in Melanie's chest. Teo must have seen her reaction because he put a gentle hand on her shoulder.

"Melanie?" her father said. "The man also knew *you* were there."

"How..." she began but then she knew. Carlos must have seen her in the plaza yesterday when she had tried to follow Cecily.

"Are you sure this isn't some crazy prank? I mean..."

"It's no prank." She paused. "What in heaven's name are we going to do?"

There was silence on the hissing line for a minute. "I'm going to pay it," he said gravely, his voice tense with fear. "I have to."

"Dad, I need to think."

"There's no time. Listen, I'll wire the money to this bank in Pamplona. You'd better get a pencil . . ."

Melanie took a deep, quavering breath and looked over at Teo. "Can you get me a pencil and paper?"

He rose swiftly to his feet and walked to the desk, opening a drawer, taking out a notepad and pen. Somewhere in Melanie's mind, she registered that Teo was half dressed, wearing only a pair of white slacks—no shirt. She had an impression of his broad, naked back, of the muscles across his shoulders. "Here," he said quietly, handing her the items.

Melanie wrote down the name of the bank and the location of a telephone booth in Pamplona where she was to be at 5:00 P.M. on Friday evening, July 9. Unconsciously, she underlined the date over and over while her father talked.

"The man expects you to have the money when he calls you at that phone booth," he explained. "It's only two days, Melanie. I'm going to have a hell of a time . . ."

"Can you get that much money, Dad?"

"Yes. But it'll be hard."

"My Lord," Melanie whispered. "I'm so sorry."

"Your mother and I are terribly worried about you, too, honey. You've got to do *exactly* what this man tells you. I'd fly over immediately to help you, Mel, but I can't leave your mother alone like this and she couldn't collect that much money without my help, anyway. I'm stuck here."

"I understand. Is Mother all right?"

"Neither of us is all right," he replied in a strained voice. "I'm dreadfully worried and I'm sorry you have to be the one to face this . . ."

"I'll be okay," she said miserably, feeling alone and far from home as the fear tightened in her stomach.

"You just make darn good and sure you're careful, Mel. This Esteban—is he trustworthy? How well do you know him?" Her father's voice was taut with worry.

Oh, how she wanted to blurt the whole thing out, her fear, her suspicions, the awful spot she was in. But she couldn't; she knew Esteban and Teo were listening. Cecily's life depended on her.

"He's fine, Dad. Yes, very trustworthy. I'm in good hands."

"And let me tell you something else. If there's even a *hint* that this isn't going as planned, I'll call Interpol and the CIA and King Juan Carlos, if I have to!"

"It'll work out, I know it, Dad. Just don't do anything yet, until I have the money," she said hastily. "I can handle everything at this end."

"That's our girl. And, Melanie, I'll keep you informed about the money transfer."

"Okay."

"I wish I was there with you."

"I know."

"Just keep your head, and for the love of God, honey, don't do anything foolish."

"I won't."

"And remember it's only money. We'll all pray for Cecily."

"Yes...pray."

"Goodbye, Melanie. I'll be in touch as soon as I've arranged the transfer."

"Goodbye, Dad. Tell Mother everything is going to be all right. And...I love you both."

When she'd hung up, Melanie sat for a long while, holding back tears and staring blindly into the distance. How had Cecily got herself involved with this...this kidnapper? Oh, there was no doubt that Carlos was involved in the kidnapping; he might even have been the caller. Her stupid, *stupid* sister!

A painful sob escaped Melanie's throat and then the tears came. She finally hid her face in her hands and cried miserably, without restraint. She was vaguely aware that Teo and Esteban were trying to comfort her, but she could barely understand what they were saying.

"I was afraid of something..." Teo said before his words trailed away.

"My dear, sweet woman." Esteban placed a warm hand on her other shoulder.

She suddenly wanted to scream. They were both too close, touching her, crowding her, offering her words of comfort. How dared they!

Feeling claustrophobic, Melanie jumped to her feet. "I'm all right," she said quickly. "Please...I'm all right." She paced the library floor, back and forth, back and forth. The room was silent except for the ticking of the clock and the muffled sound of Melanie's footsteps; no one spoke.

Melanie stopped pacing suddenly and turned, looking carefully from Esteban to Teo. On their faces she saw lines of deep concern, but neither of the men seemed truly surprised.

What had Teo said a few minutes earlier? "I was afraid of something..." She stared at him.

Eventually they moved to the kitchen, while Esteban brewed a pot of coffee. Melanie was calmer but still unable to focus her thoughts. What a mess Cecily had created! And now, all Melanie had was a scribbled note with a time and a place to receive a telephone call and her father's assurance that he would have the money at the Banco de Navarra as fast as possible.

What if he didn't?

But Melanie would face that grim prospect if and when it happened.

She looked up from her place at the polished table. Teo was speaking to his uncle in a low voice while taking coffee cups down from a cupboard. It struck her again and again:

they weren't in the least bit surprised by the news of Cecily's kidnapping. They'd known...

She studied the men. Tall and distinguished Esteban with his silvering hair and his expensive, burgundy satin robe. Teo, the portrait of masculinity, his naked sun-dark back toward her, his white trousers, loosely fitting over his lean hips, the long taper of his legs. They had both known. She was convinced of it, though how they'd known, or why, Melanie could not say. But that didn't matter. The only important thing was that these dashing Basques were at the root of Cecily's horrible situation.

She recalled with complete and sudden clarity Teo talking harshly to the stranger in the café yesterday. Sevé. That was his name. She'd bet he was involved in this. Maybe it had even been Sevé and not Carlos on the phone to her father. How many were involved? Half a million dollars was a lot of money....

Teo handed her a cup of coffee and sat down on the other side of the table.

"It's shocking," he began.

"Yes," Melanie said, her golden-flecked eyes watching him cautiously. Her brain was beginning to function, grudgingly. She could not put the suspicions out of her head. She tried to keep her wits about her, tried not to spit out the accusations that were on her tongue. But she could test him. Of course she could. "Teo," she said, her voice still breaking slightly, "I think I should call in the police."

She could see a dark shadow cross his handsome features. He turned his head, met his uncle's intent gaze for a moment, then looked back at Melanie. "No. You must not call the police."

"Why, Teo?" she pressed.

He regarded her closely for a long moment, his liquid brown eyes traveling her face; uneasily, she pulled the loose folds of her rosy silk kimono together at the throat. "I believe you told us that your father was instructed to keep the authorities out of this matter."

"He was," she said in a controlled voice. "But of course the kidnappers would say that."

"Naturally."

"I simply think the Guardia Civil could handle this better than I."

"Perhaps. But you would be taking a great risk with your sister's life, Melanie."

"How? I can even give them Carlos Echeverria's name."

"You are so very certain Carlos is involved?"

"Quite certain. And I think—" she started to say, but prudently she cut herself off.

Teo's dark brow was drawn into a deep frown. His eyes never left her, and Melanie felt a spurt of fear. She'd said too much.

"What do you think?" Teo asked with deliberate calm.

Melanie stared down at her folded hands. "Nothing."

"I see." He sat silently for a time. Finally he said, "If you believe Carlos is involved, you obviously assume that Cecily is being held by Basques. In that case, to contact the police would be very dangerous, indeed." He paused, then reached across the table as if to place his hand over hers. But Melanie quickly picked up her coffee cup, avoiding his touch. Teo shrugged eloquently. "So be it," he said. "The issue is this. The Guardia Civil and the Basques have long been enemies. Trust me in this. And believe me, the Basques have ears everywhere. Call it an intelligence network, if you will. Whatever. But rest assured, if you should contact the police, word will spread throughout the city as if on wings. It is clear that this man means business. I would not cross him, Melanie Royce."

"Teo is correct," Esteban put in. "Be this man terrorist or a member of a known violent faction or even if he is working on his own, such a move on your part would be too great a risk.''

Melanie sat very still. ''I understand what you're saying.'' She glanced from one to the other. ''Only too well.''

''Then you will not contact the authorities,'' Teo said.

''No, I won't.'' Melanie lied. She knew that she would not call them at present, but as for the future... She would just have to wait and see.

She finally disengaged herself from their observation and returned to the solitude of her bedroom. Nevertheless, she suspected that Teo would not let her stray too far from his watchful eye.

She was a prisoner in a strange land. She was completely out of her element, yet she couldn't leave, no matter how much she wanted to. The day before, she'd been hypnotized by the magic of the *feria*, the running of the bulls, the powerful and eloquently beautiful bullfights, the moments with Teo under the cloudless Spanish sky. She'd submitted, half willingly, to the thrill of primitive emotions, to the strange enchantment she felt in Teo's presence. Now she was a captive of that same lure, but the mood had turned sinister and ugly. How could she have let herself be touched by Teo, be charmed by his soft words, be held spellbound by the fascination of his dark eyes? *How?*

She took a shower, unnecessarily; she'd showered the night before. She walked out onto her balcony and gulped deep breaths of air, then strode angrily back into her bedroom. Her cell. She sat on her bed and tried to comb her damp hair but tears, hot and stinging, came to her eyes. She cried until she was exhausted with it, then slowly she got up, and slowly began to dress.

Wearing tan slacks and a loose, dark green shirt, Melanie finally reappeared downstairs. She needed to get away, to think by herself. It was unbearable to be constantly un-

der guard, so to speak. She'd drive into Pamplona, anywhere, and think out this whole confused mess on her own.

"You're going where?" Teo exclaimed when Melanie de-
fiantly announced her intention.·

"For a drive. Perhaps to Pamplona. I'm not sure."

He came to his feet. "Well, I am sure, Melanie. It is
enough that Cecily is in danger."

"Am I your prisoner?" she demanded outright.

"Certainly not." His tone was wounded and tinged with
anger.

"Then let me go without an argument."

"I cannot."

Melanie drew in a breath of frustration. "I'm going for a
walk, Teo. I've got to be by myself."

He strode over to where Melanie stood. "You must be
careful." And she could almost believe the concern in his
deep voice. Almost.

"Just don't crowd me, Teo," Melanie said deliberately,
then turned and walked away from him, like a child rebel-
liously disobeying a too-strict parent.

She went in no particular direction. It didn't matter. But
she did stay away from the winding road and walked instead along the ridge of a sloping meadow far above the
valley's basin.

Beyond her on the slanting lea, goats and sheep were
grazing, but she could see no shepherd. Somewhere in the
distance, however, a dog barked occasionally.

It was lovely, serene country. There were stands of tall fir,
their prickly needles thickly covering the ground, and inter-
mingled with the firs, Melanie saw oaks and some kind of
ash tree. It was damp and cool in the meadow; a light
morning mist still hung in the ravines and twisted under
trees.

From the hillside she could look out over a series of
mountains that climbed away from her, one overlapping the

other. Far off, on the crest of a hill, stood an old castle with turrets and towers. An enchanted castle. Melanie thought of ancient times, when the Spanish of Navarra fought the invading Moors from Africa. Perhaps, long ago, an armor-clad knight had come out of that castle on his great steed to ride among the hills, to make war on his enemies. She could almost envision the warrior, the sun glinting off his helmet and shield.

And then centuries later, these hills had seen the Spanish Civil War. Hemingway's Robert Jordan in *For Whom the Bell Tolls* had roamed these Basque forests, rifle in hand, his young face windburned, his feet moving noiselessly in his rope sandals.

Robert Jordan had made love to the beautiful shaven-headed girl, Maria, in a place like this, under a blanket. Her mind stopped dead at the inadvertent thought. Why had she thought of that? But she could almost see them in her mind's eye—the American guerrilla and the girl, Maria. They'd been so happy during their brief idyll.

But Robert Jordan had given up his life on the prickly floor of a forest like the one right over there, trying to save this land for its people.

A proud and secretive land.

And to Melanie, a land now filled with shadows and faceless fears.

Cecily. She had to think about her sister's predicament. Should she go to the police? Of course the kidnappers had instructed Oscar Royce to do no such thing. Of course Teo and Esteban backed them up. But Melanie *could* give the police the name of Carlos Echeverria.

She stood at the point where the meadow touched the forest. She looked down into the valley below and saw a narrow, twisting river, the summer sun white on the rushing water. She took a few pictures.

Where was Cecily? In Pamplona, roped to a chair in some dingy, dark room? Or in the mountains somewhere? Were her abductors feeding her, allowing her to go to the bathroom?

And then Teo Sanlucar's face superimposed itself upon the ghastly images. A darkly handsome face with those beautifully sculpted features and the strong, square jaw. It was difficult to believe the worst of him, but more and more she felt that she had no choice. It hurt, because Melanie had to admit that Teo Sanlucar was beginning to obsess her.

Eventually Melanie turned, her exploration finished, and began heading back toward Esteban's. Back to her jail.

It was as if the valley narrowed as she walked, as if the house summoned her against her will. She couldn't bear it. Everything was too close, pressing on her mind and her body. It had to stop. She would confront Teo and Esteban. Both of them. Oh, she'd be careful for she couldn't let them know how much she suspected. But they had to stop... guarding her.

Her legs were tired from the downhill hike by the time she reached the house. Yet she did feel slightly better. Getting away for a couple of hours had been the right thing to do. And she knew that, somehow or other, she was going to rescue Cecily. She would dance their dance, do whatever it took, but Melanie was not going to let anything happen to her sister.

She saw that Teo was breakfasting on the patio. She walked directly to him.

He stood up in one fluid movement. "Melanie," he said, "I'm glad you are back. We were becoming worried."

"You needn't have concerned yourself."

"Where did you go for so long a time?"

"Teo, look," she began.

"Sit down, please, Melanie. I did not mean to pressure you."

Melanie sighed and sank wearily into the wrought-iron chair that Teo held for her. "I took a walk up into the hills. It was lovely."

"Yes. The quiet forests. They are lovely." He passed her a basket of rolls. "Do you feel better now?"

"How can I feel better when Cecily is being held somewhere? Probably starving..." She eyed the basket warily. "I don't even feel like eating."

"Of course not. But you must."

He was being so infuriatingly reasonable. His attitude only served to heighten Melanie's already aroused temper. "Will you stop doing that?"

"What, Melanie?" Teo sat forward, leaning his elbows on the table, and in his habitual manner he clasped his hands and rested his chin on them.

"Stop...stop patronizing me!"

"I apologize—"

"And stop apologizing!" She knew her behavior was hardly that of a grateful guest. *But let's face it,* Melanie reminded herself, she was more prisoner than guest.

"Would you prefer," he said slowly then, "that I be blunt with you?"

"Yes." Her gaze snapped around to his.

"All right. My uncle and I have decided that you must leave the Basque country and go back to Madrid. From there you can fly to the States—"

"You and Esteban have decided! You're joking, of course." She smiled at him disdainfully.

He looked at her with somber eyes. "I make no jest of this, Melanie. Every minute you remain here is dangerous for you. These men—"

"Men," she fired back at him. "How would you know that there's more than one?"

"I make the assumption only. This man, if you will, must be desperate to have kidnapped your sister. What if he thought two hostages better than one?"

"You forget one thing. Who would take him his money?"

Teo shook his head. "Melanie...Melanie," he whispered gently, "you are so blind. Don't you think he already knows that you stay here with us? Can't you see that he merely has to instruct me or my uncle to make delivery of the ransom?"

"Anything is possible," Melanie said carefully.

"Then fly back to your family where it is safe."

And get out of your way, she thought. "No. I'm staying. And frankly, Teo, if I could find a room anywhere in Pamplona, I would leave this house instantly."

He looked as if she had physically slapped him. "Are we such ogres. Do you really believe we mean you harm?"

She didn't answer, didn't meet his eyes, but her lips closed in a firm line.

"Yes? Well then, Señorita Royce, you are a fool."

Melanie rose to her feet. "Now that we each know where the other stands, Professor Sanlucar, I think I'll take my leave." She began walking across the verdant lawn. Then, as if his stare were a hand pressing at her back, she turned to look at him, to catch the expression of fury she expected to find on his face.

Yet he merely sat, quiet and unmoving. He was watching her, yes, but there was no malice or anger in his eyes. Instead, he looked at her with a kind of wistful regret.

Chapter Seven

He found her later that afternoon on a nearby hillside, taking pictures of a flock of sheep and the young Basque shepherd boy who guarded them.

"Melanie," she heard him say, and as she turned her head toward his voice, she saw that he was walking up the hill toward her—a stranger really, a straight slim dark man with a handsome face and unreadable eyes.

"Checking up on me?" she asked sarcastically, putting the lens cap on her camera, her concentration gone.

He ignored her question. "I want to apologize for speaking so harshly to you earlier. I was worried about you. I still am."

"Don't start in on me again. There's nothing to discuss. I'm staying."

"*Bueno* . . . good, so that is settled then. But you cannot be left alone to worry so much. There is nothing you can do until Friday evening. Please, let me make amends for my bad temper."

Slowly and deliberately, Melanie put the camera in its case without answering. When she'd finally finished, she looked up at him and said sarcastically, "And just how do you propose to do that? I'm not exactly in the mood for dining and dancing."

"I thought I would take you into Pamplona. There are many diversions there, things that might cause you to forget—for a time."

"That's hardly likely," she said with studied coolness.

"But there is nothing you can do. Waiting is a hard thing," he said gently, "and sometimes a friend can help."

She stared at him. "A friend? Are you my friend, Teo? I hardly know you."

There was not a flicker of change in his face; the black eyes were calm, the mouth unsmiling. "Yes, Melanie, I am your friend. Believe me, please."

His voice was convincing and Melanie felt torn between her desire to believe him and her decision to distrust him. He seemed sincerely concerned and yet…there was so much he wasn't telling her, so much hidden behind the facade of gentility and good manners.

"Well, do you give your consent?" he asked.

She turned away from him and began to walk down the hill, angry at her own weakness, her impulsive attraction to this man. Angry at his insistence. "To what?" she asked. "Another tour of Pamplona? Another friend's balcony and cousin's restaurant? Should I be impressed?"

She was aware of him falling into step with her. She walked faster. His hand touched her arm then, bringing her to a stop. She refused to face him, however, and stood there with her head down, her shoulders tense.

"You are angry with me. A very American anger. Very open. A Spanish woman would hide her temper," he said pensively.

"I am not in any mood to hide my temper, Teo. Why don't you level with me?"

"Level with you. I like that. Do not the cowboys say that?"

"Amusing," she said dryly, still not looking up.

"Come into Pamplona with me," he urged softly. "I will show you our cathedral. Fifteenth-century. You might find some marvelous pictures."

At last she looked up into his face. He was smiling down at her, like a doting parent amused by his child's temper tantrum.

"Teo," she sighed, "I'm really not in the mood."

His lean dark hand cupped her chin and tilted her face up to his. "Moods can change."

"Please..." She didn't know what she meant exactly, what she was asking, but his face was so close, his hand so warm and strong on her skin. She could smell the faint aroma of his after-shave. His eyelashes were black as ink and very long. The sun glinted off one smoothly shaved, finely molded cheek. She tried to pull away but his touch left her in a kind of paralysis. For one sudden, dizzy, horrifying moment she thought he was going to kiss her. Panic and wonder burst within her. It struck Melanie shamefully—she wanted Teo to take her in his arms, to hold her and kiss her and make love to her. She wanted to feel those long-fingered hands on her flesh, stroking her hips and molding her breasts, preparing her in every way for love.

Yes, she was aching for this man. And she knew that he could tell. Her gaze was still locked with his: her breathing was shallow, as if a fist were squeezing her lungs, constricting them. He wasn't the dark, shadow-filled man she had thought him to be. No, Teo was kind and sincere and caring. Warm. Hadn't he shown that side to her many times already?

But he didn't kiss her. He released her and she stepped back, shaken.

"You will come to Pamplona, then?" he asked.

"Yes," she said breathlessly. "I'll come."

He drove expertly, taking the curves with perfect timing. She could not help but notice the sinews in his arm tight-

ening as he shifted, or the bulge of his thigh muscle under
his pearl-gray slacks as he pressed the accelerator and the
brake. Her awareness of his beauty and her reaction to his
nearness made her feel furious with herself again. He was a
stranger, a Basque, somehow involved in Cecily's kidnapping. She must keep her distance from him. Yet she had the
impression that he was deliberately forcing his presence on
her. She wondered why he was being so kind, so attentive.
What did he want from her?

As usual, the streets were filled with crowds. The same
people, their faces slack with wine, still grinning, shouting,
laughing. But now it seemed like a sleazy carnival to Melanie, a city of sideshows, grotesque and almost repulsive. Her
constant, gnawing worry about Cecily was too strong a
counterpoint to the joviality she saw around her. The bota
bags were repeatedly raised to greedy mouths. The dancers
moved with wild, lewd gestures, their faces distorted as the
sun beat on them mercilessly. Yet somewhere, Cecily was
being held, perhaps tortured or hurt...

"Try to forget," Teo said.

She merely looked at him and shook her head silently.
They walked down a narrow street; deftly he shielded her
from the worst of the revelers, as if he understood her pain.
She felt stifled and panicky, her whole world stumbling toward destruction. What to do? Where to go? Whom to
trust?

It suddenly seemed to Melanie that there were policemen
everywhere, on every corner and walking down the streets
in pairs, ever vigilant during this week of craziness. The
Guardia Civil. Everyone had heard of them—a paramili-
tary police force, controlled from Madrid, uniformed in
green with black patent-leather hats and tall boots. The ul-
timate symbol of strict law and order.

Did she dare go up to one and tell her story? Could they
help? Somehow she sensed that Teo would never allow it—

but what if she managed to steal away? Then she recalled his warning. If Cecily's kidnappers found out, if there was one slip, her sister would be dead. No, she couldn't take the chance. Another pair of policemen came by just then, so close she could have touched them as they passed her in the narrow, ancient street. She only had to put out a hand or call to them. But they were already gone, their boots thumping away from her, out of reach.

"The cathedral," Teo said.

She looked up at it, a huge brown mass, thick and solid in the Spanish style. Not graceful like French cathedrals or stately like English ones, but with the strength of piety in its very walls. She automatically readied her camera, automatically chose angles and composed her shots. She took a few pictures; Teo seemed to expect her to. But her heart wasn't in it.

Inside it was dark and the pillars seemed to ascend endlessly. People kneeled before candles in the cool hush. Incense wafted in the air, reminding her that San Fermín was a religious festival, too.

Teo pointed out the huge leaded-glass windows. Silently, she prayed for Cecily's safety. Somehow the atmosphere allowed her to do that, even though she wasn't Catholic.

And then Teo knelt down for a few minutes and bowed his head in prayer. Melanie waited in the rear of the church, studying him, thinking about him. She acknowledged to herself that he was a very complex being, an intelligent man, sensitive and gentle. There was no denying it. Whatever his involvement in this mess, whatever his reasons for keeping the truth from Melanie, he was nevertheless filled with concern for her and Cecily. But the contradiction between what Melanie assumed about Teo's actions and the impressions she had of his character and his feelings, refused to give her peace.

Finally he was beside her once more, his compelling eyes
soft in the dimness, his mouth curving into a friendly smile.
"I hope I did not keep you waiting too long?"

She shook her head. "No. The cathedral is lovely. I feel
peaceful in here."

"I do, too." Then he took her hand for a moment and
squeezed it tenderly. "I am certain peace will be yours again,
Melanie," he said, "when your sister's ordeal is over."

"When it's over," Melanie whispered, desperately longing to believe Teo. Longing to believe that it would soon be
over. Her thoughts were with Cecily, when Teo raised her
hand to his lips, catching her by surprise. Suddenly she was
in the grip of pure sensation, alone in the dim sanctuary with
Teo, his mouth touching her hand, sending tingling waves
up her arm. For a moment, she wished she could simply give
herself up to his strength. For a moment, she let herself believe that this man could become her lover, that she could
find love and peace and trust with him.

He lowered her hand but did not release it. She felt his
warmth surging through her and yet his touch conveyed
something else now, a reluctance, a hesitancy not present
before. His mind was pulling away from her; she could see
it in his eyes. And then, for an instant, she saw pain there
but he covered it quickly, smiling down at Melanie, squeezing her hand once more.

"Shall we go?" he asked quietly.

"I think we should," was all she could reply, and then he
released her and she felt almost as though a safety line had
been severed.

When they emerged into the bright sunlight and heat, the
atmosphere took Melanie's breath away. The noise was
overwhelming, the music harsh and relentless.

"Something to drink?" Teo suggested.

"Is there someplace quiet?" she asked ruefully.

"Quiet is only relative in Pamplona this week," he said with a laugh. He took her back to Jaime's bar. They sat toward the rear, in the dimness, and she sipped on soda water while Teo had a beer. Jaime spoke to him across the nearly empty bar. "It is quiet at this hour," Teo said, "but later Jaime will be very busy."

They were served tiny plates of *tapas*, Spanish hors d'oeuvres. Normally one ate them standing up at the bar, but Jaime honored his old friend. There were a dozen delicacies: squid and octopus, tiny smoked shrimp, cheese and bread cubes, olives and marinated vegetables.

"You must have a decent meal," Teo said. "This is not enough."

"No, please, I'm fine. I couldn't eat—really, I couldn't."

He ordered something for himself and Jaime served him, then sat down and helped himself to the bread, talking and chewing. He murmured something close to Teo's ear, all the while grinning at Melanie. And then some other comment, this time in Basque.

"He says you are as pretty as a star," Teo translated. "I can only agree."

"What else did he say?"

"It is untranslatable." Teo smiled maddeningly.

The bar began to fill up. A group of American girls were herded in by two young Spaniards. The girls were being plied with wine and the *feria* week's specialty—a sheep's head, roasted whole. The girls shrieked and laughed and delicately picked meat off the skull. Melanie shrank back in her corner; she couldn't bear to talk to them.

"Please, can we go?" Melanie whispered. "Can we go back to Esteban's?"

"But of course."

Jaime bowed them out, grinning and chattering. Teo guided her through the streets quickly; she was glad for the strength of his hand on her back. The streets were like a nightmare to her: too hot, too crowded, too wild with self-indulgent debauchery. The cries and music and laughter tore at her; the colors and faces streamed together into a terrible blur. She realized abruptly that her eyes were filled with tears.

They finally reached Teo's car, and as he held the door open for her she ducked thankfully inside. To be cool and quiet once more, to be able to think . . .

"Are you all right?" he asked with concern, sliding into the driver's seat.

She was digging in her purse for a tissue, embarrassed, unable to speak. Hysteria welled up inside her. She could do nothing but shake her head.

"Here." Quietly he handed her a clean handkerchief.

She pressed it to her eyes and wiped her sweat-dampened neck and blew her nose. "Thanks," she managed.

"My poor little lost American. I'm so sorry you had to become involved in this thing. You should be safe at home in, where did you say? Ohio." He took the handkerchief from her hand and with a clean, dry corner dabbed at her forehead and upper lip. "You need to rest. I was wrong to bring you to the city. I thought perhaps it would help." He leaned over her, so close that she could see the whorls his whiskers made on his smooth tanned cheek.

"I'm okay now. It was just the heat, really."

He put the top down on his sporty car and drove slowly, so that the wind cooled her cheeks and fanned her hair. She leaned her head back and closed her eyes, feeling the hysteria fade. The money would arrive, she would deliver it and Cecily would be freed. Very simple. She could do it. And when Cecily was safe she would walk boldly into the headquarters of the Guardia Civil and tell them everything. Even about Teo and Esteban Sanlucar. Until then, she would bide her time and wait and not arouse their suspicions. She could do it if she had to.

Esteban was gone for the evening, Lucia told Teo. She had prepared dinner and would return at nine to serve them. Esteban had insisted.

"But I feel like I'm causing so much trouble," Melanie protested.

"Not at all," Teo replied gravely.

She sank into a chair on the cool patio and accepted a brandy from Teo. It made her feel relaxed and a bit disjointed.

"Better?" he asked.

"Yes, thank you."

"Try not to worry about your sister. She will be fine. Your father will send the money and then they will release her."

"Do you know the story of the Lindbergh baby's kidnapping?" Melanie asked, leaning her chin on one hand. "They found him dead after they'd paid the ransom. I keep thinking about that. Don't kidnappers usually kill their victims? Even when they're paid?"

"Melanie, you must not think such things."

She continued stubbornly. "I seem to remember some statistics I read somewhere. Most kidnap victims—I can't recall the exact number—are killed. No matter what you do."

"That will not happen, Melanie, believe me. The men who have your sister want money, not blood."

"How do you know?" Melanie's eyes swung around to meet his; her tone sharpened. "Do you know who has her?"

"Of course not. I am merely guessing. I am attempting to relieve your anxiety."

But she looked at him searchingly. Was he lying?

The sun slipped deep into a valley beyond them. Long golden strands of light filtered through the tall mossy trees lining Esteban's patio; crickets chirped in the freshly mown grass and the earth smelled damp and fertile. Everywhere Melanie looked she saw serenity; in spite of her anxiety and depression, she saw the profound beauty, the enchantment of this land. How differently she might have viewed it if...if what? If she were sitting on the patio that evening with a close friend, a lover perhaps?

She stared down into her brandy glass, absently twisting it in her fingers, lightly sloshing the amber liquid against the curved crystal sides. The brandy, the glass tabletop, the walls of Esteban's house all glowed with the gold of the setting sun. She looked up into Teo's eyes. They too were gilded. And as always, he was watching her.

She took a long bath that evening, trying to soak away the desperation and the fear that hounded her. She dozed off in the bathtub, then jerked awake to the image of someone, some indistinct figure, pointing a gun at Cecily's head. Melanie thrust the picture of a cowering Cecily from her mind and quickly stepped out of the cooling water.

She dressed in a white skirt and turquoise blouse and wound her hair up into a knot. Her face in the mirror was pale, washed out by the bright blouse, shadowed under the eyes. Her freckles stood out sickly against the whiteness of her skin. But what did it matter?

She found Teo in the living room, reading a magazine. He wore his glasses, which somehow made him seem milder, less dangerous. She remembered having the same reaction that last night in Torremolinos, at the restaurant.

He removed the glasses and stood up. "You look lovely."

"I look like a hag," she replied scornfully.

"Never."

He was elegantly dressed in pleated white linen pants, a white shirt open at the throat and a beige nubby silk sports coat. She was forcefully reminded that he belonged to an ancient culture, one that was at its peak when America was a wilderness. A man who was utterly foreign to her yet in a curious way, familiar. She couldn't explain it, but she felt that something bound them together.

The table was set perfectly, even to the candles that flickered and touched the silver and glass and china with points of light.

"All this just for us?" she asked. "We could eat in the kitchen, for goodness' sake."

"Esteban would be scandalized," Teo said, smiling.

There was soup, then *calamare en su tinta*, squid in its own ink. Lucia's specialty, he told her. It was served with saffron rice and followed by flan, a creamy custard. Melanie's sincere and effusive appreciation delighted Lucia, who cleared the dishes, then quietly slipped away.

Teo poured a brandy for each of them. "Tell me about your family," he said. "I'm curious."

"Oh, we're very ordinary. My grandfather made a lot of money in steel during the war—World War II, that is. And we live in a comfortable Georgian house that isn't the least bit ancient. In a suburb of Cleveland. An ordinary city."

"You are somewhat older than Cecily. Are you close?"

"I practically raised her. My parents are very social, very busy. There were always live-in baby-sitters, but I guess I felt responsible for Cecily. Then I got married—"

"You are married?" he interrupted quickly. "But I thought...Señorita Royce..."

She was curiously embarrassed by his sudden reaction. "It is Miss Royce. The marriage didn't work out. I was very young. Oh, you don't want to hear that stuff."

"Ah, but I do. It may help me to understand you a little."

"It was eight years ago and we were only married for two months. My father had it annulled."

"Did you love this man?"

"I thought I did. I decided afterward that I had no idea what love was." She shrugged.

"And nobody has taught you since?"

"I haven't let anyone near enough." She wondered, distantly, whether her unwonted frankness was due to the several glasses of brandy she'd had. Or was it the intimacy of the situation? Or perhaps just her exhaustion, her emotional vulnerability.

He sat forward, silent, his hands clasped together in his habitual manner.

She had no idea what he was thinking and whether the fact of her brief marriage left any impression on him. Why should he care, this strange, dark man who made her so uncomfortable, who attracted her so much against her will?

"What about you? I thought Spanish families arranged their sons' marriages—at a young age," she dared.

"I'm Basque, not Spanish," he reminded her gently. "The simple truth is I refused to be pushed. And somehow time ran away and here I am, still single. There was a girl in England when I was at school. But she refused to consider living in my country, so nothing came of it. I expect by now she's fat and motherly. Of course, I could be wrong." And he smiled, as if mocking his own judgment. "My mother still nags me about it constantly even though she has several grandchildren already."

"My mother does the same thing. Luckily she's got Cecily—" Then the horror came back to her, bursting with immediacy, and she could feel the color drain from her face.

Teo rose and hurried toward her, pulling an empty chair next to hers. "No, *querida*, do not think of it." He put his hand over hers comfortingly.

Who was this man sitting so close to her, touching her? His expression was one of concern, his voice gentle. The candlelight flickered on his dark eyes, on the soft fabric of his jacket strained by his broad shoulders, on the mouth that was made to give a woman pleasure.

Who was he really? Friend or foe? Criminal or protector? Scholarly professor or proud Basque? How could a man dance with so many shadows?

She turned her head and looked into his eyes for the answers. She saw none. She pulled her hand away from his, on the pretext of smoothing back her hair.

They were both silent for a time, silent in the eloquently hushed dining room that seemed to be growing smaller by the second. Teo was utterly relaxed, so close to her that she was sure he could hear her heart beating, could sense the tension writhing in her stomach. She took a breath; it quivered in her chest, and she reached for her brandy glass, accidentally knocking it over.

"Oh, no," she said, mopping the linen with her napkin. "I've done it again. I'm so clumsy."

Once more he covered her hand with his. "Lucia will get it," he said, his breath brushing her neck. "You are nervous this evening. Is it something I have done?" He sounded so sincere.

"No," Melanie replied too quickly. "I mean yes. You do make me a little edgy."

"I am sorry for that. I have seen you happy and laughing. Worry does not suit you."

"It doesn't suit anyone, Teo."

"And do you worry about being alone in this house with me?"

There was that constricted feeling in her chest again. She tried not to look at him. He was so close, so very close. "Should I worry?" she managed.

He didn't answer, not immediately. In his eyes she could see indecision; she also thought she saw desire. Finally he said, "You are safe with me," and she was a little disappointed in spite of herself. But Teo wasn't finished talking, not yet. "I think you have a certain—what shall I say—fear of men, Melanie."

"That's absurd," she began.

"And you are so young," he went on, undaunted. "It is a tragedy. Wounds of the heart must be allowed to heal."

"There are always scars," she threw out defensively.

"Scars, yes, but something tells me you view these scars as more significant than they really are."

"That is none of your concern." Her voice shook. Her stomach knotted. In her heart she knew he was right; it was just that no one had ever put it so bluntly. No one else had ever bothered to look beyond her defenses. She wasn't used to this kind of probing. She added more words to her description of this complex man—exasperatingly honest.

"I feel somehow," he was saying, "that you are my concern, Melanie. You must realize that I would like to..."

Instantly Melanie pushed back her chair, making a terrible scraping sound on the polished tiles. "I'm going to bed now," she said shakily.

He turned in his seat to look up at her but all he said was, "Good night, Melanie. Rest well."

Sleep eluded her. She was too overwrought, too tired to sleep, her nerves jangling, her body trembling with exhaustion. Eventually she rose and slipped out through the curtains, onto the stone balcony. The night breeze lifted her hair and molded her nightgown to her body. She stood, as if on the prow of a ship, her hands on the railing, her eyes closed, feeling the fresh damp soothing air. A lopsided moon, a day or so from fullness, silvered the mountaintops, glimmering on the mist crawling in the hollows.

Now, perhaps, she could sleep. As Melanie turned toward the doorway, she heard a sound below her, the quiet shuffle of a footstep. Was it Esteban returning?

A ghostly shadow detached itself from the blackness. She saw that it was a man, dressed in white with a black Basque beret on his head. He moved stealthily toward the cars, obviously trying not to awaken anyone.

Instinctively, Melanie shrank back into a dark corner of the balcony. Was it a thief? Should she alert someone? The man looked up just then, as if to search her out in her dark corner, as if he knew she was there.

It was Teo.

She stifled her gasp of shock. He turned and moved on, away from her, and soon she heard the quiet *chunk* of a car door closing and the crunching of wheels on the gravel driveway.

Long moments later Melanie realized she was still standing there, her fingernails digging into her palms, her knuckles white.

Where was he going secretly in the night? Where? Her heart raced in agonized confusion. What should she do?

Then, as if a voice had spoken aloud in her brain, she knew. She made her way into her room, found her kimono and threw it over her shoulders. She walked resolutely down the deserted hallway, her bare feet clammy against the cold smoothness of the marble floor, halting outside his room. She boldly pushed open the door and entered, then sat down in a chair and settled herself for a long wait. Her eyes scanned the room in a cursory inspection, but something kept her from searching his dresser drawers or looking through the books and letters piled beside the bed. Something stopped her from violating his privacy in so complete and final a way. Yet she couldn't have said exactly what it was, or why she flinched from such an open expression of her distrust. Was she still harboring hopes—or illusions—about Teo Sanlucar, despite what she'd just seen?

Somewhere in the darkness a clock intruded upon the silence. A beam creaked. As Melanie sat waiting, she suddenly remembered what Teo had called her earlier that evening.

Querida, he had said. *Querida*. Melanie knew what that word meant. It meant "beloved."

Chapter Eight

Thursday, July 8

His voice nudged her into wakefulness.

At first she was disoriented and sat up too quickly, her back and neck aching from her fitful sleep in his hard chair.

"Melanie..." he was saying in a soft and caressing tone. "What on earth are you...?" He crouched in front of her on his haunches, and his hands rested on either arm of the chair, imprisoning her. "Are you all right?" he asked.

"Yes...I just..." How to put it? She had planned to confront him, not to fall asleep in his bedroom.

"I wanted to talk to you, Teo. I fell asleep," she explained lamely.

"So I see." He was so close she could detect an odor on his clothes; it was a familiar smell, conjuring up some vague, pleasant association from her past. She finally grasped the elusive memory; it was wood smoke that she smelled.

"Couldn't whatever you wanted to talk to me about have waited until morning?" he asked.

"No," she said quickly. "I mean, yes, of course it could have." She looked at his face in the semidarkness, at the long shadows that cut grooves in his cheeks, at his dark eyes glinting in the lamplight. His hair was unruly, as if stirred by the night wind, his lean body, although outwardly relaxed, was nevertheless poised in readiness. She was acutely aware of him and knew then what a foolish mistake it had been to come to his room.

"If you'll move," she said carefully, "I'll leave now."

"And our talk?"

"In the morning, Teo." She could see those intelligent, long-lashed eyes studying her, boring into her, probing her hidden fears. Inadvertently, Melanie pulled the folds of her robe together.

"You are here now," he said. "Perhaps in the morning you will have changed your mind."

"Changed my mind?"

"About telling me what was so important that you felt you had to come to a man's room, in the middle of the night, in a state of..."

It was what he hadn't said that caused the tension to coil in her stomach. "It's not what you're thinking."

"Then pray enlighten me."

She edged back in the chair as if the few inches more she put between them would protect her. "All right, Teo. I came in here to wait and find out exactly where you'd gone at so late an hour."

"I see." A slow smile gathered at the corners of his mouth. "Would you believe that I went to visit a village maid?"

"I find that unlikely."

"Ah...then perhaps I merely went for a long walk in the moonlight?"

"You smell of wood smoke, Teo," she observed dispassionately. "Did you build a fire for warmth?"

He came smoothly to his feet and backed a step or two away from her. He stood as if in thought, his head cocked, his hands resting on his hips. "Should I tell you? Do you trust me at all, Melanie?"

"Yes." But she was answering his first question, not the one about trust, she thought.

"I was visiting friends in the hills. I was simply trying to pursue information about Cecily."

Melanie rose too, but veered away from him and walked to a window. "Let's say I believe you. Why couldn't you have visited these friends of yours at a more suitable hour?"

"For the obvious reasons, Melanie. Had I been seen at their houses by anyone who held sympathy for Cecily's abductors, I could have placed my friends in a compromising position."

"Is everything everyone does around here so well-known? My," she said sarcastically, whirling around to face him, "but you Basques are a suspicious lot."

"You are exactly correct. I told you once before that the Basques are an insular race. They feel it necessary to have an excellent network of information."

"They are not the CIA, Teo."

"No. They are more skilled, in some ways. More cunning, Melanie."

"Nice country..." she reflected, a hint of bitterness in her voice.

"My people have been forced to be wary and therefore close-knit."

"Maybe... And did you find out anything?"

Teo's face was impassive. He walked slowly in her direction until he stood only inches away. "First you must answer a question for me, Melanie," he said, speaking so quietly that she was forced to lean toward him.

"What?" she asked, trying with all her strength to resist his compelling voice.

"Tell me what it is you think I have done."

"Done?" Her heart was in her throat, and her knees felt suddenly weak.

"Yes. Why is it you have no trust for me, Melanie?"

GIVE YOUR HEART TO HARLEQUIN®

FREE!

Mail this heart today!

AND WE'LL GIVE YOU
4 FREE BOOKS, A FREE PEN AND WATCH SET, AND A FREE MYSTERY GIFT!

·≈ It's a ≈·
HARLEQUIN HONEYMOON
A SWEETHEART
OF A FREE OFFER!

FOUR NEW "HARLEQUIN AMERICAN ROMANCES"—FREE! Take a "Harlequin Honeymoon" with four exciting romances—yours FREE from Harlequin Reader Service. Each of these hot-off-the-presses novels brings you all the passion and tenderness of today's greatest love stories...your free passports to bright new worlds of love and foreign adventure!

But wait...there's <u>even more</u> to this great offer!

HARLEQUIN PEN AND WATCH SET—ABSOLUTELY FREE! You'll love your personal Harlequin Pen and Watch Set. Perfect for daytime...elegant enough for evening. The watch has a genuine leather strap and replaceable battery. The watch and the stylish matching pen are yours free with this offer!

SPECIAL EXTRAS—FREE! You'll get our free monthly newsletter, packed with news on your favorite writers, upcoming books, and more. Four times a year, you'll receive our members' magazine, Harlequin Romance Digest!

<u>Best of all,</u> you'll periodically <u>receive our special-edition "Harlequin Bestsellers," yours to preview for ten days without charge!</u>

MONEY-SAVING HOME DELIVERY! Join Harlequin Reader Service and enjoy the <u>convenience</u> of previewing four new books every month, delivered right to your home. Each book is yours for only $2.25—25¢ less <u>per book</u> than what you pay in stores! Great savings plus total convenience add up to a sweetheart of a deal for <u>you</u>!

START YOUR HARLEQUIN HONEYMOON TODAY— JUST COMPLETE, DETACH & MAIL YOUR FREE OFFER CARD!

HARLEQUIN READER SERVICE

⊷§ FREE OFFER CARD ¿∞

PLACE HEART STICKER HERE

FREE PEN AND WATCH SET

FREE HOME DELIVERY

PLUS AN EXTRA BONUS "MYSTERY GIFT"!

4 FREE BOOKS

☐ **YES!** Please send me my four HARLEQUIN AMERICAN ROMANCES™ books, free, along with my free Pen and Watch Set and Mystery Gift! Then send me four new HARLEQUIN AMERICAN ROMANCES books every month, as they come off the presses, and bill me at just $2.25 per book (25¢ less than retail), with no extra charges for shipping and handling. If I am not completely satisfied, I may return a shipment and cancel at any time. The free books, Pen, Watch and Mystery Gift remain mine to keep!

154 CIA NA7J

FIRST NAME_____ LAST NAME_____
(PLEASE PRINT)

ADDRESS_____APT._____

CITY_____

PROV./STATE_____ POSTAL CODE/ZIP_____

PRINTED IN U.S.A.

"I...do trust you." Her gaze fell away from his. "I guess I'm so worried about Cecily that I must seem suspicious of everyone."

"You do."

"Well, I'm not." Even to her own ears the lie sounded unconvincing. "Tell me what you found out."

He watched her for a moment, then shrugged. "It could be that your sister is being held by the Cax Carot." He put a silencing finger to her lips. "Allow me to finish. I do not know this for a certainty, but there is reason to suspect it."

"Who are they?"

"I must consider how to describe these youths." He searched for words. "They believe that one must protect oneself from a dangerous world, in which the bomb may be exploded at any moment. A world where greedy nations and men take whatever they wish from one another. The Cax Carot ready themselves for the worst..."

"Survivalists."

"That, I assume, is what you would label them."

"They're not...terrorists, are they?"

He shook his head. "They do not believe in such things. Only, as you put it, survival."

"Why would they want so much money?"

"Who can say? Perhaps they buy food and weapons."

"Half a million American dollars can buy a lot of food and guns, Teo."

"One might say these boys have grown too big for their trousers..."

"Their britches," she corrected automatically.

"Yes. Whatever."

"And Carlos Echeverria? Is he a survivalist? In the Cax Carot?"

"Perhaps."

She turned away and gazed out over the moon-bathed hills. "You haven't told me much."

"There is little more to tell."

"Do you have any idea if this Cax Carot has a headquarters or something?"

"Again, I can be of little help. I can only assume, as do you, that they hide out in the mountains. Is that not where a survivalist would feel most safe?"

"Perhaps," she agreed warily. Yet what Teo had said did make sense. Certainly the theory of survivalism described in part her sister's current outlook. Was it possible Teo was telling her the truth? Was he just an innocent bystander, like herself? Could she be so mistaken about him? After all, a man who was so obviously wealthy did not need to kidnap someone for a ransom. If he were guilty, it must be for some other reason. Idealism? Thrills? A history professor grown bored with the classroom, perhaps. What *was* his motive?

And Cecily. Melanie wondered again whether her sister was entirely innocent. Certainly she'd been kidnapped, but had she knowingly involved herself with the very man—or men—who were now holding her captive?

Questions flew around in Melanie's head. She felt that she was getting closer to some truth but its core still eluded her. And yet, if what Teo said was true, shouldn't she feel hopeful? Young, idealistic survivalists did not kill naive American girls.

But then there was Sevé. He was neither young nor, Melanie was sure, an idealist.

Teo took a step toward her and caught her hands in his, clasping them with a gentle strength. "I hope you can find it in your heart to believe me," he said softly, his breath warm on her forehead.

She couldn't answer. Instead she was held immobile with indecision and the exquisite agony of his touch.

"It was a mistake to have come to my room, Melanie," he said slowly. "It was also a mistake to have come to Pamplona."

"You're wrong on both counts," she said. "It was very right for me to have come to Pamplona, and as for your room—"

"As for my room," he broke in harshly, "I am only too human. You cannot be so blind as to think I do not desire you. My bed is but a few feet away, and all you need do is walk there with me, Melanie. But you won't. I know that. You are too afraid of me and too afraid of your own responses."

Her eyes flew up to meet his, and she saw a kind of pain and warning there and felt weakened by the evidence of his undisguised torment. She wanted suddenly to draw him toward her. To be surrounded by those beautifully formed arms. And yet all her instincts told her to flee from him, to run for her life.

She pulled back from his closeness but paradoxically tightened the clasp of their hands.

"I have to . . . go, Teo," she whispered.

He held her a moment longer, and his quiet strength seemed to flow into her body. Then he let her go. "Leave me," he said, the lines in his face suddenly stern. "Leave me and go back to your room before I forget what a poor liar you are or that you are a guest in this house and I am a gentleman."

Somehow she managed to cross to the door, to pull it open and walk down the dim hallway to her own room. She even managed to sleep but she couldn't escape Teo. Even in her sleep, in the privacy of her dreams, he was there.

THE NEXT DAY, Thursday, seemed to drag. Once again, she'd been awakened early by Esteban with a call from her father—an unsettling call telling her that he was wiring the money through New York to Madrid that afternoon.

"There'll be a rush order put on it, Mel," he'd said, "so it should be in Pamplona on Friday."

"Should be?"

"I've pulled every string I know to hurry this up, honey. You sound as if you think we're not worried sick over here."

"I'm sorry," she'd said, "I know how upset you are." Then she'd reassured him that she was safe and being watched over every minute. What Melanie could not tell her father was that her bodyguards might very well be involved in the kidnapping. Esteban had been standing over her the whole time.

She breakfasted with Esteban. Teo was nowhere to be seen. Afterward, Esteban offered to take her into Pamplona, but Melanie had no heart for the fiesta that day. She simply moped around the huge house, taking an occasional photograph, tormented continually by a single thought. What if the money didn't arrive?

It rained lightly in the valley that afternoon. She sat in the living room, mutely staring out of the windows at the quiet drizzle. Was it raining in Pamplona? She could imagine the thousands upon thousands of tourists all jamming into the shops and restaurants. An ugly vision.

She tapped a finger absently against her chin. What if the money didn't arrive by tomorrow? The police. She'd have to think about getting in touch with them somehow. She remembered all the reasons Teo had told her not to, but those reasons might be utterly invalid. She wished she knew. And then, even if the money arrived on time, Cecily's life might be forfeited anyway. The Lindbergh baby pattern . . .

She watched the gray mist cloak the mountains and her stomach twisted in anguished indecision: what should she do?

She heard Teo finally return to the house in the early evening. Melanie was in the library, leafing through books and magazines, feeling edgy and irritable and bored, almost as if she were crawling out of her skin.

She could hear Esteban's low voice coming from the living room, but he and Teo were speaking in Basque.

She walked purposefully into their midst. "Good evening, Teo," she interrupted.

He looked over to where she stood, and Melanie was surprised at the weariness she saw in his face. "Good evening, Melanie."

The men continued their conversation as if she weren't there at all. It infuriated her. She began to pace the room, feeling like an outsider, feeling like...a prisoner. Yes, she felt a resurgence of that earlier emotion, that sense of being imprisoned. She fingered an ashtray, looked at a photograph, sat down, then stood up. She walked to the French doors that led out onto the lawn and turned around to face Teo and Esteban, still engrossed in conversation, still ignoring her presence.

"It's stopped raining," she said and they looked over at her, surprised, as though they'd forgotten she was there. "Lovely evening, isn't it?" Melanie said firmly.

"Beautiful," Esteban replied. He glanced at Teo. "You are tired."

"*Sí.*" And Teo rested his gaze on Melanie. "Please excuse my appearance." He was wearing white cotton trousers and a white shirt. Both had dried, muddy smudges on them as did one of his unshaven cheeks. "I will go clean up now, if you do not mind." He gave a slight bow in Melanie's direction.

"Of course," she said loftily.

He was singularly quiet at dinner. His eyes would meet Esteban's, then he would stare off into the distance. He seemed preoccupied, his brow creased by a deep frown.

Melanie picked at her food. She had little interest in dinner. But it was a perfect opportunity to study Teo, and she took full advantage of his curious lack of interest in his surroundings. He'd washed and shaved and donned a clean white shirt and trousers. His shaving lotion clung to him softly, tantalizing her senses. The silver at his temples seemed to stand out that evening, and the lines of concentration on his face somehow aged him. He would always be a handsome man, she guessed, but the loss of tenderness in his expression made her annoyingly anxious.

Who was he? How many different faces did he show the world? There was the tender, caring side of him. The intellect, too. She'd heard him speak sarcastically, though never cruelly; she'd seen him pray. He was a gentleman, through and through. Hadn't last night proved that much? And he could show pain, could bare his soul to her, could risk her rejection and withstand her distrust.

And now who was this Teo sitting silently at the table? Something was troubling him—that showed plainly on his face, in those dark, long-lashed eyes. But what?

What was he thinking? Where had he been all day?

"Teo," she said, "were you at the fiesta?"

He shook his head. "I was visiting some people."

"Was it about Cecily?"

"Yes."

"Did you find out anything?"

He glanced at Esteban, then at her. "Nothing more."

Melanie leaned back in her chair and fell silent.

Over brandy, he said to his uncle, "I'll be going out again tonight." That was all. No explanation whatsoever. Melanie guessed that Esteban already knew Teo's destination. If only she could...

A thought struck her. Of course she could! But how?

She remembered watching Teo the previous night from her balcony. It wouldn't be so difficult to follow, would it?

Melanie waited a few minutes then yawned. "I am dreadfully sleepy tonight."

Both men turned their dark heads toward her. "Please," Esteban said, "if you are tired, take your rest, Melanie."

"Maybe I should," she agreed smoothly.

It seemed so easy. She walked up the stairs as if weary to the bone and closed her bedroom door gently. Then she began to rush. First she stripped off her dress and threw it on top of her suitcase. Then she put on chocolate-brown slacks and her dark green shirt. Camouflage. She even pulled down the covers on her bed and shoved some bunched-up clothes underneath to make it look as if she were asleep—just in case. She tied her hair back in a practical ponytail and even considered blackening her face, the only part of her that might reflect light. What could she use? Mascara? It would take forever. No, she'd just have to chance it. No one would get that close to her, anyway, not if she could help it.

She was ready.

Melanie turned off the lights and stepped onto the balcony to wait in the shadows.

She had it all planned. At the far end of the hall was a set of narrow stairs leading to the kitchen. From there, she could get to the back door. Of course, Lucia might still be about, but dinner was long over. Surely the cook had retired by now.

Her car! Would Esteban or Lucia hear her start the engine? Most likely not. She'd parked at the far end of the circle; surely the lawn and the trees and the stone walls would muffle the sound. Besides, Esteban would have no reason to be listening for her. She was certain it wouldn't occur to either of the men that she might follow Teo.

She was pleased with her cleverness. Let Teo sneak off to his "friend." Soon enough, she would know exactly what he was up to.

The mist eddied around her, causing her hair to spring into curls. She was pressed back against the stone wall and could feel the cool dampness seeping into her clothes, chilling her skin. She wished he would hurry.... Then finally, she saw a rectangle of light on the lawn below—light spilling from his bedroom window. Shortly after, it was dark on the lawn once more. She listened but could hear nothing. So she imagined his progress, down the hall, down the front stairs, to the door.

She crossed her fingers, took a deep breath, then made her move.

Peering out of a crack in her bedroom door, Melanie saw that there was no one in the hallway. She rushed as silently as she could toward the back staircase. The floor creaked beneath her sneakers once, and her heart sank.

Hurry! she thought. Or she might miss him . . .

The kitchen was dark and empty. Thank God! Gingerly, she closed the back door, careful not to lock it. Then she paused. What if Esteban checked it before he went to bed?

But she couldn't worry about that now. That was a problem she'd just have to deal with if and when it came her way.

She peeked out across the lawn from around the corner of the house. Teo's car was still there. Then she heard the front door of the house, its sound echoing off the hillside as it was firmly closed.

Yes! There he was!

She waited as he stepped into his car and turned on the motor. He began to pull away and she ran quickly across the lawn toward her car, crouching, using the trees and the night shadows to hide herself.

Oh, clever, clever!

She started her car, the quiet little engine sounding to her like a Concorde jet.

Oh, my Lord, she thought, cringing inwardly, her knuckles white on the steering wheel, what if Esteban discovered her ruse? But what could he do now? Drag her out of the car and lock her in her room?

She pulled away from the curve of the lawn, leaving her lights off, and steered down the long drive. Which way had he gone—left or right?

Yes! There were his lights bouncing off the trees a couple of hundred yards down the road to the right. Then his car disappeared around a bend.

She switched on her own headlights and followed. Then, when she came to the same bend in the road, she turned them off, slowed down and strained to see in the pale moonlight.

His taillights showed in the distance; at least they were something to follow, a moving beacon in the night. Then they disappeared. She turned her lights back on. Over and over again, Melanie followed the same routine, finding it amazingly easy. The roads were not all that dark, especially with no other cars to blind her and a liquid moon to brighten the way.

The road led in the opposite direction from Pamplona—or so she assumed. It twisted through the tall hills and once over a bridge. Always, she could find his lights in the distance, however, and frequently she was able to turn hers on.

It was deserted country. Deserted and a bit frightening with the mottled moonlight on the twisted road, forming eerie shadows.

Very seldom did Melanie pass a house, and only once did she drive through a tiny village, where she deemed it safe to turn on her parking lights, the accepted European custom for driving in cities at night.

She had driven a little over eight kilometers when she saw Teo's brake lights illuminate a straight stretch of road ahead of her. She pulled to the soft, muddy side of the road and came to a stop a few hundred yards behind him. Then she could make out his interior lights switching on and off as he opened the door to step out of his car. Silently, she opened and closed her own door and began walking swiftly in his direction. He couldn't conceivably see her in her dark clothes from that distance, but still she clung closer to the trees than to the road.

As he was once again dressed in the familiar white of the Basques, Melanie could easily see his pale form moving ahead of her. She saw that he'd turned off the road and entered a meadow.

Where was he going? She could see no houses anywhere; there were only sloping meadows and steep hills on either side of the road. Very curious indeed.

She made her way into the meadow and discovered that there was a rocky path to follow. She stayed at least a hundred yards behind him, losing his shadow every so often but always finding him again, still ahead of her.

The low, sweeping meadows ended abruptly and the path began to climb sharply along the ridge of a mountain. She grew tired and drew deep breaths into her lungs. If only she could rest a bit.

Above her was a forest; below, a slope fell away gradually. Then the path switched back, rounding onto the hidden side of the mountain where it continued to climb. Once, she missed Teo's figure for a few interminable minutes and fear swept over her. What if she had lost him? Or worse, what if he'd stopped and she bumped right into him? But then finally, mercifully, she saw Teo again, coming out of the thick pines and beginning to cross a wide expanse of meadow.

There were other pale shapes in the clearing—sheep—but more important, there was a cabin on its far side. Light spilled out from two tiny windows. She stood still at the edge of the forest for a moment, speculating. Smoke rose from a stone chimney into the night sky. Of course, the wood smoke on Teo's clothing.

She saw him enter the cabin and close the door. Melanie began to move again across the grassy meadow, startling a sheep once and frightening herself out of her own wits as the ewe jumped across a ditch, giving Melanie a wide berth.

She was terrified that someone might see her approach. There was no cover whatsoever. And the moon kept emerging from the patchy blanket of clouds. She saw a boulder near the cabin and crouched as she came up behind it.

She was so close now. The light from one of the sooty windows fell softly onto the meadow in front of Melanie, laying a small, hazy square on the ground. Then she could see a figure—a man's figure—through the window, his white-clad back leaning against the pane, blocking her vision.

Was it Teo?

No matter. This was a perfect moment for Melanie to sneak up to the side of the cabin undetected. She took the opportunity, ducking low, finally pressing herself up against the rough stones of the wall.

She caught her breath and suddenly wished she were back at Esteban's safe and sound.

But you're not, she told herself and she knew she had to summon the courage to peek into that window. She could do it. She could!

Holding her breath, Melanie tried to see if the man's back was still partially blocking the window.

Yes.

She took advantage of the inadvertent shield he provided and moved slightly so that she could see a portion of the cabin's interior. Her heart was in her throat.

Then she could see three men sitting around a peasant table, a kerosene lamp in its center.

She almost gasped aloud; one of the men was the one who'd argued with Teo at the café. Sevé. She didn't recognize the other men or the one whose back hid the rest of the room from her vision, but she had an impression of youth. Then her eyes were drawn to the opposite wall and the hair rose on her arms. There were two rifles leaning against the stones. *My God* . . .

The man at the window moved suddenly into the room and Melanie quickly ducked her head. It was long minutes before she braved another look. The entire room was visible now. There was Teo, standing in the dimness on the far side of the cabin, across from Sevé and the youths.

He was looking down at a cot . . .

He shifted his weight.

And there, lying on the cot, looking pale and exhausted, was Cecily.

Chapter Nine

Melanie only became aware of her surroundings when she tripped on a rock and fell to her knees. She stayed there for a minute on all fours, gasping for breath, sobbing with fear and horror and a terrible certainty. Slowly she stood, brushed the dirt off her knees and the grit and gravel from her hands. One of her palms stung; she must have cut it in falling. It didn't matter.

Teo Sanlucar had lied to her from the beginning. Suspecting him had put her on edge, but knowing he was involved twisted like a knife in her heart. All those lies, those caring looks. *Querida.* It meant nothing; it was just part of his role—and he'd played his role well. Of all the men in the world, how had he got past her ironbound caution and touched her heart?

She began walking down the path again, feeling her way. She had a desperate urge to run, but it was too dark and the mountainside was too rough. She had to be gone before Teo returned to his car. If he discovered that she'd followed him...

She must never let **him** know what she'd done or that she knew he was involved. To do so would put Cecily, not to mention herself, in even greater danger. Melanie knew she had to remain free in order to plan, to get the money, to call the police if need be. Somehow she had to make sure those men did not kill Cecily. How?

Once, she was afraid she was lost; a huge gnarled tree with twisted branches like grasping arms suddenly stood in her path. Had it been there before? Or had she been too intent on following Teo to notice it? She wished she had a flashlight but where could she have got one? The entire time she'd been in that house, she'd been watched. Oh, how conveniently she'd fallen into his hands!

She could, of course, get in her car and simply leave, leave the Basque country behind and fly home. Which was what Teo had told her to do. But that wasn't even a remote choice, not with her sister all alone in that awful hut... Who were those men? Which one was Carlos? What exactly did they want the money for?

She stumbled on through the shadowed night, down, down. Her car was there, just out of sight, some hundred yards behind Teo's. She'd been deathly afraid it would be gone and she'd be left alone in the night where those men with their wicked-looking guns would find her.

She stopped and listened for a few minutes in case Teo had left the cabin after her. But there was only the rustling of the trees and the sound of a stream somewhere. A night bird called softly and in the underbrush a small animal disturbed some branches. It was quiet, and utterly peaceful, with the scent of green growing things and the damp night air.

Starting her car, she winced as the noise broke the silence, but then she was away, driving back along the twisted road, praying she remembered how to get to Esteban's, praying no one noticed the unlocked door or her missing car.

It was nearly three in the morning by the time she turned her lights off and pulled up into the driveway. She slumped over the steering wheel, resting her head on her hands, too tired to think or plan anymore. She dragged herself to the back door. What if someone had awakened and locked it?

It was still open. But Melanie was too drained to rejoice in the fact. She crept wearily up the back staircase and to her room, closing and locking the door behind her. Then, carefully, she closed and locked the patio door and drew the curtains together. When she turned on the light, she saw that her one hand was raw with a slash of dried blood on the palm. The knees of her pants were muddy, grass-stained, torn. Her sneakers were muddy, too. She scraped off the mud and flushed it down the toilet. She cleaned up as well as she could in the bathroom and hid her muddy, blood-stained clothes in the bottom of her suitcase.

Then sleep, blessed forgetfulness. Not even the sound of Teo's car, slipping quietly up the drive, wakened her.

By ten the next morning she was downstairs, trying to ask Lucia when the banks in Pamplona opened.

There were many, Lucia told her, misunderstanding her Spanish.

In her limited Spanish, Melanie tried again, impatiently.

And finally, Lucia understood; she grinned widely, using the kitchen clock to indicate what time *el banco* opened.

"Nine-thirty. Tell *los señores* I go *banco*," Melanie said, gesturing in the vague direction of Pamplona.

Her father had wired the money yesterday; perhaps it was already there. She doubted it, because overseas money transfers usually took several days. But her father had specified a rush order.

Lucia asked whether she wanted coffee, but Melanie politely declined. "No, *gracias*, no coffee. Later."

To her relief no one was about. Teo undoubtedly was sleeping late, if indeed he had returned. But his car was there, pulled up near the house; its tires were muddy.

Her heart clutched in fear. She glanced quickly at her own car. Its tires, too, were muddy. Had he noticed them last night? She bit her lip and hoped not. She'd get into Pamplona and wash them off somehow.

"Going somewhere so early?"

She whirled around at the sound of his voice, dropping her car keys. "Oh, you startled me!"

He stood before her, looking as fresh as if he'd been in bed asleep all night. His white sport shirt was crisp and clean, his khaki pants pressed and immaculate.

"Sorry. But I repeat, are you leaving us at this early hour?" Were his eyes more hooded than usual? Did he see the mud on her tires?

"Yes, I'm going to the bank to see if the money has arrived."

"Let me drive you. The fiesta is still going on, you know. You'll never be able to park."

"I'll take my chances."

"I insist," he said quietly.

He couldn't know, could he? Her skin crawled with fear. She bent down to pick up her keys, trying to hide her face, wondering if he saw the truth in it. But he moved faster than she did, scooping up the keys and handing them to her, his eyes dark and unreadable, his touch electric. Then he took her hand in his and turned its palm up.

"What is this? A nasty cut. But, Melanie, how did this happen?"

She shrank inside her skin. "Oh, that? Oh, it's nothing. I cut it on a broken mirror in my makeup case."

"Why on earth didn't you ask for a bandage?"

She shrugged. "They never stay on your hand, do they?"

His acute gaze seemed to reach inside her as they stood there silently, her hand still held in his. Again, his glance fell to the cut, then swung sharply back to her face. His touch was cautious. She thought inanely that he might hold an injured bird in the same manner as he did her hand: gently, carefully... reverently.

Melanie's heart felt squeezed. She tried to smile, to show her gratitude for his concern. Wasn't that what he would expect?

"You can let me go now," she said quietly.

He looked at the scrapes on her hand once more, saying as if to himself, "A cut from a mirror..." before he freed her. For a moment neither of them spoke. Uncontrollable panic rose in Melanie's breast. Any second he was going to tell her that the game was up and that he knew she had followed him.

"Have you eaten?" he asked suddenly, his voice shattering the tense quiet.

She swallowed hard. "No, really, I'm too nervous. I'd like to get to the bank."

"Of course. Come then. I'll buy you breakfast in town."

Did he notice that she pressed against the car door, as far from him as possible? Did he see her hands tremble with nervousness? Did he believe her lie about the cut on her hand?

On the drive to Pamplona, Teo was his usual, open self. He made casual conversation, pointing out things on the way—a fourteenth-century castle on a distant hill, a sheep herder driving his flock to greener pastures.

"Over there, near the river—" he nodded "—is an old wool mill. It's still in use."

"Interesting," Melanie murmured distractedly.

He went on to regale her with local Basque legends concerning the surrounding countryside; he seemed to be trying especially hard to entertain Melanie, or was he really the kind, generous man he seemed to be? From time to time, she asked herself if she could have been mistaken about Teo. And then she would remember him standing in the cabin with those men, dressed as one of them, and she would feel a surge of fear. If Teo Sanlucar knew she'd followed him—what would he do?

Still, his conversation kept her mind occupied, kept her from thinking too much, from imagining unknown horrors.

She watched him out of the corner of her eye, as she held her whipping hair out of her face with one hand. Teo seemed almost to be enjoying the drive; the Mercedes' top was down, and his black hair was blowing wildly in the wind. He looked young and carefree and innocent. But what had Cecily thought when her brilliant Professor Sanlucar had turned out to be a common criminal?

As she'd expected, the streets were already swarming. It was excruciatingly slow going and Teo had to practically push his way through the crowds. He pulled up right in front of the bank, double parked, and stepped out of the car.

"You're going to leave it here?" she asked in amazement.

"Of course. We won't be long."

He ushered her into the bank, his hand on the small of her back. "Please wait here. I will be just a moment."

He returned with a short, distinguished-looking man whose formal black suit and small brush mustache proclaimed him a banker.

"Señorita Royce," Teo was saying to the man, "is expecting a wire. Quite a large sum, as I was telling you."

"*Señorita*, it is my pleasure," the man said. "Please allow me to introduce myself. I am Diego Pacheco." He spread his hands in a Latin gesture. "However, I am sorry to inform you, Señorita Royce, that there is no wire for you."

Melanie's heart sank. Señor Pacheco was saying something to Teo in Spanish. Teo answered and the man's face registered astonishment, then consternation. He spoke rapidly.

"Señor Pacheco says that such a large sum will take time to collect, if you want cash," Teo told her. "His bank does not have such amounts on hand."

"I doubt the . . . people I'm doing business with will accept a check," Melanie said dryly. "How long will it take?"

"A few days, *señorita*," the banker answered. "Monday, Tuesday, I do not know."

"I see." She fought to keep the panic from her voice.

"I will watch for this wire myself," Señor Pacheco assured her. "I will expedite the collection of cash."

"Thank you," Melanie said faintly. "I appreciate your help."

"There is something else," Señor Pacheco explained, his brow creased in a frown. "A sum this large will attract attention in Madrid when it comes through. Our government, you understand, may be interested—for tax purposes." He spread his hands to express his helplessness and shook his head apologetically. How much did he suspect?

"If anyone asks," she said firmly, "this money is meant to buy a house, a summer home."

"Ah, *sí*, I understand. A property. Of course."

He didn't believe her, but never mind. By the time anyone could start to look too closely, this whole nightmare would be over.

As they left the bank, Teo's hand was at her back again. She wanted to knock his arm away, to scream at him: *"Let my sister go!"*

"We will check with Señor Pacheco this afternoon," he said quietly. "And then you will know what to tell them when they call you at five."

"It's not my father's fault," she insisted breathlessly. "It's not. You know that. He wired the money yesterday. Surely those men will understand. They have to."

"Of course they will. Don't worry."

"Don't worry! With my sister held prisoner up there—" She clamped her mouth shut instantly, cutting off her sentence.

He seemed not to notice. She watched his face carefully, but he looked as worried as she felt. Sincerely worried. He took her to a café near the outskirts of town, which was not quite so crowded as those in the plaza, and they sat under a vine-covered trellis. The tables were spread with checkered oilcloth and the floor tiles were cracked. A working man's place. She refused his offer of breakfast, but agreed to a cup of coffee. It was hot and sweet and she immediately felt somewhat revived.

"They will wait, won't they?" she asked again. "I mean, if the money isn't here, what can they do?"

"Nothing, I expect."

"By the way, did you find out anything more last night?" He'd made no secret of his nocturnal journey; why not ask?

"No, nothing more. Except that Cecily is well."

"Did you see her?" she burst out.

"No, Melanie, I merely heard that. How could I see her?"

Lies! How dare he sit there and lie to her like that? How dare he dirty himself with such low deception? What kind of man was he?

Teo deftly steered the conversation away from Cecily. He began talking about the factory district of Pamplona and the modernization being carried out there. There didn't seem to be much that the professor didn't know something about— he was a veritable book of knowledge, she thought sarcastically to herself.

How did he manage to continually put up that congenial facade of his in the face of Cecily's predicament? What did he really feel, Melanie wondered. Did he care what happened to Cecily—and to her?

After reading the menu, he asked again if Melanie was hungry. When she again told him no, he removed his glasses and smiled. "You do not eat enough. Through such an ordeal you would be wise to keep up your strength," he said.

"I don't have much of an appetite these days," she replied.

Still smiling slightly, he shook his head and studied her openly. There it was again, she realized uncomfortably, that charm, that look in his eyes that told her he was thinking of her in more than a casual way. Desire. He didn't even bother to hide it.

She squirmed in her hard chair, avoiding his gaze, trying to quell the tingling in her stomach.

It's not fair, she thought. Teo had no right to be so damned appealing, to turn on his charm, to try to lure her. And what could she do to stop him—tell him she knew he was involved in the Cax Carot? She had to sit there and fight the attraction. It simply wasn't fair.

They left the small café and Teo, as always, handed her into his car. His Mercedes. Once more, she asked herself why a man as obviously well-off as Teo would need money? But then, perhaps neither he nor Esteban was really all that well-off. Perhaps their creditors were breathing down their necks at this very minute. What kind of factory had Teo told her his family owned? Machinery, parts for ships? Was the Sanlucar family in dire financial straits? It was possible . . .

On the drive to Esteban's, he parked in a small shopping area near the factory district.

"I will only be a moment," he said, stepping out of the car.

She watched his ease of movement as he entered a store. Then he was back, sliding into his seat, turning toward her. He produced a box of Band-Aids and a small bottle of iodine, then took her hand in his to doctor her scrapes. But all she could think was that he had obviously not forgotten her cut. Did he suspect something? Or had she convinced him with her story about the broken mirror? Was he merely being the ever-conscientious host and protector?

At three, just before the Banco de Navarra closed for siesta, Teo phoned Señor Pacheco. When he hung up and slowly turned to Melanie, she could tell by his expression. "It's not there," she said flatly.

"No. Señor Pacheco even phoned the main office in Madrid. Nothing yet. It may take until Monday."

She covered her face with her hands. "Will they believe me? Will they kill Cecily?"

"No," he soothed. "They must believe you. It is the truth."

Pulling her face from her hands, she cried bitterly, "The truth! Since when has the truth meant anything!" But he only stood there, a look of sympathy on his face, his eyes clouded with anxiety.

When they arrived back at Esteban's house, she phoned her parents again.

"Hell, Melanie, I wired that money yesterday, like they said! It has to go through New York and Madrid. And there's a weekend coming up. What do they want? I'm not a magician!"

"I'll explain it. I'll make them believe me, Dad. They'll wait."

"Hang in there, Mel. Thank God you're there."

"Right, Dad."

Hang in there. Well, she was trying.

She went to her room and attempted to sleep after the phone call, but she kept remembering the interior of that ugly little cabin. She had a clear image of its few shabby furnishings and the terrible bilious light that had made everyone there look drained and sickly. And the guns... Would those men really harm Cecily? What about Carlos, her sister's erstwhile lover? Even if he had deliberately lured Cecily into this thing, surely he would not let them hurt her.

In her mind's eye, she kept seeing clocks, all different sizes and shapes, each one, however, reading the same: 5:00 P.M. She went over again and again what she would say to this man when he called her at the phone booth. She must make the caller believe her sincerity. It wasn't her fault the money wasn't there. It wasn't her fault!

Then she would see Cecily, her sister's pinched, pale face, the suntan gone, the freckles standing out as if she were ill. And her own pallid face, Melanie thought, must look the same as Cecily's—worried, sickly and white. How long could she keep up this facade for Teo and his uncle? How long before she broke down and the accusations poured from her lips?

Punctually at four-thirty, Teo knocked on her door. "Melanie? Are you ready?"

Naturally, he insisted on driving her into the city for the phone call. She was not allowed to go anywhere alone. And how convenient an excuse it was to say she must be protected! Yet, she thought, what would she do if he'd let her go alone? Nothing.

The phone booth, an old-fashioned wood-and-glass one, was on a corner near the central plaza. How would she hear? The noise all around her was deafening. The hollow drums thumped, the flutes wailed, the dancers' heads went up and down, up and down above the crowd. A young man lay rolling on the ground in the plaza, laughing hysterically, his shirt stained with wine.

She could do nothing but stand there, waiting, with the crowd jolting and shoving her. The minutes crawled slowly by. And then the phone rang. Melanie leaped for it.

"Pronto," a voice called. *"¿Pronto?"*

"Hello? This is Melanie Royce..."

The voice said something, then the line went dead.

"Who was it?" Teo asked.

"I don't know. A wrong number maybe." She fought a growing hysteria.

They waited. Three minutes past five, four minutes, five. At eight minutes after five the phone rang again. Melanie stared at it, afraid for a moment. Then she snatched it up. "Hello? Don't hang up, please. This is Melanie Royce." She held her breath, aching inside with fear.

"Señorita Royce?" A harsh, heavily accented voice. Sevé? "You have my money?"

"No, not yet. But it's coming. My father wired it yesterday. It'll be here very soon." Her words tripped over themselves, rushing to get out.

There was silence on the line.

"Hello? Hello?" cried Melanie. "Please!"

"It better be here. *Mañana.* Tomorrow. Or your sister may get hurt."

"No, please! Don't hurt her! The money will come. And…and how do I know you really have Cecily? How do I know she's still alive?"

"You must take my word on that. The word of a gentleman." He laughed hoarsely.

"Let me talk to her, please."

"Tomorrow at five at this same *teléfono.* No more time." The line went dead.

"Hello, hello! Oh, please!" But there was no one at the other end.

She hung up the phone and turned to leave the booth, swaying as if drugged.

"Melanie, what happened?" Teo asked anxiously.

"I have till tomorrow at five. He'll call again." She shuddered. "I guess I should be relieved."

He put a hand on her arm. "You are very brave, Melanie."

She withdrew from his touch. "Me? I'm scared to death, Teo."

"That is nothing. Like the matador. He is afraid, but still he does it. He faces his worst fear. That is true courage."

Dinner at Esteban's that night was a sad charade. As always, the table was beautifully laid, and the candlelight winked cheerfully off the crystal. To Melanie, the whole scene was a bitter parody of ease and well-being. Esteban spoke gravely, trying to draw her into the conversation, but she found it difficult to respond graciously. The food stuck in her throat while Teo offered the best morsels off the serving platter or another glass of wine or a particularly ripe peach. She wanted to scream "Stop it!" She wanted to run from the room, to knock the exquisite lamps off their tables.

She looked up once to find Teo's eyes on her. "Your sister will not be harmed," he said softly.

"Can you promise me that?" she pressed.

He smiled sadly. "Would that I could. But nevertheless, I am sure. Alas, poor Melanie, this is hard on you."

"A brandy," suggested Esteban. "That such a thing should happen to a guest of mine! A brandy, and you will sleep."

Her room was a kind of haven, a place where she could let out the sobs of frustration and pummel her mattress in impotent fury. A place where she could sink down onto her bed and cry and feel herself safe from prying eyes.

Then she rose, her fists clenched at her sides. She would have to keep her wits about her. Neither Teo nor his uncle must ever know her fear and her loneliness; she would have to conceal the strain she felt at deceiving them, the tearing worry over her sister. She must stay strong for a few more days—until the money came. She must lie and hide her true feelings and let them see nothing, *nothing* of the truth.

The curtains were billowing at the balcony doors. Melanie was drawn to the cool moist air, scented with the fragrance of the overhanging trees. A breeze, almost a wind, blew from over the hills, from the ocean, fresh and bracing. She took a deep breath and leaned on the balustrade, looking up at the starry night sky. The moon hung like a huge blank eye, faintly veined. Its light would be bright enough to reveal anyone leaving the house that night. Was Teo going out again? And why did he go? Did he need to reassure Sevé that the money was truly on its way?

There was a noise behind her, footsteps, a low voice calling her name. "Melanie?"

Her breath caught in her throat.

"Melanie, are you there?"

Oh, God, please let him leave her alone.

Then he was behind her on the balcony, the familiar, faint smell of after-shave reaching her nostrils. "I was worried. You weren't in your room." He paused. "I knocked."

"I was out here."

"Yes."

He was standing too close, and suddenly the night was sultry. Melanie's breath came too quickly and a pulse beat strongly in her neck, jumping against her hot skin. She could sense him moving even closer; if she didn't turn around maybe he'd leave, maybe—

"Are you all right?" he asked quietly.

She laughed then, a short, nervous sound. "All right? No, I'm not all right. I'm worried sick, I'm half out of my mind—" Her strained torrent stopped short and she drew in her breath with a gasp as he stepped even nearer. She felt trapped, like an animal, her heart leaping in fear, her breath coming fast, her body taut with adrenaline. She had to run, to escape; her muscles tensed involuntarily.

But his hand was on her shoulder and he was turning her toward him, slowly, slowly. His dark head bent and his eyes, glittering like black coals in the night, were fixed on hers and his mouth descended. Melanie was frantic. Where did the game end? His lips were on hers, warm and firm. She could taste him, smell him. Her head whirled with the explosion of sensation: the touch of his mouth, his hands hard on her shoulders, the heat of him.

She closed her eyes and let him kiss her, let him open her mouth and find the honey inside, let him knead her shoulders with his strong brown hands. She could only close her mind to the sweet torment and endure it while her arms hung limply at her sides.

But her resolve waned, and slowly and inevitably her arms slid around his back. How could she! her mind screamed even as his mouth moved from her lips to her throat and waves of raw pleasure coursed through her veins.

Teo took his time, as if they had all night to stand on the misty balcony, embracing. If he had pressed her, she might have summoned the strength to repel him. As it was, her response grew until her mouth opened willingly to receive his and her hands began to massage the long muscles of his back.

She wanted him. And yet the wild notion of fully submitting to his caresses was abhorrent to her sense of right and wrong. She couldn't believe she was standing there in her scant silk nightgown, allowing him to pull her against his chest, to feel his male hardness pressing into her leg.

He moved his hands from her shoulders and touched the swell of her breast, feather soft, reverently. The pulse in the hollow of her throat leaped compulsively, and she gasped as his mouth moved over hers with more demand. Then suddenly his lips left hers, and his head bent and he was kissing the curve of one breast through the smooth peach-colored silk. Her nipples grew taut. He kissed each slowly, with infinite patience. She tried a thousand times to say no.

But his careful ministrations, his gentle, giving caresses made her heart cry, *yes, take me. Teo. Let me take you.*

He kissed her earlobe and whispered, "I want you," and her stomach rolled over and the agony of indecision held her silent. "Let me love you, Melanie."

She said yes. She told herself that it was all part of the game—Teo mustn't suspect. But she knew it was a lie. God help her, she wanted him, as much as he wanted her. She ached to feel his warmth, to rise to his passion, to welcome sweet oblivion.

His nakedness in the sultry night was beautiful, making her feel lovely herself as the thin silk gown slipped from her body and dropped in a circle at her feet by the bedside.

He kissed her everywhere, in sensitive places she'd never realized she possessed. Her spine, the white curve of her hip, behind her knees, even her ankles. Every inch of her flesh was ripe, ready to be plucked by his mouth, to be savored by his tongue. Gasp after gasp escaped Melanie unashamedly. Once she breathed, "I never knew it could be this way."

Still he did not poise himself above her. He waited. He drew her out until she was pulling at his shoulders with her hands, dizzy with urgency.

Finally he entered her, ending her suspense. Melanie instinctively moved to his rhythm, responded to his quickening thrusts. Almost immediately she felt a deep physical release, a sensation so unexpected, so exquisite that she cried out, her head thrashing from side to side, her mouth moving as if in prayer.

His soft laugh reached her consciousness. She froze.

"Melanie," he said, "do not pull away. That was but the first pleasure. Let me show you, please," and he began caressing her again, slowly, slowly, until she relaxed beneath him and at last, amazed, she felt desire rekindling.

It was impossible, but he brought her to a fever pitch once more. Her flesh began to burn, her movements matched his, faster, faster, and then she was moaning and gasping and kneading his back with her hands and the fire raged until it exploded in brilliant flashes in and around her. It had been so beautiful, so wonderful, that her tears mingled with their sweat.

She'd thought, she'd hoped, he would stay with her in the big bed, but after kissing and stroking her lovingly he shifted away from her and groaned.

"We'd be doing this all night," he said softly, "and you must rest."

"You're right, of course," she said, just as softly, and he turned once more and kissed her.

"Are you afraid I might lock you up and keep you my prisoner?" he said against her lips.

"Am I your prisoner?"

"Only if you want to be." He rose then and dressed in the darkness. His words rang in her head: only if she wanted to be. And when he was gone she cried into the pillow and wondered how it had all happened, how she had let herself go like that. And she wondered if she did want to be his lover, his prisoner. If somehow he had just removed her shackles, and the choice, now, was hers.

Chapter Ten

Melanie was puffy eyed when she descended the stairs the next morning. It had been a long, image-filled night in which sleep had come only in brief, restless spurts. She'd lain in the bed and cursed her weakness, cursed the flaw in her character that had allowed her to yearn for a man who had betrayed her. And not only had she yearned for him, she thought in shame, she'd willingly surrendered her body to his.

She looked into the living room. No Teo or Esteban. Then she glanced through the French doors onto the patio. They weren't there, either.

Why did Teo have to be a traitor? Couldn't she have awakened that morning and found it had all been a dreadful mistake and Teo was innocent? And yet she'd seen him in that cabin, standing watch over her sister. A sinister and devious man—and her lover, she thought, heartsick.

Teo Sanlucar. He was like an itch under her skin, a roar in her head, a knife thrust in her breast. He'd become the nucleus of her existence. And she'd let it happen.

No, Melanie thought, she hadn't just let it happen. She had wanted him all along, secretly gloried in his dark watchfulness on the beach even while she'd been afraid. She had asked for it.

Of course she knew that when she did find Teo and Esteban their faces and their words would be solicitous—poor dear Melanie. She suddenly felt she couldn't bear it, couldn't enact the disgusting farce for even one more minute.

Much to her surprise, neither man was at home.

Lucia smiled warmly and handed Melanie a note from Teo. It read: "Esteban has gone to Bilbao for the day and I have gone out on business." *Business,* she sneered. "Please wait with Lucia and I shall return and drive you to the bank this afternoon. Teo."

Melanie sat in the kitchen and sipped coffee and envisioned him with her sister and those awful men. How had Cecily got herself into this fix? Had her sister actually been so blind where Carlos was concerned that she hadn't seen what he was doing or where he was leading her? How else could it have happened? Cecily wasn't selected at random to be kidnapped. Her foolish, naive sister...

Nine o'clock came and went. Melanie telephoned Diego Pacheco at the bank, for the second time in an hour.

"It is Saturday," he tried to explain, "and even though we remain open this day until one, the banks in New York, I fear, are closed." But a wire transfer could come in from Madrid, he told her in a kind voice. She must, of course, try again later.

It won't come, Melanie thought as she hung up. What would the Cax Carot do to her sister? How could Melanie make them understand that the transfer was complicated by a weekend now? But any reasonable person knew that.

Reasonable? A kidnapper?

There was a hope. Teo. Surely he would explain the situation to his comrades. Teo would not let them harm Cecily. He might be greedy and deceitful, but a killer? And he was still a man of learning and culture, a professor of history... he could not be a murderer!

By ten the waiting had become intolerable. How could she just sit in this elegant house and do nothing?

It came to Melanie suddenly. The money most likely was not going to arrive on a weekend. She had to accept that. And there was no guarantee that Teo could keep Cecily from harm. But perhaps the police could.

She dashed up the stairs to her bedroom two at a time and collected her purse and camera. Then she turned and stared mutely at the unmade bed. A shiver crawled up her spine. Had she really made love there with Teo only a few short hours ago? Could it have been as wonderful as she remembered? A disturbing thought insinuated itself into her mind. Was it possible that, in spite of the guilt she was feeling, she had come to care for her treacherous Basque? That she felt not only an intense attraction but something deeper? She couldn't think about it now.

She turned from the bed and walked quickly to a small inlaid desk in a corner of the room, where she scratched out a note for Teo. "I have gone shopping. The waiting is driving me crazy. Melanie." Downstairs she handed the note to Lucia.

"Por Señor Teo."

"Sí, señorita," Lucia said, nodding and smiling.

Then Melanie hurried out to her car. The drive was becoming familiar. She took the curves along the winding road smoothly, if a little too fast, but at least this time there were no animals to bar her path.

On the outskirts of Pamplona she found a parking place near an ironworks factory and locked her car. The police station, she recalled, was close to the older part of town, perhaps three or four blocks west of the square. She didn't know its exact location, but that didn't matter. She began heading in the direction of the plaza. There would be a policeman on every corner and all she needed to do was ask directions.

Melanie had plenty to tell the Guardia Civil. She knew the kidnappers, and she even knew where they were holding Cecily. Why hadn't she gone and done this before? Could it be that she dreaded giving the police Teo's name?

She stopped short. What if these Basque kidnappers really did have a pipeline to the police? What if the very policeman she spoke to was a Basque infiltrator?

She began to walk again. But if the police acted quickly, surely no one could get word to Teo or Sevé in time for them to react.

The element of surprise would be on the side of the Guardia Civil.

As she approached the plaza the crowds were frenzied, shoving and elbowing her, making it impossible to hurry. She spotted one of the ever-present policemen in his formal, polished attire and walked toward him. If anyone were following—which was always a possibility—she'd pretend to photograph the officer.

She received the directions, and just in case, she took his picture.

Clever, she was so clever!

Then she headed in the direction he had indicated but stopped once or twice to take a few more pictures. *Act normal,* she told herself.

There it was, the station house. Just down the street now, so near. And yet, would she be seen by someone as she entered? If she hadn't been followed, did the kidnappers perhaps have someone watching the station?

She stood at the corner and took a picture of the cathedral's steeple, which emerged between the buildings. Then she moved her camera up and down the crowded street as if looking for another shot. She scanned the many faces. She did the same thing two more times, viewing the entire block to her satisfaction. There were no strange men watching her. She saw only *feria*-goers and tourists.

She took a deep breath and crossed to the other side of the street, two buildings away from the station house. Someone offered her wine and Melanie took it, smiling, trying to appear as if she were joining the gaiety of the crowd.

She moved on down the block, stopping to look in a shop window. She was nearly there.

A moment before she was going to turn and head up the steps of the police station, she caught a reflection in the windowpane. Her heart jumped in fear.

There, on the other side of the street, was a young man in a black beret. He was standing still, out of time with the flux, facing in her direction.

Melanie kept her back to him, pretending to window-shop. The hordes of people moved past the man in both directions but he remained rooted to his spot.

He was watching her.

Melanie made a quick decision and began strolling very slowly in the opposite direction from the police station; her hands were fumbling with her camera.

She stopped, keeping her head turned away from the man in the beret. She lifted her camera and shot a picture of God knew what, then very slowly she swung it around, aiming in his direction. She swept the camera slowly past him, as if looking for something photogenic; she saw his dark head turn quickly. Her heart leaped wildly and her hands began to tremble.

Dumb! She had been so stupid! She should have known they'd either have someone tailing her or someone watching the police station. Now she was a prisoner of her own audacity.

What was she going to do?

She was so painfully conspicuous, standing one building away from the police station. If she walked in, would the young man rush to tell Sevé? Then they would kill Cecily and disappear into the hills, as Basques had done for centuries.

Move, think!

She spotted a group of student types nearby, drunk as lords. She made an elaborate production of taking their picture.

Not good enough. She was standing there like a criminal caught in the act, next to the police station!

She began walking again. To head in the direction opposite the station was so open a ruse that surely he would spot it and report to Teo or Sevé that Melanie had seen him, then fled.

She turned around again and pretended to be searching the street for something specific. Then she set off with a purposeful stride to the corner directly in front of the station. She stepped off the curb and walked diagonally across the road, weaving through traffic, bumping into people.

Then she stood in front of the shop—a shoe shop—and looked in the window. She couldn't see him because the glass was facing the wrong way, but Melanie sensed he was still there. She could almost feel his dark eyes following her every move.

She entered the shop.

Shoes. She didn't need any, but she knew she had better walk out with a package and a contented look on her face.

Melanie spent a long time selecting a pair of Italian pumps. Finally she paid the clerk with a traveler's check, at a terrible rate of exchange, and left with her package.

There he was. Studiously nonchalant, positioned across the street from her, his head turned away. All he needed was a newspaper to hide behind, she thought.

Melanie began walking in the general direction of her car. There was nothing more she could do to allay his suspicions. It had been foolish of her to consider going to the police in the first place. And God help Cecily if the young

Basque reported Melanie's suspicious movements to his superiors. But he had no reason to, did he? She had played it wisely. So what if he'd seen her on the same street as the police station?

Melanie drove out of Pamplona barely aware that she was operating a vehicle. She was thinking of Teo, trying to imagine his reaction to her note. Shopping. He'd never believe it! He'd put one and one together and know that she was up to something.

Foolish!

Perhaps she could beat him back to Esteban's and destroy the note.

She drove too quickly along the narrow road; once, she nearly collided with a goat. Her blouse was sticking to her back with nervous perspiration.

When she pulled up the long drive her heart sank—Teo's car was already there.

She entered the house, feeling both guilty and frightened. As she passed the two stone lions, she took a deep breath and told herself to act normal, to calm down. Whatever Teo might suspect, he couldn't prove a thing.

Peeking into the living room, she saw that he wasn't there. She looked out the French doors onto the lawn. Not there, either. Finally she spotted him in the library, deep in concentration. He hadn't noticed her yet. She stood motionless, gripping her shopping bag, watching him. He looked like the professor again, with his reading glasses on and the papers scattered across the desk. The house seemed suddenly too hushed, and she felt as if she should go back to the front door, bang it open and shout, "Hi! I'm home!"

But she had to face him. Melanie squared her shoulders, walked to the library door and cleared her throat. "Hello." She forced a smile to her lips. "What are you doing—correcting papers?"

He looked up finally, his train of thought broken. "Hello," he said, "and yes, that is exactly what I am doing. Summer students, Melanie."

"Don't you find it hard to concentrate with everything that's happened?"

"Yes. But that does not excuse neglecting my work."

"I see." She wondered, inanely, if Cecily had a paper in that stack.

He removed his glasses then, rubbing his eyes before he looked back up to Melanie. "Where did you go?"

A chill crawled across her flesh. "You got my note, didn't you?" she asked levelly.

"Yes. But I found it difficult to believe you could shop under such pressure, Melanie. You amaze me." His dark eyes rested on her.

She looked away and shrugged. "I called the bank several times and the money had still not arrived. I was so nervous..." She smiled weakly.

"Of course."

"So I had to go somewhere, do something, anything..."

"Shopping."

"Yes." She looked back at him and held up the plastic bag that was sticky and warm in her hand. "Shoes."

"Shoes. I see."

"I killed some time." She tried to smile again but her face felt as though it might crack with the effort.

He was silent for too long a time. Finally he said, "You did not do anything...foolish, did you, Melanie?"

"Foolish?"

"Yes. Such as contact someone...say, the *policía*?"

Melanie did her utmost to appear surprised, adding a touch of wounded pride to her expression. "I would never do anything to compromise Cecily. How could you even think such a thing?"

He was not very quick to answer. "I merely asked." Then he placed his elbows on the desk, hands folded under his chin in that familiar pose, and he sat there silently, studying her. The moment stretched out agonizingly.

Deliberately she changed the subject. "Is Esteban home yet?"

He shook his head. "Still in Bilbao, I assume."

"Oh..."

"And," he added, "Lucia is also gone for the afternoon."

He was letting her know how alone they were, and a picture flashed into her mind: Teo standing behind her last night on the balcony, turning her to face him, his mouth descending...

"Have you eaten?"

"What?" she asked breathlessly.

"Eaten?"

She shook her head.

"Well, then, we must be in Pamplona at five. Perhaps I could take you for the afternoon meal..."

"No, thank you. I'm really not..."

"I insist. You see, I am a poor cook and without Esteban or Lucia, I am afraid we wil' both starve."

Melanie shook her head again. "Please, not Pamplona. The crowds..."

"I understand." He sat for a minute more, thinking. Then he looked at his watch. "Could you prepare a basket of food? Things that are left from before?"

"Leftovers."

"Yes. Then perhaps we might drive somewhere. I have a place in mind."

"But the bank?"

"We shall telephone Señor Pacheco first. The money will come when it comes. We cannot make it arrive any sooner. I will not allow you to sit here, worrying so."

"I'm not sure..."

He got to his feet, pushing papers together, leaving neat stacks for later. "I shall telephone the bank now. Could you attend to the basket?"

"I guess so," she said listlessly, "but where are we going?"

He looked up from the desk. "Allow me to surprise you, Melanie."

She found a basket covered in cobwebs in the laundry room and cleaned it carefully. Then she wrapped cheese and bread and placed them inside, together with several bunches of plump green grapes. Teo walked into the kitchen with two wine glasses and a dusty bottle.

"I am no cook, but I would make an excellent wine steward." He smiled charmingly.

A picnic, Melanie thought, feeling suddenly restless. "Maybe we should just eat here. I'm not in the mood..."

"Nonsense. We will steal a few hours from your worries. I absolutely insist."

She was a prisoner, a prisoner of his deceit, his lies and his overbearing charm. She hadn't the heart to fight him.

"Come, change your clothing and perhaps this afternoon will be a pleasant surprise for you."

For a moment as their eyes met and their gazes locked, Melanie thought that he might take a step toward her, pull her into his arms, bring his mouth down on hers. It all came flooding back, his embrace, his artful hands, the thrust of his powerful male body against hers.

"Aren't you going to change?" Teo asked then, his mouth curved in a small knowledgeable smile.

"Change," she breathed. "Of course." She tore her stare away in embarrassed confusion.

She changed into slacks. Then they were off on a mysterious jaunt, Teo's so-called pleasant surprise.

They took his Mercedes and he put the top down as they headed north on a winding mountain road that Melanie didn't recognize.

"Where are we going?" she asked curiously.

"Back to the past," was all he would tell her, but his voice was teasing.

"Well, that's fine," Melanie said, "but don't forget, I have to be at that phone booth in Pamplona at five."

"You will be at the telephone on time. Now relax."

"Relax . . ." she mumbled to herself.

Any other time, it would have been a beautiful drive up through the foothills of the Pyrenees. Teo was charming and Melanie repeatedly had to remind herself that he was the enemy—he was *not* a handsome, debonair Basque taking her for a romantic drive in his sporty convertible.

It was very difficult for her to hate him.

The road began to rise into the higher mountains. As they ascended, Melanie noticed a kind of mist covering the countryside, lying low in the ravines and sneaking up into the forests. It was by no means a cold fog, but it was heavy, blotting out the sun, muffling all sound. They came to a stop at a crossroads in the dense forest once, and Melanie could hear the twittering of birds from deep within the misty woods.

They drove on. As the fog thickened, the valley seemed to grow darker and the foliage greener. It was breathtakingly lovely. Haunting, Melanie thought.

"You could at least tell me where we are," she said over the soft purr of the engine. She was a little nervous. Did this trip have anything to do with the kidnapping? Some rendezvous?

"Roncesvalles Pass," Teo said. "Does that sound familiar?"

It did, indeed, but Melanie had to search her memory. "I know," she said, a bit irked that he was testing her. "The song of Roland," she put in smugly.

"Yes. Very good," said the professor as he pulled off the road at the crest of a lofty hill. He turned the car off. *"Le Chanson de Roland."* He stepped out of the car and came around to open her door. "From here we must walk."

Melanie swung her legs out and hesitated a moment, finally taking his proffered hand. "I don't remember a thing about Roland," she admitted. "There's an old legend, isn't there?"

Teo shrugged as he began to lead her along a mossy path heading into the shrouded forest, away from the roadside. "Myth? Fact? It really does not matter."

"That's a very strange thing for a history professor to say."

"Perhaps I am a romantic at heart." His smile was tender, yet she could not believe this was merely an innocent jaunt into the past. Why had he really brought her there? To keep her off guard, to lull her suspicions? Or did he have a different motive in mind? Was he trying to seduce her in yet another way?

Melanie could almost imagine their lovemaking, the tidy picnic basket beside them, a mossy bed beneath, the mist soft and dewy on their naked flesh.

Stop this, her mind commanded. She must not think of him in that way. It was too dangerous; he made it too easy for her to let go, to forget. Hadn't she found that out already?

She glanced at their surroundings, so alien, so unearthly, on that fog-shrouded mountainside.

She moved away from his side as they walked and watched him carefully from the corner of her eye. The hills seemed to encroach upon them, so thick with tall mossy trees and the clouds of mist that she could see only a few yards in any direction. She looked nervously around. Were the kidnappers hidden in the fog somewhere?

The path finally brought them out into a small clearing. Below was the spectacular view of a deep valley, half-hidden now in fog. Surrounding them were dark forests, the trees vague shapes in the mist. There was utter silence and Melanie had the disconcerting feeling that they were the only two living creatures on the mountainside. What did the mist hide?

Teo stopped and stood still, his hands on his hips, as he turned to look in all directions. "Roncesvalles Pass," he said quietly, reverently. He kneeled down on the moist grass and looked up at her. "It's damp and I forgot a blanket, but we'll survive. And we have food."

She knelt down alongside him and opened the picnic basket. Wine, grapes, cheese and bread. Even Esteban's crystal glasses. So very charming...

"Hungry?" He looked at her with concern.

"A little. What was the legend of Roland, by the way?" she asked.

"It is difficult to pry the truth from lore." He smiled and cut her pieces of bread and cheese. "Legend has it that thousands of Moorish Saracens attacked Charlemagne and that one of his many knights, the fairest knight of all, Roland, blew his horn on this hill to warn his uncle who was riding far ahead on the point. The infamous mists of Roncesvalles, however, swallowed the sound of Roland's horn and the knight, who turned his face to the south so that his uncle, Charlemagne, would know of his brave confrontation with the Saracens, perished boldly."

"It's a very heroic tale," Melanie said, sipping wine.

"Very," Teo agreed. "It was even written that when Charlemagne returned safely to France and told Roland's fiancée, she dropped dead on the spot."

Melanie grimaced. "A dreadful ending."

"Quite." He laughed lightly. "But then there is the story, probably far more historically accurate, that Roland did not perish at all."

"I see. And no doubt Charlemagne was not in Spain to rid Europe of the dastardly Saracens, either."

"No," said Teo, "it is believed that he was not. He apparently rode to Spain to make a pilgrimage to Santiago de Compostela and encountered a handful of Basques on his way back into France. There was, of course, a skirmish here, but to what extent it was important, who knows?"

"I like Roland blowing his horn with thousands of bloodthirsty Saracens at his heels."

"So do I."

Melanie took some more bread and glanced around. It was so lovely and quiet in this unearthly forest with the cool, damp air caressing her skin. She could almost see the knights on their great horses, their heavy armor dull in the hazy light, and hear the ring of their swords before the sound was lost in the mists.

She glanced at Teo; he sat close to her on the damp grass, beads of moisture on his dark curling hair. What did he want with her? Why were they here on this deserted pass? Uncomfortably she shifted her position a little farther away from him.

"You do not eat much," he said gently.

"I'm worried, you know that, Teo. I've been worried for days now. It's sort of hard for me to enjoy myself..."

"Of course, I understand."

She looked at him narrowly. He sounded sympathetic, but she didn't believe a word of it. With her own eyes she'd seen him standing in that hut, talking to the kidnappers.

He ate a grape, his pensive gaze resting on her. Then he seemed to give a slight shrug. "Still, it is an interesting spot, is it not? Esteban is far more familiar than I with the many romantic legends of the Pyrenees. I wish you had the time..." Then he paused. "But, no. Once your sister is safe, you will, of course, leave this land of mine."

"Of course," she said boldly. "What would keep me here? This place will never hold fond memories for me, you know."

He looked suddenly wounded, suddenly boyish and alone and hurt. And an unaccountable feeling of guilt swept over her.

"I could not hope that you might remain for a time?" he asked.

"I don't think so," she began.

"Even after...last night?"

Melanie's eyes dropped to her lap abruptly. "I think we should...forget about last night." Her heart thudded heavily; she wanted never to forget, never.

"It will stay with me always." Teo's voice was gentle and sorrowful. He reached out a hand and tilted her chin and she could no longer avoid his gaze. *Oh, God,* she cried inwardly. *I still want him.* And then his hand was behind her head, his long fingers moving through the knot of her coppery hair, loosening it, tenderly urging her toward him.

She responded to his touch, and even as she damned herself she let his lips move over hers and her mouth parted. But there were tears burning in her eyes this time. They spilled finally and Teo tasted them.

He drew back. "You're crying."

"Yes," she whispered.

"Why?"

"Because I'm hurting, Teo. Because I want you to kiss me, but I'm afraid."

"I don't understand..."

Melanie could say nothing. What could she have told him—that she knew he was involved with Cecily's kidnappers?

"You have shut me away," Teo said long moments later.

She nodded, wiping at a stubborn tear.

"And so you will find your sister and merely leave the Basque country. Forever?"

"Yes," Melanie said, "once Cecily is safe..."

"I wish you could have seen another side of life here. It can be very wonderful."

"I'm sure you're right," she said stiffly, as the fog crept silently around them, wrapping Melanie and Teo in an eerie embrace.

They left the magical mountains, driving down toward Pamplona, which lay to the south. Suddenly the sun was on Melanie's shoulders once more, and perspiration dampened her neck. She took a deep breath of relief, put on her sunglasses and repinned the knot in her hair.

She looked at her watch. It was four o'clock. Had the money arrived in Pamplona? Well, if it hadn't, then Teo could just go tell his comrades that she had done everything humanly possible. Was it her fault that wire transfers could not be made on a moment's notice? Perhaps if they hadn't been so greedy...

Teo was quiet as he drove smoothly and expertly along the twisting road. She could see the plateau of Pamplona ahead, baking beneath the Spanish sun.

She looked again at Teo, at his slightly graying hair, at the strong, chiseled profile and the sun-darkened forearms flexing as he steered. They should be driving in to celebrate the *feria*—to drink and dance and cheer the bull and the matador. But that was impossible.

Teo drove as near to the bank as possible and parked, wedging his car between two very old, beat-up Volkswagens.

"Your car will be destroyed," Melanie said, and she felt a perverse sort of satisfaction.

He shrugged. "This will only take a minute. Señor Pacheco is waiting for us."

Melanie knew that in Spain banks closed at 1:00 P.M. on Saturdays. She was grateful to Señor Pacheco for remaining there, just for her. Still, when he unlocked the door and let them both in, his expression told her the worst.

"As I explained," he said with deep concern, "I placed a telephone call to Madrid but my…tracer, you say? has gone nowhere." He spread his hands helplessly. "Perhaps Monday, your American money arrives. ¿Sí?"

Melanie sank into a chair in the lobby. It would take until Monday. Dear God, how was she going to explain it to this Sevé? He'd never believe her. He would think that she was just stalling.

But then—and she glanced up from her folded hands— there was always Teo to explain on her behalf. He could sneak off from Esteban's tonight and tell Sevé what had happened.

Oh, wasn't she lucky, Melanie thought sarcastically, to have Teo on her side?

They left the bank with Señor Pacheco's assurance that he had already spoken to several other banks in Navarre and that as soon as the wire did come in, the large amount of cash would be made available.

At least it was one less thing to worry about, she supposed.

She dreaded the telephone call. It wasn't fair that she had to be the one to tear out her hair worrying. Why couldn't her father have flown over? So what if her mother, the delicate and ever-social Muriel, couldn't possibly stay alone during the ordeal. So what!

How about me, Melanie railed inwardly as they walked. What about her ordeal?

She was deep in thought when Teo placed a hand on her arm; surprised, she came to a halt. "What is the matter?"

"It's not fair," Melanie said sharply.

"I see." His dark brow creased in a frown. "Seldom is life fair," he said pensively.

"Is that so?" Melanie fired back. "It seems to me that everyone around me has control of his life. Everyone else has choices. Everyone but me. I'm the prisoner of all this." And she made an angry sweeping gesture with her hand. Even Cecily had made her own choices—she'd chosen to take up with Carlos, hadn't she? And it seemed safe to assume that was why both she and Cecily were in this mess now.

He softly touched her arm. "I know, but it will come out all right, Melanie. We will find a way."

She only shook him off and walked ahead swiftly, pushing through the happy, laughing, heedless mass of people.

The telephone booth sat ominously at the end of the block. Someone was using it. The time was now four forty-five. Surely the man wouldn't talk all night.

At five o'clock however, he still had not hung up.

Melanie panicked. "Tell him to hang up, Teo!" she pleaded.

Teo walked to the booth and rapped on the glass door, speaking to the occupant in Spanish. She caught a few words; Teo was telling him that they were awaiting an important call, *vida y muerte*. Life and death.

The man looked at them both, shook his head, said *adios* or some such thing, and hung up.

Melanie sighed with relief.

Still, it was three minutes after five by her watch. Had she missed the call? My God.

At ten after, she was twisting her hands nervously, her dark red hair wringing wet at the nape of her neck.

"Why doesn't he call?" she said over and over.

Teo had no explanation. "He must call, Melanie, if he wants his money," he reassured her. "Please do not worry."

"Worry?" she hissed, half out of her mind. "Why would I *worry*?"

It was twelve after five. The street was crowded and noisy with hordes of fiesta lovers, pushing and bumping into one another, offering their bota bags, laughing and cheering, arms around shoulders, dancing and bobbing up and down, up and down.

There were always cars jamming the narrow street. It would momentarily clear to the tune of many horns, then jam up once again.

Melanie never saw the nondescript auto that pulled up near them, blocking traffic. She was looking at Teo, trying to avoid the crush of the throng, when suddenly Teo's face darkened at something he saw over her shoulder.

Melanie turned around quickly. Two men in white shirts and black berets had disengaged themselves from the crowd and before she had time to react, they were standing on either side of her, each taking an arm.

"What do you think you're—?" she gasped, then felt a cold, hard object shoved into her ribs. Disbelieving, she looked down. Half-hidden in one of the men's hands was a gun. "No," she breathed, too terrified to move.

"Vayate," one of the men said. "Go. The car." He flicked his head toward the curb.

"I . . ." Melanie tried to turn her head. Where was Teo? Why didn't he stop them?

"Go," came the other man's curt command and suddenly they were pulling her toward a car.

She was shoved into the back seat before she could think, and in the madness of the fiesta, no one had noticed, not a soul.

"What are you doing!" she demanded.

The driver turned around. It was Sevé. "Keep quiet," he said in a low, threatening voice, and Melanie's heart flew into her throat. She looked at them, panic-stricken, helpless.

Teo? *Where is he?*

She twisted in her seat to stare out the window, ignoring the young Basque who sat tensely beside her. The car was already moving, but she could still see Teo standing there, utterly motionless, buffeted by the revelers, his hands shoved in his pockets and his face totally devoid of expression.

She turned around again. Damn him to hell, she thought. How very proud of himself he must be—he'd delivered her straight into this madman's hands.

And then Sevé moved his head slightly, his dark eyes catching hers in the mirror. "You have played games with us, Señorita Royce." He grinned slowly. "Now it will cost you greatly."

Chapter Eleven

The car swerved around a corner too fast and threw Melanie against the man on her left. Her mind was spinning in futility and confusion, unable to absorb what had happened. It seemed so unreal that she was sitting there, in this car, being driven out of Pamplona. She was aware of faces flashing by the window, of Sevé pressing on the horn again and again, scattering people before him, jerkily stopping and starting the car.

The men on either side of her smelled of sweat and wood smoke. They were dressed in dirty white with the inevitable black berets giving them an air of rakishness. She looked again, closer. Why, they truly were boys! Not even twenty. One watched her as a rodent would watch a snake about to strike, in paralyzed fascination. The other had turned his head away—unable to meet her eyes? They each carried ugly black handguns stuck in their red sashes. The one in the front passenger seat turned and smiled sickly at her, as if in apology. He was so young he had pimples on his face. What was going on? These kidnappers were practically children. Except Sevé.

And Teo.

Had he known this was planned? Had he led her to the phone booth, as a lamb is led to slaughter, and calmly handed her over to these men? Or had he, too, been surprised by Sevé's coup?

What were they going to do with her? She was afraid to speak, but she forced herself to lean forward and ask Sevé, "Where are we going? What do you want from me? If anything happens to either me or my sister, you will not get the money."

But Sevé never turned his head. He laughed, a low harsh chortle that made Melanie shiver. He was evil, pure evil.

She fell back against the car seat, weak with fear, her heart pounding drumbeats inside her head. Her parents would call . . . They would be frantic with worry. And there was no one now to help either her or Cecily. No one. They were alone, prisoners of this insane Sevé and his protégés. It was only too obvious that he was their leader, that the boys were afraid of him. But where did Teo fit in to this mess? And what, exactly, had he and Sevé argued about that night in the café?

Melanie could only sit there and endure the bumpy ride, the proximity of the boys with their guns, the evil aura of Sevé. She clung to the belief that they were taking her to Cecily and that they could not harm her—or Cecily—until they got the money.

But what would happen then?

Eventually she leaned forward and tried once more. "My father wired the money two days ago. You must believe that. It had to go through New York and Madrid. I've checked with the bank many times. The money has not arrived yet."

Sevé said nothing. The boy in the front seat turned, though, and stared at her gravely. Did he understand?

"Please, we've tried to do what you said. But it takes several days for a money transfer. Believe me, I would give it to you if I had it."

The boy with the bad complexion said something to Sevé in Basque. There was a grunt in answer. Then silence.

It suddenly occurred to Melanie to pay attention to their route. Most likely they were taking her to that cabin where she'd seen Cecily. But Melanie couldn't be certain, so she tried to mark her surroundings, just in case the information came in handy at some point. Sevé was driving up into the hills, along a road that twisted and turned. What direction from Pamplona? She craned her neck around to look at the sun. It was behind them. They were going east then, perhaps northeast. How long had they been driving? She glanced surreptitiously at her watch. Five forty-three. They'd abducted her a few minutes after five. She estimated that they'd gone maybe thirty kilometers—twenty miles or so. She'd keep track.

Sevé followed the rough road until it ended, then pulled up and parked at the edge of a path that led up the mountainside. It seemed vaguely familiar to Melanie. Of course, this was where she'd followed Teo; the path led to the hut. But it had been dark then, and everything had looked different.

When she got out of the car, Sevé snatched her camera bag; he removed the camera, clumsily yanking off its case. He pried open the back with uncaring fingers and pulled out the film, deliberately exposing it. He tossed the ruined film aside and removed the unopened rolls, grinning as he flattened them with a boot heel. Then he threw the empty camera into the bag and handed it to Melanie with a mocking flourish. After that he searched her shoulder bag. Her traveler's checks he leafed through and put back. The same with her car keys and some pesetas.

What was he looking for?

Finally, he seemed satisfied and returned the purse to her. There was much talking then, as if Melanie's four kidnappers now felt safe. Pointing toward the path, the pimply boy said, "You walk." The other two nodded, their hands on their guns.

"And do not try to run," said Sevé harshly. "There are bullets in these guns."

They walked. The hike seemed much shorter in the sunlight than it had at night. The gnarled tree was there, but it no longer looked so ominous. The meadows alternated with evergreen forests; Melanie recalled the smell of pine in her nostrils that night.

The hut looked smaller and more insignificant by daylight. A shepherd's cabin. It was made of stone and wood and its roof was thatched. Sheep grazed beyond it, their plump white forms like dirty powder puffs dotting the green field. Smoke rose in a lazy spiral from the stone chimney.

Sevé shouted across the meadow. The plank door opened inward and a man stepped out and waved, then shouted something back.

Cecily must be in there, Melanie thought. Was she all right? She'd been held prisoner in that place for days—it must have been close to a week. Did they feed her? Let her sleep?

Sevé pushed Melanie unnecessarily, so that she stumbled through the low doorway.

"Melanie!" she heard, "Oh, Mel!" And then Cecily was hugging her fiercely, crying, sobbing hysterically with fright and relief.

She shook her sister sharply. "Stop it, Cecily." Then, holding her at arm's length, she asked, "Are you okay? Did they hurt you?"

"No, I mean yes, I'm okay."

"Did they..." Melanie hesitated to put her fear into words, but Cecily caught on.

"They're not into rape," she said disdainfully, "only kidnapping."

"Well, I guess that's something. Oh, Cecily, how did you ever get yourself into this?"

"Oh, don't, *don't* be superior. I couldn't stand it, Mel. I've been so bored and scared and I was so worried..." And she burst into tears again. "I was afraid... They threatened to get you, too. The money... What did Dad say? Oh, Mel, I'm so sorry..."

"What's going on, Cecily? You disappeared in Madrid. I was half out of my mind... What is going on?" Then she looked around at the dirty, unkempt cabin, at the young boys who stared at them as if they were strange beasts of some sort, at Sevé who smiled gloatingly and stood leaning on a long black, wicked-looking rifle.

"Can we go outside?" she asked.

Cecily shook her head, wiping away tears with one grimy hand. She was dirty and pale, her jeans were wrinkled and spotted, her T-shirt stained. "They won't let us." She gulped back tears. "Except to go to the outhouse. Under guard."

Melanie closed her eyes and swallowed hard. They were truly prisoners.

"Come on, let's sit down on your bed, at least. Tell me, from the beginning. I have to know what's going on, Cecily."

"Oh, Mel, it's such a mess." She sniffed. "You know, in Madrid, how I didn't want to go home with you?"

Melanie nodded.

"It was because Carlos and I and his friends... They call themselves the Cax Carot. That's Basque for some kind of dance. Anyway, this group...I thought...oh, gee, Mel, they sounded so wonderful, so, so idealistic, I thought..."

"Go on. What were you going to do?"

"You see, they believe you have to have someplace to go, all ready with food and weapons and medicine and books and stuff. For when the bomb falls and destroys civilization. A place like this, up in the mountains where it'll be safe. That's what they wanted to do, to supply this cottage and build another. They needed money."

Melanie sat very still, listening.

"And Sevé taught them all kinds of things, like hunting and tracking and fishing and survival. So we decided, Carlos and I, that we should pretend I was kidnapped and Mother and Dad would send some money and then I'd pretend to be freed but the Cax would have the money. It was only pretend, Mel, and Mother and Dad can afford it. They have so much..."

"Sort of instant socialism," Melanie said pensively. "So what happened?"

"Oh, God, it all went wrong." She looked around and lowered her voice. "It was Sevé. He went along at first. He said what a good idea it was. That they'd buy guns and a generator and dried food and stuff. Then at the beginning of the *feria*, he turned all hard and...and vicious. And he made them...Melanie, they didn't want to, but he threatened...Oh, I don't know, they spoke Basque, then Carlos was afraid to talk to me. Sevé threatened them, said they were already in so much trouble and he'd kill them—and me—if they didn't do as he said." Cecily hid her face in her hands. "And then he called Dad and asked for five hundred thousand dollars! Mel, I swear, I didn't know! The guys, Carlos, they were only going to ask for two or three thousand. Melanie, I swear, they didn't know, they didn't mean...!"

"Shh! I believe you." She thought for a minute. "So the boys knew Sevé before?"

"Yes, see, they're all from around here. They've known each other for ages. Sevé was, well, sort of their idol." She lowered her voice. "He's a mercenary. He fought in Africa and South America. He's scary, Mel, real scary. But at first he was fun and he knew so much about survival and weapons and stuff. They were like Boy Scouts, you know. At first—''

"How did Sevé know our family could afford such a big ransom, Cecily?''

"Well,'' she said, shamefaced, "it was because I bragged to Carlos. It was when we first had the idea and I thought the money was just going to be a small amount. And then Sevé found out.''

"I see. So he realized he could use you to get a lot more. And you walked right into it, made it real easy for him,'' Melanie mused, shaking her head.

"We didn't *know*!'' Cecily wailed. "And then it was too late. Oh, I'm so sorry! It's turned out to be a horrible nightmare. Oh, Mel . . .''

"Carlos. Which one is he?''

Cecily answered sullenly. "He's outside. The good-looking blondish one. I thought he loved me. I loved him...'' She sounded bitter. "But he's so scared of Sevé he'd wet his pants if Sevé told him to!''

Everything made sense now—her own foreboding in Torremolinos, Cecily's abrupt disappearance... And Teo's attempt to convince her to go back home. Of course he'd wanted her out of the way. Then he could have picked up the money and there would have been no complications. Nobody would have been looking for Cecily, nobody would have suspected him, nobody would have been around to call in the Guardia Civil. Oh, Lord, no wonder he'd been so adamantly against her calling the police. Melanie sat for a minute, staring off into the distance, thinking. Gullible. There was no other word for it. She'd been utterly taken in by Teo. She'd known all along that he was involved in this— with her own eyes she'd even seen him in this very cabin. And yet she'd blinded herself and hoped like a fool. A decision of the heart, certainly not the brain. Her skin felt hot and feverish, burning with shame and humiliation.

She'd slept with him, acquiescing fully to his every whim. Dear Lord in heaven, she'd even come up with a few whims of her own during their lovemaking!

Stupid, she thought, naive and stupid. Well, she was paying for it now.

"What is it, Mel?" Cecily asked, putting a tentative hand on her sister's arm.

"Nothing." Melanie shook her head irritably.

"I know something's bugging you. Come on."

"Don't you think being kidnapped is enough?"

"Yes," Cecily admitted in a small, chagrined voice.

Melanie looked at her sister for a long moment. She shrugged. "Something *is* bothering me. It's Teo. I want to know what he's got to do with all this. Did you have any idea he was involved in this group?"

"Well, yes, I knew he was part of the Cax, sort of an intellectual leader. He knows Carlos very well. I think their families are old friends."

"Isn't that cozy," Melanie muttered darkly. "Did you and Carlos tell him your plans back in Madrid?"

"Well, you see, he used to invite us over to his apartment, you know, on Saturday nights. We'd all go there and—"

"All?" Melanie interrupted.

"Most of the Cax Carot are students, Mel. Anyway, we would go over there and drink wine and talk about things."

"And he filled your heads with all this survivalist stuff..."

"Well, no, he didn't. That was Sevé. We all went to Teo's because everyone thought he was such a great guy and besides that, he's a Basque and they really stick together. Carlos said it was the only place he felt comfortable in Madrid. There's some hard feeling between the Basques and the rest of Spain, you know."

"But he went along with this Sevé. He used you students," Melanie insisted angrily.

"I don't know. He may have heard what we were planning. I'm not sure. We knew he would have disagreed, so we didn't tell him but he may have caught on," Cecily explained.

"Don't be silly. He set it up. He knew from the beginning. He knew Sevé. They probably grew up together."

"Teo wouldn't—"

"Then why was he here, Cecily? I followed him the other night and saw him right here, dressed like one of them!" she stated scornfully. "Your brilliant nice-guy professor!"

"He is nice!" Then she looked down at her hands. "He was," she said more softly. "Oh, I don't know . . ."

"Well, I do. He took a bunch of easily influenced students and used them."

"I really liked him . . ."

Melanie said nothing, afraid she might betray her own strong feelings, her own blind spot where he was concerned. She had been no better than those students of his . . . She looked at Cecily. "Did you kids know Sevé well in Madrid?"

Cecily shook her head. "I didn't. But Carlos would tell me once in a while that Sevé was around. He talked like he was a hero or something."

"Of course. A great man, a mercenary. For God's sake, Cecily, he's a killer! Hanging around a campus—it's sick!"

"But the professor wasn't like that. Honestly."

"Oh, no? Have you forgotten that he was in Torremolinos?"

"Well, yes . . . But I don't understand . . ."

"Simple. He was there to watch us. To make darn good and sure you didn't hop on a plane and leave Spain. He either did it on his own, or maybe it was Sevé's brilliant idea. Who cares?" Melanie suddenly felt like crying. "You do understand now that these men are evil, don't you, Cecily?"

Cecily nodded slowly. "I really thought Teo was wonderful, a really great guy, a good teacher. I'm so scared. I'll never be able to trust my judgment again, Mel. I've been making mistakes all along."

So Cecily thought they were going to get out of there. Melanie wished she herself felt so sure. Kidnappers could be caught afterward if there were witnesses who could identify them. These boys—and Sevé—had no masks on. Melanie and her sister would be those witnesses—if the Cax Carot released them. The thought chilled Melanie to the bone. No masks. Then they didn't care! Or rather Sevé didn't care that they knew his name and his face. And then Melanie knew, as surely as she knew her own name, that Sevé meant to kill them both as soon as he got the money. The boys, perhaps, weren't part of the murder scheme; but Sevé—what had he to lose?

And Teo Sanlucar? Did he know what the future held for the two sisters? Had he planned with Sevé? Or maybe that had been the real issue of their argument that night . . .

"What are we going to do, Mel? I heard them saying the money wasn't here yet and I got so scared. The way Sevé looked at me. And then you—they got you, too. Why? What happened? Oh, I've been going crazy up here. How did you even know I was going to Pamplona?"

Melanie thought for a minute before answering. "First of all—" she lowered her voice "—we're going to see if we can escape. If we can't, we'll wait for the money. The bank won't give the money to anyone but me."

"Hey, gee, that's right." Cecily brightened.

"As for why I'm here, I don't really know. Maybe they were afraid I'd go to the police."

Cecily shuddered. "Sevé told me what they'd do if you went to the police, or if Dad did. He's a terrible man. I think," Cecily whispered, "I think he'd kill someone without blinking an eye. He's killed hundreds of men—he brags about it.''

"Did you know I've been staying with the Sanlucars?" Melanie asked.

"Sevé told me you were in Pamplona, but not that. I knew Professor Sanlucar was from here and had family—but how did you find him?''

"Oh, it wasn't hard. He followed me from Madrid. I went to see him there—at the university. And then in Pamplona, well, there wasn't a hotel room and he conveniently came along and offered me his uncle's house. It was all a setup. Do you know his uncle, Esteban?''

"No. I knew he had someone here, that's all.''

"How well do you know Teo? I mean, could he have been a mercenary at one time, too?'' Melanie asked. "Maybe he was in the Spanish military once...''

"Hey, he was just my professor. As to that, Mel, I have a feeling you'd know better. You've been staying in the same house for—how many days?'' Cecily remarked dryly.

"Well, I don't have a clue. He's not exactly easy to know,'' she replied sharply, then asked, "Would Carlos help you secretly, if you asked him?''

"No, I tried. Oh, how I tried. I even tried, well, you know...'' Cecily looked away, embarrassed.

"I can guess. No go, huh?''

"He's too scared. I think Sevé really would kill someone who helped us.'' She shook her head miserably.

"How many are there?''

"Six including Sevé. Two are always on guard—with guns. The door is locked. The windows are locked. I thought of breaking them, but the noise would alert the guards. The walls are stone. The roof is too high. Mel, I've been studying this place for days!''

"The outhouse, then.''

Cecily shook her head. "How?''

"A loose board? A window?"

"The window's tiny and up high. Loose boards, I don't know. And anyway, there's always a guard."

Melanie stood. Boldly she turned and went toward the door. She called to Sevé, "I have to go to the ladies' room, please. The Damas, you understand?"

"Sí." He said something brusque to the pimply boy who stood just outside. "Follow him," Sevé said, "and no forget he has a gun and he know how to use it."

The foul-smelling little building was about a hundred feet behind the cabin. Her heart sank; it was made of stone. She went inside, horribly aware of the boy just a few feet away. Quickly she stood on the seat and felt around the roof. Thatch. It could be pushed aside. She could probably crawl out. But the noise she'd make... And how would she be able to free Cecily? Perhaps if she came up with some excuse for them to be in the outhouse together? How? She'd have to think. It was a possibility.

Then, on the way back to the cabin, Melanie thought of another possibility. She could try to escape when they took her into town to get the money. In the city she could run and get lost among the crowds. But Cecily would be left behind. No, that wouldn't do. But she still had time. The next day was Sunday and the banks would be closed. She had at least until Monday. She'd think of something by then.

She'd have to.

On the way into the cabin she looked carefully at the youths who lounged around the door. There was one who was tall and slim as a reed; his hair was dark blond, thick and wavy. His eyes were green.

"You're Carlos, aren't you?" she said, standing right in front of him. "Aren't you ashamed of yourself?" She paused. "Will you help us?"

He didn't answer; his eyes slid away. Did he understand English?

"Listen, Carlos, if you help us, my parents will pay you for it. We won't tell the police. Do you understand? You can't get away with this. You're ruining your life. Your parents…" She was sure she saw a painful shadow cross his face. She put a hand on his arm, and lowered her voice. "He'll kill us, you know. That Sevé. He'll shoot us like he'd shoot rats. And you'll be guilty, too."

No response.

"You're all cowards!" she shouted then, turning to the others. "Don't do this! There's only one of him and—" she held up her hand, fingers spread "—five of you!"

They shuffled nervously, fingering their guns. Afraid.

Sevé burst out of the cabin and grabbed her arm, dragging her over to the rough wall and slamming her against it. His face was contorted in rage. "What? You try something? Stupid! They no listen!"

The stones hurt her back. Sevé's grip numbed her arm. She felt her stomach clutch with fear. He was going to kill her right then!

But he only spat on the ground at her feet and grated out something in Basque to the others. Then he pulled her inside, flinging her onto the cot where Cecily sat. She lost her balance, half falling on her sister. Tears of fear and anger and humiliation welled up inside her.

"Melanie, I heard you," Cecily was saying. "Wow, I'd never have had the nerve! What did they do?"

Painfully, Melanie pulled herself upright and rubbed her sore arm. She was shaking all over. "Nothing," she said woodenly. "They did nothing."

They could hear Sevé talking to the men outside, haranguing them. Cecily ran to the window and tried to see what was going on. Suddenly they heard two gunshots. Cecily jumped back from the window with a cry; Melanie felt every muscle in her body go rigid.

"What?" she rasped to her sister.

"I . . . I don't know." Cecily's face was as white as snow.

The door flew open and Sevé swaggered in, banging it shut behind him. He laughed coldly. "Don't worry. I no shoot anybody. Not yet. Only to warn them. And you, too."

He approached Melanie, thrusting his face close to hers. She could smell the odor of his sweat and the sour wine on his breath. He was unshaven and the red kerchief about his weathered neck was twisted and filthy. She shrank back.

"Señorita," he said hoarsely. "Tomorrow you will call your rich parents and tell them I want twice the money! For two daughters! One million I want now because I do not get it soon enough. You hear? And I want it all by *el fin de la feria*. In four days, *señorita*. By the end of the Fiesta de San Fermín."

Chapter Twelve

Sunday, July 11

Melanie was wakened sometime after midnight by the sound of two men speaking outside the cabin door. They seemed to be arguing, their voices alternately raised and lowered. She propped herself up on an elbow, shifting in her cramped space on the narrow bed next to Cecily, and strained to hear.

They were speaking Basque.

What was going on? she wondered, feeling apprehensive. Who was it? Was Sevé tongue-lashing one of the young boys, berating him for some error?

It was cold in the cabin. She looked toward the fireplace; the logs had burned down to a few glowing embers. There was wood next to the hearth, but for some unaccountable reason, Melanie hesitated to rise and rekindle the fire. It was because of those men outside, because there was something intimidating in their tones and she felt it safer to shrink back into her corner with Cecily.

The arguing halted abruptly. Melanie looked at the door through the darkness and wished that whoever had been quarreling would start again. It suddenly seemed entirely too quiet.

She lay there, cold and shaking, watching the door. She could feel the harsh roughness of the filthy wool blanket that covered her and smell the stale odor that permeated it. Her skin crawled from its touch, and she wondered if they'd both get vermin from the bedding. It was awful, she told herself, that she could think of such inconsequential things when her very life was in danger.

Her eyes fastened on the door again. The latch rattled a little. Was Sevé coming to kill them in their sleep? Or had one of the boys decided that he needed a little amorous diversion? Her muscles tensed and she looked around desperately for a weapon—a stick, or a heavy pot, a chair— anything she could grab. She willed the door to stay closed. But she saw the latch slowly move, raised as if by an invisible hand. The door creaked, then swung inward. Her heart quickened and she gently nudged Cecily. Her sister was asleep.

What did this intruder want?

A lone man, a tall shadow filling the portal, stood silhouetted in the moonlight for a long time. Then the figure began to walk toward the cot.

"Get out of here," Melanie hissed.

He stopped and stood over her, large in the night.

"Get out!" she whispered harshly.

"Do not be afraid, Melanie."

"You . . ." Her voice was very quiet, disbelieving. "What nerve . . . showing up here."

"Melanie, I—"

"No. Don't say anything. One more word and I'll scratch your eyes out."

"I see that you are unharmed. I will leave you, then," Teo said, but he hesitated, and Melanie could feel the tension emanating from his body, could see the rigid set of his shoulders against the diffused light from outside.

She felt brittle and close to tears, caught between outrage that he would have the nerve to let her recognize him and a pathetic relief that he had come at last.

"You are unharmed," he'd said. And she despised herself for the fatal weakness that let her still care—and still look for signs that he cared.

"Wait!" she cried softly.

He turned, pausing, a tall shadow in the musty cabin.

"Can you get us out of here? Will you help us? Teo—" Her voice choked and stopped.

His silence was oppressive. Finally he spoke and his voice was harsh. "I cannot. The men outside have guns and will use them."

"You could, I know you could!" she whispered, heartbroken. "You won't do it. Teo, how can you be part of this? How can you?"

"I must go," Teo said in a strained whisper. "But when I am gone, ask yourself, didn't I tell you to leave Spain? Did I not warn you over and over?"

Her lips compressed into an unforgiving line.

"So be it."

She could not see his face, but she wondered if it was pain she'd heard in his voice. He stood unmoving, a dark, shadowy form in the moonlight. "For your own sake," he said, "do not anger Sevé, Melanie."

"So good of you to worry about us."

"Just remember. That is all." He turned on his heel and left, closing the cabin door softly, and the latch fell back into place with a quiet click.

"It was Teo, wasn't it?" Cecily spoke in the darkness. "I'm so scared," she whimpered.

"So am I," Melanie said softly, "so am I."

She lay awake for a long time, listening to the night. Somewhere, far off in the deep timber, an owl hooted. There was the sound of trickling water that she hadn't noticed during the day. The silence seemed unearthly without the noise of a passing car once in a while. She felt more alone than she ever had since coming to this country of the Basques.

She grimaced, knowing why she had felt more secure before her own kidnapping. Teo. He had kept her his prisoner, yes, but his hand had always been at her back and the strength of his dark eyes had watched over her. He'd been her protector, just as he'd said. And now she had no one.

Cecily had fallen back to sleep and was taking up most of the narrow cot they were forced to share. Melanie shifted her carefully and tried every technique she could think of to get to sleep. It was exhaustion that finally won out.

At dawn she and her sister were roughly awakened by one of the young Basques. "Food," he said, nodding toward the cabin door.

Melanie looked at him curiously.

"He wants us to cook," Cecily explained, sighing wearily.

"Us?"

"Yes. It was Sevé's idea. A few days ago. I guess he thinks women should be slaves."

"Not this one," Melanie murmured.

But in the end, after the young guard had reported that Melanie refused to do the cooking, Sevé entered the cabin and dragged her out, shoving her toward a fire, pointing at the greasy tin plates and crusty pans.

Under great protest, Melanie cooked.

Teo was nowhere to be seen. Melanie supposed he had returned to Esteban's, to his creature comforts, his comfortable bed and elegant meals. Or perhaps he had been an apparition, dark and ghostly in the night; perhaps he had not been there at all.

She scrambled eggs in a charred iron pan and looked around the campsite in the light of day. There were sleeping bags hanging out on branches to air. A couple of army-style pup tents sat in the woods and the familiar outhouse was behind the cabin. She glanced at the thatched roof of the latrine and once again thought of escape.

Everything seemed sharper, purer, more defined, in the clear mountain air. It was fresher in the woods. A ridiculous thought, Melanie decided, and quite irrelevant, considering their situation. And yet her senses were keen with the smell of burning wood and brewing coffee, the sound of squirrels chattering, the warble of a bird nearby, the touch of the hot iron pan in her hand.

She thought of taking a few pictures then almost laughed. Take a picture of her kidnappers? Besides, Sevé had ruined her film.

She was busy slicing ham when she felt her skin begin to crawl, as if she were being watched. She straightened from her crouched position, spinning around to look behind her. Teo was leaning against a tree near the camp, his eyes fastened on her.

A gasp caught in Melanie's throat. She'd thought him gone. Where had he been earlier? Standing there, watching while Sevé dragged her out of the cabin?

Her eyes narrowed. Teo, her self-proclaimed protector. What a laugh!

He moved then, striding over to one of the guards, saying something she couldn't hear to the boy, who seemed to be listening respectfully. Even as he spoke, Teo's pensive gaze still rested on Melanie. Then when he was done talking, he headed away from the camp, along the path Melanie knew so well.

He was leaving. Going, undoubtedly, for a decent meal or a bath or whatever. Leaving them in Sevé's hands.

Damn him, she swore under her breath even as her heart was squeezed by a terrible anguish.

When he was gone from her sight, a white form disappearing into the depths of the trees, Melanie turned back to cutting the meat, hacking at it, wiping the treacherous tears from her eyes.

The men ate piles of eggs and ham and stale bread. They all still wore their grimy clothes and dusty black berets. Two of them—Carlos was one—sat on rocks near the cabin, sharpening hunting knives. Another was sitting close to the fire, cleaning a rifle, polishing its stock with an oily rag, over and over again.

These kids were so stupid and blind, Melanie thought. She felt sorry for them, but her pity was vastly overshadowed by her own anxiety.

And where had Sevé gone?

As if in response to her question, he emerged moments later from the dusky forest, carrying a dead rabbit in one hand, brandishing a long knife in the other.

He grinned widely, revealing his ugly, broken teeth. "Supper!" he shouted gleefully.

Melanie turned to her sister. "The big man," she sneered, "the Great White Hunter."

Sevé approached the women and tossed the pathetic little carcass at their feet. "Clean it."

"You must be—"

But Cecily interrupted Melanie quickly. "Here, I'll do it." She gave Melanie a warning glance.

Maybe it was wrong of her to harbor such vengeful feelings, Melanie reflected, but she swore to herself that if and when they got out of this ordeal, she was going to see Sevé pay.

It was midmorning when he barged into the cabin. "Come," he ordered, looking directly at Melanie, "we call your father now."

"Go on," pleaded Cecily, "don't make him mad. He's crazy," she whispered fervently.

Grudgingly, Melanie picked up her purse and her camera bag and followed Sevé out. The hike down the mountain was growing familiar—the meadows and forests, even her giant old tree. She would have delighted in the splendid country had Sevé not been right at her heel, his hot breath on her neck.

"Must you walk so close?" Melanie asked once.

He merely grinned, his dark eyes traveling leisurely over her body.

She turned and began walking again, more quickly, vowing to keep her opinions to herself.

"Remember," Sevé said from behind her, "twice the money." They trekked to a village some four kilometers from where Sevé had parked the car. It took over an hour to make the overseas connection, and when Melanie was finally on the line to Ohio, she was horrified to find out her father wasn't home.

"A million dollars!" Muriel cried, aghast. "Are these men insane?"

Melanie felt like crying. "Mother," she said, "didn't you hear me? This is no joke, for God's sake! They're holding me now, too! *Please*, just tell Dad. Tell him to wire the same amount as before. Tell him to do it as fast as possible. *Please*."

The line went silent for a minute. "What if he doesn't have it?"

"He'd better have it," Melanie choked out. "Believe me, Mother, Dad can get his hands on it somehow." She could almost see Muriel biting her lower lip, hand pressed to her heart.

"All right, darling. Your dad will handle everything. Is Cecily okay?"

"Yes. We're okay, for now. But, Mother, these men mean business. You must get the money sent as fast as possible."

"Are those men . . . bothering you?"

"No, Mother—all they want is money."

"I'm so afraid . . ." Her mother's voice trailed off.

"Tell Dad. He'll handle everything. And don't . . . worry, Mother."

When Melanie finally hung up, Sevé pulled her out of the phone booth and held her arm in a vicelike grip. "Problem? There is a problem?"

"No," Melanie said wearily. "My mother is just very upset."

"What?"

"Nothing."

The hike back up to the cabin tired Melanie. Sevé, as always, stayed right on her heel, prodding her, rudely laughing when she stumbled once, not even offering to help her to her feet.

Melanie shot him a hateful glance. "You're a vicious man."

"Veeshus," he mispronounced it. "What is the meaning?"

"Look it up," Melanie retorted, hastening her footsteps.

Carlos and the others were sitting outside when they returned. She might have happened on a student outing, Melanie thought, but when the young faces looked up and saw Sevé, their expressions became blank and guarded.

The fools! Hadn't they realized yet where Sevé was leading them? There were five of them. Sevé was only a man, one single man!

But it was useless. Admittedly, he possessed a certain power, a charisma of some sort. His mere presence seemed to quell any thoughts of disobedience or rebellion.

Melanie walked inside the cabin, threw herself down on the cot and fought back tears of frustration.

It must have been several hours before she opened her eyes again. Pale light slanted through the cabin's sooty window, and dust motes danced in the panel of brightness.

Melanie looked at her watch. Six o'clock. How had she managed to fall asleep? She sat up and felt a little dizzy. Was she getting sick? But no, she always felt lightheaded after a nap in the afternoon.

An idea came to her. Maybe she should get sick... Where was Cecily?

She walked to the door and pulled it open. Cecily was cooking something over the small camp stove. She looked up and smiled. "You're awake."

"Yes," Melanie said. "Could you come here? I feel kind of...ill."

"What's wrong?" Cecily asked as she closed the door behind her.

Melanie put a finger to her lips. "Shh...nothing's wrong."

"But you said..."

"I know what I said, Cecily. Look, I've got an idea. Now hear me out before you go off in a panic. Okay?"

Cecily nodded. "Sure."

Melanie explained her plan to her sister.

"That's nuts, Mel. I mean, you'll get us...killed," she whispered.

"They won't kill anybody until they have the money," Melanie hissed, "and then it may be too late."

"I think you're crazy. The money will come and they'll let us go."

"Maybe," Melanie said darkly, "but I refuse to let that criminal get away with a million dollars!"

"But won't the police catch him someday?"

"Maybe, and then again, maybe not. He could hide in these hills forever."

Cecily was silent for a long minute. "Okay, let's go for it. I've been sitting on my butt long enough."

"Good girl. It's a deal." Melanie stuck out her hand for Cecily to shake.

"Oh, wow..." She grasped Melanie's hand. "This better work."

They waited until dusk. Melanie made it look good by staying in the cabin while Cecily cooked outside. She refused to eat any of the meal, and she even made sure Cecily told Sevé in Spanish that her sister was not feeling well. And then after the sun had disappeared behind a ridge and it grew dark in the east, Melanie stuffed her passport and some pesetas in her pocket, glanced wistfully at her camera and let out a huge moan. "Cecily! Oh, Cecily, come here quick! Ohhh!"

Cecily helped a staggering Melanie out of the cabin and into the outhouse. The men stood mutely watching; what was wrong with the *americana*, their faces warily asked. Even Sevé stayed away after he'd heard Cecily call over her shoulder in Spanish that her sister had female troubles.

No man on earth knew how to cope with that circumstance.

Behind the closed door, Melanie whispered, "If I have to stay in here, I *am* going to be sick."

Cecily went to work on the roof, tugging away thatch, while Melanie made all sorts of moans and groans to her sister's signals. And then finally there was room for them to crawl out.

Darkness fell over the camp. The fire would help, too, Melanie hoped, as the men standing around its warmth would be partially blinded by the bright flames. Cecily, younger and more agile, had no difficulty pulling herself up through the roof and letting herself down behind the outhouse.

It was Melanie's turn. She made a few more retching sounds and tried to pull herself up. No way. She tried again. Dear God, she wasn't going to make it. It was like trying to chin herself. Melanie hadn't chinned herself since high school!

"Come on," she heard Cecily's whisper. "Think of Sevé catching us . . ."

Catching and killing us, Melanie thought. She tried again, finally able to get a foothold on a loose stone. A little more! Yes! She was up, pulling her legs through the hole, sucking in fresh air.

"Ooh," she groaned from behind the outhouse. "Ooh, Cecily... I'm so sick," and they both crouched, lying low, then rushing for the cover of the trees.

They had only minutes before the men would notice that there was silence from the outhouse. "Hurry," Melanie gasped, pushing Cecily along, putting distance between them and the fire's glow.

Melanie's plan was simple: skirt the meadow by using the forest to conceal themselves, find the path, run as fast as possible down to the road. If Sevé and his men chased them, surely she and Cecily would hear the noise and could duck into the woods until they passed.

They did stumble onto the path, but it took them twice as long as she'd expected to get there. Melanie tried to peer across the grassy field toward the fire, but she couldn't hear anything. She listened hard for voices or cries of discovery, but the wind was blowing away from them and the trees were rustling all around her.

"They must know by now," Cecily said breathlessly.

Melanie nodded. "But I don't know where they are. Maybe on the path ahead of us? I don't know."

"What do we do?"

"Follow the trail down as quietly as we can. We ought to be able to hear six men, no matter where they are. Right?"

The path was bathed in moonlight where it crossed the clearing but in the depths of the forest it was completely dark. The trees were eerie shapes against the sky and their roots seemed to twist grotesquely on the path, reaching out for Melanie's legs.

"Where are they?" Cecily panted when they stopped before dashing across yet another clearing.

"I don't know. Behind us, maybe."

"What if they reach the road first, though?"

"We'll leave the path before the road, then. We can find our way out somehow." She gave Cecily's arm a reassuring pat in the darkness. "Come on. The coast looks clear."

The question of the men's whereabouts beat at Melanie relentlessly. It was like being chased as a kid and almost wanting to be caught, just to end the agony of the suspense. Melanie had never been very good at those games. Neither, she remembered, had Cecily.

Her legs were tired and her lungs ached. Even when they stopped to catch their breath and listen, Melanie's heart pumped furiously. They had to be getting close to the road, they had to be!

There was that giant gnarled tree. Oh, yes! They were going to make it!

Melanie held her sister back for a moment and listened again. She could hear nothing, only an owl hooting in the night somewhere. As she recalled, ahead of the tree there was one small clearing, then forest again, then the road. If they made it across this last meadow lying before them, and into the cover of the forest, they could leave the path at that point and wind their way through the timber until they came out onto the road somewhere below where Sevé kept his car.

They started across the clearing, crouched low, rushing, feeling exposed. They were so close now...

Ahead were the trees where they could safely leave the path without getting lost. She could see that it was dark and tunnellike, spooky, where the trail entered the forest again. But Melanie reminded herself that there was more protection among the trees.

Stepping from the moonlit path into the darkness, Melanie let out a tentative sigh of relief. Almost there...

She turned to Cecily. "A few more yards and we'll get off the path," she whispered, then forged ahead once again.

It was very, very dark. She tripped over a rock, caught herself and kept going. Up ahead was a bend in the trail. They'd leave it there. She could feel Cecily's hand groping at her back, then her sister's sharp intake of breath. "I hear something!" she whispered desperately.

Melanie froze. There was a cracking sound just ahead of them, a twig snapping under a foot, the beam of a flashlight spearing through the trees. She spun around to reach for Cecily but it was too late. The light touched her and she froze in horror.

"¿Qué diablo?" came a voice she knew too well. He grabbed her arm, steadying her, and Melanie struggled in fright. "Melanie? What on earth...?"

"Let us go!" she gasped. "Oh, God, let us go!"

Then there were voices on the trail behind them.

"Teo! *Please*..." But already it was too late. She could hear the men's feet, crunching through the undergrowth, rushing toward them. "No..." Melanie sobbed, sinking to her knees. "No..."

Sevé was violently angry, raging at his men, at Teo, then standing over Melanie and Cecily and hollering in their faces, shaking his rifle at them. Cecily clung in terror to her sister.

"Stop it!" she was crying. "Make him leave us alone!"

Something in Melanie finally gave way. She raised herself to her full five feet seven inches and faced Sevé.

"Leave us alone!" she shrieked. It was the wrong thing to have done. Sevé grabbed both her arms and began shaking her and then Teo was there, pulling him away, shouting at Sevé in Basque.

Finally Sevé let her go and stood glaring at Teo. They exchanged a few more heated words, then Teo turned to Melanie.

"Get going back up the trail," he ordered. *"Now."*

She would have confronted him, too, but what would it get her? More bruises on her arm?

Feeling utterly defeated, Melanie helped Cecily to her feet and began to walk. One foot in front of the other. Her strength was depleted, her head pounding with rage and frustration.

The men pushed them hard. A sick little punishment, Melanie observed with a strange sense of detachment. She just kept going, trying to hold her head up, trying to ignore the ache in her muscles.

They passed her twisted tree. She looked into the moon-lit sky and felt a hand at her back, helping her gently along.

She turned around. It was Teo. "Get your hands off me," she said in a deadened voice.

She could feel him stiffen as he pulled his hand away. "Have it your way," he said simply.

The incident was not lost on Sevé. He said something obviously crude to Teo in Basque and laughed. "*La señorita* no like you, either, eh, *mi amigo*? Cold, she is, like ice. And even if you are so fine she no like you to touch!" And he kept laughing, a bloodcurdling cackle that filled the night.

"I warn you, Melanie, do as you are told," Teo said quietly. "It is all I can tell you."

"And what if I don't?" she shot back in challenge.

"The price will be greater than you can afford."

Later, after they had finally reached camp, and she lay on the hard, narrow bed, staring into the blackness, Melanie could still hear Sevé's laughter as it echoed through the secretive mountains of the Basques.

Chapter Thirteen

Monday, July 12

The morning was overcast and gray, as somber as Melanie's mood. The fog rolled in from the ocean and hung on the hillsides, tattered when the wind blew, solid when it was still. Everything seemed to close in on her: the walls of the cabin, the sky itself. A damp chill made her shiver incessantly.

If they had planned their escape for today, the fog might have hidden them. But now it was too late. And Teo, not Melanie, was to phone the bank that morning, so there would be no chance to escape in the village.

Teo appeared from out of the mist at midmorning but did not immediately enter the hut. He spoke to Sevé first. Their voices went on for a long time, Sevé's shouting and frenzied, Teo's calm and even. Melanie's heart clutched with fear. What was wrong?

Finally Teo came inside. His face was drawn and tired looking. "The money is here," he said flatly.

"Thank goodness," Cecily breathed.

How innocent she was, thought Melanie. Once Sevé had the money, their lives were forfeited. And Teo knew it as well as she did. But did he even care?

"There is a small problem, however," he went on.

"Oh, Lord, no!" Cecily wailed.

Melanie merely sat, staring at her dirty fingernails.

"It will take another day for Señor Pacheco to gather enough cash."

One more day. Then what?

Cecily buried her face in her hands. "I can't stand another day! I can't!"

Better another day in here—alive—than what tomorrow might bring, thought Melanie. Teo was looking at her, wondering at her singular lack of response. "Are you all right?" he asked. "He did you no harm yesterday...?"

"Nothing that matters," she bit out coldly.

"Melanie—" he started to say then cut himself off. "Only half the money is here, of course. I have tried very hard to convince him that a bird in the fist..."

"A bird in the hand," Melanie corrected tiredly.

"But Sevé, I am afraid, wants as much as he can get. He is torn between greed and prudence."

"And you? What makes you tick, Teo?" she asked.

But he only scrutinized her darkly once again.

The door burst open. Sevé. His bullet-round head was sunk between his shoulders as if he were an enraged bull. "One day more!" he shouted. "Always one day more!"

"Señor Pacheco at the bank promises it will be ready tomorrow," Melanie said. "Didn't Teo tell you? The money's here."

He lurched around, his rifle bumping carelessly against a chair. Teo lashed out a warning in Basque. Sevé growled back. A rabid animal, a cold-blooded killer. Then he whirled to face Melanie. "*You!* So smart! Always one day more! This is your trick! And tomorrow it will be there. If not—" He shook his fist threateningly.

"If not what, Señor Sevé?" Melanie asked coolly. She sat motionless, looking squarely at him, her gold-flecked eyes narrowed and flashing with defiance. There was a core of strength in Melanie that she had never suspected. It seemed to grow inside her, taking on a will of its own. A reckless-ness.

Sevé glared at her hotly, then his eyes fell and he paced the floor. A perverse satisfaction surged through Melanie—she'd stared him down, the great dangerous mercenary. At her shoulder, she could feel Cecily shrinking away from the tension between Melanie and her adversary.

Finally Sevé turned on her. He shouted in Basque. Spit-tle gathered at the corners of his mouth in his fury. Teo tried to say something but Sevé ignored him.

Then, abruptly, Sevé stopped ranting. He smiled evilly and Melanie thought that was worse than his anger.

"Ay, the *señorita* is very brave. Yes, very brave." He strode over and jerked her to her feet and pushed his face close to hers, holding her arm with one iron-hard hand. "Do you know what I do with a woman like you? I *tame* her. Yes. I will enjoy to tame you. So rich, so clean, so cold. Yes."

Melanie's nerve fled and she was paralyzed with horror in his grasp. The room turned black in front of her eyes. She never even heard Teo shout at Sevé. She only knew she would die if this animal touched her. But she would not beg. No, she would never lower herself to beg him. She closed her eyes and gritted her teeth.

He was shoving her into the wall with both hands, his gun slung on his shoulder now, his thick body grinding against hers. She turned her face away. "So, *señorita*, you no like Sevé? Eh? Maybe I will keep you until I get more money. Maybe you will learn to be more polite, *sí*?"

She was aware of Cecily leaping to her feet, her face white and scared, her hands reaching for Sevé. But he knocked her aside without a backward glance.

Thrusting his head forward, he tried to kiss Melanie on the mouth, but she turned her head away again. Then his brutal fingers were clutching her chin and he was pressing his rough, unshaven face to hers. The sour wine smell from his breath was nauseating and a scream of hysteria bubbled up inside her.

"No!" Cecily cried, "Please leave her alone!"

Then, abruptly, Sevé was yanked off her, his hold torn away. Melanie collapsed onto the floor, sobbing, wiping her mouth.

Sevé crouched, his arms in front of him, facing Teo. There was an unearthly, dangerous silence between them. It took a second for her numbed brain to register what had happened: Teo had pulled him off her.

With a roar of rage Sevé threw aside his gun and launched himself at Teo, his hands reaching for the taller man's neck. He was screaming curses and panting as they fell to the floor, locked together. They broke apart; Sevé kicked out at Teo. They rolled on the ground, slamming into the table, knocking over chairs. The thuds of blows hitting home, grunts, the terrible ferocity of two powerful men clashing.

Melanie watched, frozen, then her eyes flew up to the door, which had burst open. Two of the young men were staring in, their faces pale and frightened. They backed off and the door slammed shut; they would not dare to interrupt such a battle.

When she looked again, Teo was dragging Sevé up by his shirt. Teo was breathing hard and one sleeve was torn off, showing the lean brown strength of his arm as he held Sevé up against the wall. Teo's lip was split and bleeding, his chest heaving, his eyes storm dark.

Sevé glared at him through a swollen eye. The anger and challenge on their faces terrified Melanie. The words poured from Sevé's twisted mouth—an explosion of savagery. He shouted and Carlos and two others sprang in through the door, their guns raised.

Slowly, Teo backed off, his hands upraised, his voice cold and low. She wished she could understand what they were saying. She felt limp with relief, confused, still weak with horror. She could only think: he had saved her from that beast! He had fought for her!

They went outside, all of them, leaving the women alone in the hut. Cecily collapsed on her cot, pale and trembling. "Oh, Mel, what are we going to do?"

Melanie straightened slowly, inching her way up, using the wall for support. She felt bruised all over. "Hang in there." She tried a smile; it felt crooked and stiff.

"He's so horrible. I thought... Thank God Teo was here."

"Yes."

"It's only until tomorrow, isn't it? Then he'll let us go. The money's here, isn't it?"

"Yes, tomorrow," Melanie said. "I'm sure he'll let us go tomorrow."

The men's voices outside the hut were low, droning on and on, occasionally raised in anger. They could hear Sevé, spitting viciousness. Then Teo's voice, calm and cold.

"What are they saying?" cried Cecily. "If only they'd speak Spanish!"

The door opened once more. Both sisters watched it with dread and fascination. Had Sevé won this round? Would he now be able to do as he pleased with them?

But it was Teo. "Sevé has agreed—I think—to take the money that is here. He says he will release both of you. But if he does not receive the money tomorrow he threatens to...do you some harm." Inadvertently he touched the cut on his lip. "I only tell you this that you may realize the gravity of your situation. Do not goad Sevé again."

"You mean like I just did?" Melanie asked. "I'm sorry. I didn't think... I want to thank you..."

He turned his gaze on her almost angrily. "What did you expect me to do? Let the man maul you? Do you think I am enjoying this? Please—" he sounded tired "—just do as I say. Don't push your fortune."

"Don't push your luck," Melanie said automatically, then added, "I'm sorry, it doesn't matter."

"I think he will leave you alone now."

"Does your lip hurt?" Cecily asked. "Maybe you need stitches."

He almost laughed. "I think that can wait, Cecily. I seem to have a few other things on my mind now." He went on. "Tomorrow I will phone Diego Pacheco. As soon as he has collected the money I will return here. Melanie, you will be taken to the bank, then escorted back here. Do not push, Melanie. This man is dangerous. Now I must leave. Is there anything I can do for you before I go?"

Cecily gave a little cry. "Oh, yes! Could I take a bath somewhere, or a shower? I've been here almost a week. I'm filthy! If I don't wash my hair, I'll die!" Then she thought a minute. "And some chocolate. I'm craving some gooey chocolate."

"Gooey chocolate and a bath," Teo repeated dully. "I'll see what I can do." He stood in the middle of the room a few moments longer. It seemed to Melanie that he was hesitant; perhaps he didn't want to leave them. Her heart began that familiar, uncomfortable aching again, as if her blood had suddenly become too heavy.

She looked at Teo carefully, saw his finely chiseled features, his elegant bearing and the drying cut on his lip. He'd got that because of her; he'd fought his comrade on her behalf. Did it hurt him that she was no longer interested? Did he care about what they'd shared the beautiful night that could never happen between them again?

There was a sadness in his eyes. A look of regret, she thought. What was he thinking? She wished he would leave. The longer he stayed, the more painful it was for Melanie; he might be her betrayer, yes, but only a few nights ago, she had given herself to him willingly.

"I must go now," he said finally, and his gaze met hers for one last moment before he turned and left.

The bath turned out to be a dip in a nearby river, under guard. Carlos and three of the other young men walked the women down to the riverbank and insisted that they stay within sight of the guards at all times. An angry conversation ensued between Carlos and Cecily.

"Goddamn it! Those creeps!" Cecily complained. "Can you believe it?"

"Unfortunately, yes," Melanie said.

"Well, let 'em look then! I need a bath!" Deliberately Cecily took off her clothes and, shivering, walked down into the river. The sky was still gray, the air chilly.

"Brr! It's freezing!" she yelled. But she ducked her head and began washing her hair with the bar of soap that was all Carlos had been able to find.

The four boys looked everywhere but at Cecily. They were horribly embarrassed. Carlos blushed like a girl but held his gun unwaveringly.

Melanie shrugged and turned her back to undress. She needn't have, because the boys studiously ignored them both. The water was cold but clear. She borrowed the bar of soap from Cecily and washed her own hair, remembering fondly, ruefully, her long luxurious baths at Esteban's.

In the water Melanie took the opportunity to whisper to Cecily, "Do you think Carlos would let us go? I mean, now that they're away from Sevé's influence? Do you think it's worth trying him?"

Cecily shrugged. "I can try. But we already know what to expect—I know now that he's a coward!"

There were only the rough wool blankets for towels. Cecily marched out of the river and wrung out her hair. Water ran off her skin in sparkling rivulets and her tan line was like a stark white bikini. Eventually she picked up the blanket and draped it over herself.

"Carlos," she called, then said something in Spanish. He walked over and answered, unsmiling. Cecily bent her head close to him and spoke earnestly, quietly, for a long time.

Melanie wrapped the other blanket tightly around herself and watched. Carlos couldn't take his eyes off Cecily's damp, half-nude body. But he shook his head and said something in a vehement tone of voice.

Cecily was begging, putting a hand on Carlos's arm. He shook it off and raised his gun. Cecily stood there and glared at him, then said something angrily, turned on her heel and walked away.

"I tried," she grated out. "Now it's your turn. Think of something."

They dressed in the same grubby clothes they'd been wearing for the past days. Cecily complained about it loudly in both Spanish and English. Her suitcase had been left in the cheap hotel room in Pamplona she and Carlos had shared when they arrived. Sevé had forbidden Carlos or anyone to return to fetch it. She was sure it had long since been stolen.

"And I had one pair of really worn jeans that I loved," Cecily recalled. "All they let me keep was my passport." Then she launched into another diatribe in Spanish. One of the guards laughed behind his hand at something she said and Carlos turned on him furiously.

In the early afternoon the sun began to burn off the layer of clouds. The sisters sat on their blankets in front of the cabin, drying their hair and brushing it with the brush from Melanie's purse. How fortunate they were to be allowed to stay outside, she thought bitterly.

She wished she could have photographed the rustic scene: the green sloping meadow, the darker trees, the mountains, the cotton-ball sheep, the old stone shepherd's hut. But if she did, she would have to include the boys with their berets and guns, Sevé with his black eye, the ugly green army tents. It was truly like some kind of perverted Boy Scout camp, without the smiles and fun and comradeship. These boys were tense and afraid and utterly miserable. Melanie felt sorry for them and their misguided ideals, but she pushed the feeling aside. The most important thing was her survival and Cecily's.

If she somehow got hold of one of their guns, she wondered, could she actually shoot someone with it? She told herself that she could use a weapon on Sevé, all right, but the young boys . . . ?

And Teo. Could she shoot Teo if he stood between her and freedom? Could she pull a trigger and see bullets smash into his smooth, tanned skin, his dark handsome face? She shivered. But what if it came to a choice between her and Cecily's lives and his?

But of course it was most unlikely she could get her hands on a gun. The boys were careful. Sevé had trained them well. They all slept outside the house, one right in front of the heavy plank door. There was no way to sneak out and take a gun; besides, there were always two of them awake.

There must be a way to escape, there must be!

Cecily was chasing a late-born lamb across the grass, laughing, looking so young, so innocent. Carlos watched her, his face full of pain and regret. She finally caught the little thing and carried it back to its mother. "Isn't it cute?" she called to Melanie.

Melanie smiled and nodded and waved. If there was more time, they'd be able to work on the sympathy of the boys. She knew Carlos and the others could eventually be persuaded to let them go.

But Sevé—and Teo. Those were the two strong ones, the leaders.

Sevé left for a while that afternoon and the atmosphere lightened. Carlos made some sort of excuse to talk to Cecily. Melanie approached the pimply-faced boy casually and, pointing to the sun, asked him the Spanish word for it.

"Sol," he answered. *"El sol."*

"Do you speak English?" she asked then.

"Leetle." He gave a weak apologetic grin.

"I am Melanie," she said, smiling. "What is your name?"

"Me llama Antonio."

"Ah, Antonio. Do they call you Tony?"

"To-nee," he said and laughed.

No harm making a friend. It might come in handy. "How do you say hungry?" asked Melanie, rubbing her stomach.

He placed a finger on his own narrow chest. *"Tengo hambre,"* he said triumphantly.

"Well then, Tony, *tengo hambre*," Melanie replied.

He thought that was very funny and told all the others.

"Clever," Cecily said dryly. "Now we get to cook."

But this time the boys brought out a round loaf of bread and a chunk of cheese. Laughing and talking, they laid down their guns and sliced thick slabs and handed them around. Dark red strong wine washed down the repast. It could have been a picnic.

Then Sevé came back. He carried a dead chicken by the legs. Stolen, no doubt. He scowled and the boys jumped, grabbing their guns, their faces suddenly hard and frightened.

"The prodigal returns," Melanie whispered to her sister.

"He could use a bath, too," muttered Cecily. "Enough is enough."

The mist reappeared in the evening, necessitating a fire in the hut. Cecily struggled to kindle it, but the damp wood didn't light easily and the small room filled with smoke.

Melanie wondered if Teo was going to come back that night. Had his lip healed yet? She couldn't help remembering the vicious fight, seeing it over and over in her head. It had been a revelation to her, a terrifying revelation. Did it take so little to reduce a man, even a man as cultured and intelligent as Teo Sanlucar, to a primitive, bestial state? Was civilization, then, so superficial?

She couldn't sleep. She couldn't stop brooding on what the next day—their last?—would hold for them. How would Sevé kill them? Bullets, knives, strangling? Would Teo help or would he stand by, disinterested?

She must get away! She and Cecily must manage to escape! Tomorrow she would be escorted into Pamplona. Once she had the money, it was as good as over.

Or was it?

An idea came to her then, in the darkest hour of that night.

Chapter Fourteen

It wasn't going exactly as Melanie had expected. She'd hoped they would all leave the camp and make the trip to the bank together.

But Sevé was too smart for that. "No, *señorita*," he told her, "the sister stays. First, I have the money. Second, the girl is free. *Entiende?*"

Melanie glared at him; she understood only too well. Once she'd picked up the money, he would tell her that they were going back to the camp and she and Cecily would be set free. Of course, Sevé thought he held the trump card—Cecily—but Melanie was going to change the rules of his game.

Sevé stood in the cabin, telling her they would leave in five minutes, tossing a paper sack at Melanie's feet.

"You wear clothes in there," he stated, then stood watching as she picked up the bag and opened it curiously.

Inside were slacks and a blouse, clean. Her own clothes from her suitcase in Esteban's house. Naturally, Melanie thought, they wouldn't want her looking disreputable and attracting too much attention. She could just see Teo rummaging through her suitcase, finding the dirt- and blood-stained clothes she had worn the night she'd followed him to the cabin.

What had he thought when he found them?

"Put clothes on!" Sevé said impatiently.

Melanie looked at him hard. "Get out of here, then."

He hesitated, grinning. Finally he chortled, the ugly laugh rolling around his throat, grating on Melanie's nerves. He left.

"I want to go, too," Cecily said. "I can't bear another moment here! Oh, Mel..."

"We'll be safe soon. You'll see."

"But what if they won't let us go?" she asked.

Melanie avoided her sister's apprehensive glance. So Cecily was finally putting two and two together. When she spoke, she tried to sound sincere. "Of course they'll let us go. They'll be happy as larks to see us get on a plane and leave."

"But what if—"

"Shh." Melanie tousled Cecily's hair playfully. "There's no problem; they only want the money. You'll see."

Cecily hugged her. "I hope you're right."

"I'd better be going." Melanie couldn't stand the imploring look in her sister's eyes another second. She brusquely gathered up her purse and camera bag and took a deep breath before she marched out the cabin door. When she emerged, the heads of the men turned in her direction. Hadn't they ever seen clean clothes before?

They were waiting for her, ready to leave. Even Teo. He stood some distance from the rest of the group, his eyes always following her. She tried to decipher his expression. Was that regret she saw on his face?

There were the three men, Sevé, Teo and Antonio, and then Melanie. Teo sat next to her in the back seat of Sevé's car, but she shrank as far away from him as she could. She kept catching Sevé's eyes on her in the rearview mirror as he negotiated the narrow, winding road. He was watching her very carefully, his dark gaze prying away the cloak of her pretended indifference. Dear God, she hoped he couldn't read her mind.

No one spoke much during the drive. Melanie found that unsettling. She wondered what each man was thinking. No doubt Sevé was planning his very prosperous future, or perhaps wondering how to dispose of two female bodies. And Antonio, To-nee, what was going on in his young, impressionable head? Was he envisioning himself with all those expensive new toys he would have, the guns and knives and bombs? Or perhaps he had begun to suspect that he and his *compañeros* were in too deep with Sevé. In their early, idealistic days, had any of these young Cax Carot members realized they would end up criminals?

Teo. He was the most silent of the three. He sat in that relaxed pose she knew so well but as always, there was a watchfulness about him, an air of detached observation. It was evident in the way he held his head and the alert look in his eyes, even while he stared out of the window at the passing scenery.

She was too aware of Teo. Too aware of the scabbed cut on his lip. Too keenly attentive to his smallest movements, to each nuance of emotion on his face, the pitch of his body, the way he would upon occasion look at the back of Sevé's head and then at the scenery once again.

He never looked at her, though.

Teo Sanlucar, she thought, professor of history, was going to be in for a big surprise. Perhaps he *should* have been watching her.

It was almost the last day of the Fiesta de San Fermín. Even though they were still several kilometers from the city's outskirts, the road was already crowded with cars and motorcycles and bicycles. Pamplona, Melanie knew, would be a madhouse. Perfect. And even better than that, the bank was situated near a corner . . .

It took them almost an hour to drive the last two kilometers. Sweat poured from Sevé's body, staining his dirty white shirt. His face was set in rigid lines. Melanie could see him reach for the horn many times but then draw his hand back, clenching it into a white-knuckled fist. With the weapons they carried, it obviously wouldn't do to call attention to themselves.

The hot morning sun pounded on the car, on the stretch of road ahead, on the dark roofs of the factories. It glinted off windows, beat on uncovered heads, melted the ice cream that vendors hawked on corners. The merciless Spanish sun.

Melanie squirmed uncomfortably in the heat. Her hair clung to the nape of her neck, her hands were sticky and she could feel a trickle of perspiration between her breasts. The car was stuck in an endless line of cars, all trying to park as close as possible to the central plaza.

She looked beside her, at Teo. He was leaning forward a little in his seat, glancing out of the window at the crowds. His shirt was dry. Did nothing perturb him?

He turned his head and for a moment their eyes met and held. She thought he was going to say something but he didn't. He simply sat watching her, his expression unreadable. Melanie forced herself to look away. Would it always hurt so terribly?

It took Sevé another half hour to drive from the factory district through a maze of apartment complexes and into the old section of the city.

There was noise all around them. Droves of shouting, laughing, singing fiesta-goers blocked the streets. The din of the traffic and the crowds filled every block, every alley, every shadowy corner of the city.

Sevé steered into the block where the bank was located and finally managed to double-park. Ordinarily, letting his car sit in the middle of the narrow street, blocking traffic, would have caused a commotion. But as it was, there were dozens of stopped cars jamming the street, their occupants hanging out of rolled-down windows, laughing, sharing their pleasure with passersby. It was a scene of complete bedlam.

Sevé turned in his seat and threw an Iberia airline's bag into Melanie's lap. "Go and fill it." He grinned widely.

Melanie stared at him for a moment and then looked at Teo. "You can still call this off," she said.

"You had better go." Teo's voice was very quiet.

"Go!" commanded Sevé.

When Melanie stepped out onto the street, Antonio and Teo did the same, tailing her to the door of the bank.

At the entrance, she turned to Teo. "Aren't you coming in?" she asked sarcastically.

He shook his head.

"No? Then I'll have to say hello to Señor Pacheco for you. He'll be so disappointed." She was well aware that her voice quavered.

"Go on, Melanie. Finish the task."

She nodded sadly, then said, "I had hoped that you, of all people, would stop this madness."

"I cannot." And for once, his eyes refused to meet hers.

Señor Pacheco had everything ready. He spotted Melanie among the crowds in his lobby and ushered her into his office with a flourish.

"You have told me very little about this very curious transaction," he said as he opened a huge, sealed sack of money brought in by two cashiers. "It is none of my affair..." He began to pull out dozens of neatly banded stacks of pesetas. "But is there anything I might do?"

"Thank you, but no." Melanie shook her head.

"I know that you said the money was for a property, *señorita*, but I have wondered. Would I be indiscreet if I alerted the *policía* when you left?"

The man obviously suspected something. No one paid for real estate with half a million dollars worth of pesetas—in cash. "Please, *señor*, there is no need. This matter will be taken care of tonight." She tried to give him a confident smile. "You have been very kind through all this. I appreciate your help."

He bowed his head with dignity.

She signed the bank draft, which was drawn on the Banco de Madrid, and began to pack the bundles of money into the Iberia bag.

"Are you not going to count the money?" He looked at her in disbelief.

"No," Melanie replied.

He had a grave expression on his dark face. "This is not wise."

"It won't matter," she remarked.

Teo and Antonio stood watch outside. Melanie peered through the glass doors, took a deep breath, then pushed them open. She knew she had to move quickly. She glanced at the corner. Yes, the policeman was there.

Teo was standing on the street just outside the bank, waiting for her. So was Antonio. Sevé was still in the car.

She walked purposefully in the direction of the policeman, then stopped near enough so that the officer could see everything she did and hear her if she raised her voice. She turned then and stared deliberately and boldly at Teo.

"Melanie . . ." he said, beginning to move toward her.

"Stop right there," she ordered, clutching the bag to her chest. She could see Sevé in the car, craning his neck to watch. He spun around in his seat and threw open the car door, then instantly he was out on the street heading toward her, a murderous look on his face.

Fiesta-goers were shouldering and jostling Melanie. Their ceaseless din pulsed in her ears as she stood staring at the three men, the bag held tight against her body, only a few yards from the policeman.

For a moment, they all stood silent and unmoving like a tableau frozen in time. Then Melanie broke the strange spell.

"Don't come any closer," she told them. "If I scream from here, every policeman in this city will be down your throats in a minute." She looked at Sevé. He was crouched low, like an animal, ready to pounce.

"No," Teo ground out, putting a restraining arm in front of Sevé's body. Then he said something in Basque and Sevé glared at Melanie in rage.

She moved another step away from them. "I am going to walk away from you now," she said in a brittle voice. "I want you to bring my sister to the bullring when the fights are over, at ten tonight. You'll get this bag then and I'll get Cecily."

"I'll kill her!" Sevé's teeth were bared.

"Then you won't get your money, will you, Sevé?"

Teo was still trying to hold him back, but Antonio merely stood there, dumbfounded.

"One more thing," Melanie said, her mouth cotton dry with fear. "Tell Antonio to approach me very slowly and look into the bag. He mustn't touch me, though. Now tell him, Teo."

Teo hesitated, staring at Melanie incredulously. Finally he spoke to Antonio in Basque and the young man nodded. Melanie realized this part of her desperate scheme was risky, but it was vital that Sevé know the money was really there, in the bag.

Antonio took several steps in her direction, then looked past her once toward the policeman.

When he was close enough, Melanie said, "Stop!" He did, and she unzipped the bag and tipped it in his direction just long enough for him to view the neat stacks of money.

He turned his head and nodded to his comrades.

"The bullring at ten," Melanie said hoarsely. "You understand?"

"Yes." Teo's voice was barely audible, his lean body stiff and tensed for action.

She backed away a few more steps, then turned and hurried to the corner, rounding it, disappearing past the policeman and into the evermoving surge of bodies.

For now, she was safe. Yet her mental picture of Sevé, crouched and cornered like a wolf, his dark eyes hooded in fury, followed her relentlessly.

ANTONIO HAD TRAILED HER. Melanie, however, had expected someone to do precisely that. What she had not counted on was another of the Cax Carot joining him. She'd been sitting at a crowded table, quietly drinking her soda and lime, periodically glancing up to keep track of her pursuer. And then, suddenly, there were two of them.

Sevé must have sent someone out immediately after returning to the camp. It occurred to Melanie that she'd been unwise to come to the plaza, the most obvious of all places, and to sit at a corner café with an ever-present policeman nearby. How easy she had made it for the other man to find Antonio and join him! Stupid!

They were good—she had to give them that, at least.

She must rethink her plans, then. She had already taken into account the necessity of losing one tail but now, with the two of them...

Melanie stood near a corner, close to a policeman, and checked her watch. It was five o'clock. She had hours to kill. Hours in which to perfect her plan and make it foolproof, but she needed to lose the two men first.

She pushed her way through the frenzied crowd to another café, all the while working out an idea that had come to her. It could succeed. She studied the hotel that stood behind the café: the location of the front door, the size of the building—not too big, not too small, four stories. The crush of people could be to her advantage if she used it wisely.

She needed a cover, though, to confuse her pursuers—and for protection. Eyeing the people jammed around the tables of the outdoor café, she decided on one particular foursome.

It wasn't her ordinary kind of behavior to do the sort of thing she had in mind, but these were extraordinary circumstances. It was a question of absolute necessity, and she couldn't afford to be squeamish.

It was funny, she thought later, how easy it was—just then—for her to turn into a brashly presumptuous person. She'd chosen a table of Californians. She didn't question for a second that they were from the Golden State. Their sun-bleached hair and perfect tans and their air of youthful enthusiasm told her that. They were exactly what she needed to carry out her plan.

"Hey, you guys," she said breezily, "mind if I join you?" She leaned down to them conspiratorially. "There's this creepy Spaniard following me."

"Hey, sure, I know what you mean," said the slim blond girl. "Thank goodness I've got these three to run interference for me." She rolled her eyes. "Those Spanish guys are randy to the max."

"My name's Melanie. You having fun?"

"Wow! Fun? This place is the most!" said one of the boys. "I'm Ted. This is Buzz and Toro and Franny."

"You know we all ran with the bulls yesterday?" said Buzz. "And this guy next to me got flattened, like *that*!" He gestured with his palm. "Then I'll be a son of a gun if he didn't get right up after the bull passed and keep running!" He shook his head wonderingly and fingered his dirty red kerchief.

Melanie saw To-nee waiting for her to get up and leave the café. She was safe with her new friends, but she was impatient to lose her two young pursuers.

"Where're you from?" Franny was asking.

"Ohio."

"Oh, wow, I've got an uncle in Toledo. Dick Ledbetter—you know him?"

"Ledbetter?" Melanie thought a moment. "No, can't say I do." Where was the second spy? She had an irresistible urge to look behind her.

The group was sharing a meal of marinated mussels and olives and tidbits of octopus. Melanie ordered a bottle of five-hundred-peseta wine.

"Gosh, you can get it for a hundred and fifty," Toro exclaimed.

"Never mind, nothing but the best." Melanie smiled graciously, feeling rather like a bountiful grandmother.

Was she going to be able to lose To-nee and friend—just for those precious minutes she needed? She laughed at some asinine remark of Ted's and glanced toward the street. There they both were, standing motionless and close together, unmindful of the jostling throng, watching her carefully. Then she saw a figure approaching Antonio—a familiar figure—Teo. He had obviously been sent by Sevé to help find her. Three men after her, three men to evade and fool and deceive with nothing but her wits. She had to succeed or Cecily's life wouldn't be worth two cents.

And Teo, the traitor, the beautiful dark stranger to whom she'd given herself, willingly and lovingly. Now he was hunting her down, a hound on her trail.

To-nee was pointing her out, and Teo was looking across the crowded plaza, straight toward her. Studiously she avoided glancing in his direction and laughed gaily at something Franny said.

How was she going to get out of their sight?

Ted moved his chair noticeably closer. "So you're from Ohio," he said. "Going to Ohio State?"

She almost choked on her wine. "Well, actually I'm out of school."

"What'd you major in?" His arm was on the back of her chair.

"Oh . . . photography."

Ted nodded sagely.

It came to her suddenly, that proverbial light bulb switching on in her head. It might work!

"Do you know if there's a bathroom in that hotel behind us?" she asked.

"I guess so."

"Would you mind walking me to the lobby? I mean, these Spanish men!" She rolled her eyes.

"I'd be glad to," he said sincerely.

They both walked toward the hotel; Melanie took his arm and looked around, as if she felt anxious about being followed. Only it wasn't an act. But her pursuers couldn't do a thing, not with Ted so close—and he was close. Melanie let him guide her through the crowds, even let him press snugly against her.

Ted must have noticed her anxiety. When they stopped to allow a large group of Spaniards to go by, he said, "Boy, you really are nervous. You're as stiff as a board."

"I am?"

He nodded and smiled. "But don't worry, you're with me now. They won't bother you."

"It's just all this madness, I guess." She tried to return his smile, but her face felt brittle.

She glanced over her shoulder. There were the three men, very near, yet obviously afraid to try anything with so many tourists around. Still, Melanie was not comforted. Not with Teo so close. His face was carved in unforgiving lines, his dark eyes menacing. He looked slowly from Melanie to Ted and back, and she could almost see the muscle in his jaw grow taut and begin to twitch.

Good, she thought, let Teo think she really had picked someone up. Let him see how easy it was and that she didn't care if he saw or not.

The notion buoyed her momentarily, but her satisfaction didn't last long. It hurt terribly to see Teo looking at her with threat in his eyes.

Ted began to walk again, leading Melanie, threading his way in and out of the masses toward the hotel. Finally they were entering the lobby, and the cooler air fanned Melanie's hot cheeks.

"Thank you, Ted," she said just inside the door. "I'm fine now. Go on back to the table."

"I'll wait," he replied meaningfully.

"Oh, no, really—I'll be perfectly all right here."

"Okay," he said reluctantly, "but the next bottle's on me."

"That'll be great," she managed to reply.

He left. Melanie took a deep breath and started toward the front desk. When she was certain Ted was gone, she turned and walked quickly to one of the big windows that looked out onto the street. She wanted to make sure that Teo and his sidekicks were still there.

They were. And as she expected, Antonio was looking perplexed, gesturing to the other two, staring at the hotel, then at the alley, and back to the front door.

Teo, too, was casting about, but he didn't look nearly as disconcerted as Antonio. He appeared to be taking charge, telling the youths to calm down, assuring them that Melanie couldn't have escaped.

He nodded toward the front entrance and spoke to Antonio as if to say, You watch the front. Then Teo and the other young man began to head in the direction of the alley, no doubt to guard the rear exit.

Now, she thought, let Antonio's curiosity overcome him. Let him get itchy and begin to wonder what she was up to. Let him leave his post and follow her inside. Come on, Antonio.

Melanie left her place at the window, crossed the lobby and climbed the narrow steps. Would her plan work? There were people everywhere, bumping into her on the stairs, talking in the hallways, milling around in the corridors on the way to their rooms.

On the second landing she stopped and glanced around the hallway. Yes, there was a door marked Damas. Ladies. She pushed it—locked. Damn! *Hurry up,* Melanie prayed, *get out of there before Antonio climbs those stairs.* She rattled the door handle several times. *Hurry up!*

Finally the door was unlatched and swung open. Melanie ducked in quickly past the scowling woman, thinking furiously, trying to recall every ploy in every mystery book she had ever read. How would Agatha Christie have done it?

The light in her head flared again. Of course!

She left the door unlocked—oh, how clever she was— then went into the toilet stall and stepped up onto the seat; the stall would appear to be empty if Antonio were to peer into the bathroom, looking for a pair of feet. She could imagine him entering the lobby, desperately searching for her, then noticing the staircase. He would eventually deduce that she hadn't slipped out the back because his partners were there and she couldn't have got past them. He would know that she'd gone up the stairs.

Come on, she thought.

He'd go to the first landing, push open the doors to the broom closet, to the bathroom. He might even have to wait to see who came out of the bathroom if it was occupied. And then, still looking watchfully around him, he would assume that Melanie had gone up another flight of stairs.

The minutes ticked by. It struck Melanie that someone might come in to use the toilet. She listened and kept her fingers crossed. No one came.

More minutes passed. Had she underestimated his curiosity? Surely he wouldn't stand out in front of the hotel forever...

She felt claustrophobic in the small cubicle. Sweat burst out on her forehead and neck and under her arms. She could feel it roll down her skin beneath her clothes. The faint odor of urine, mixed with a strong disinfectant, made her stomach lurch. It seemed she was always hiding in small, smelly bathrooms!

Hurry, Antonio!

Her legs felt weak; if only she could sit down. Shifting her position, she wiped at the sweat ineffectually. She stared down at the floor. It was made of small white tiles, many of them broken. There was a pattern of cracks radiating like a star out from the toilet. The lines between the tiles were perfectly straight rows, except for one corner where they went all crooked. Melanie wondered why. Had the workman lost patience with his task? Or got lazy? Gone mad?

Hurry, hurry, Antonio. Don't you want to know where the lady went?

Suddenly she could hear voices in the hallway, men and women. Someone opened the door to the bathroom, a woman who was still talking to someone in heavily accented Spanish while she held the door ajar. Melanie sucked in her breath. The woman finally pushed on the door to the stall and found it locked.

"*Ocupado.* It's occupied," Melanie said. "I'll be a while, sorry." Then she repeated it as best she could in her poor Spanish.

The woman grumbled something in French and left.

Another minute went by, agonizingly slow.

Why didn't he come? He couldn't wait out front all day...

And then she sensed he was there. Melanie thought her heart was going to burst. She heard the outside door carefully pushed open, and there was an awful moment of silence. She imagined him crouching, looking for that telltale pair of feet. Frightening things flew into her head: Antonio had read the same book, he would wait outside the bathroom, he wouldn't check the third floor...

The muscles in her thighs were quivering; the sweat popping out on her brow was salty and blinding. But she didn't dare breathe or move to wipe it away. If he didn't leave in a moment, she thought desperately, she was going to give the game up, throw herself at his mercy.

It seemed deathly quiet in the bathroom, in the hotel. It was earshatteringly still. Until she heard the harsh whisper of a man's voice. He whispered in Basque, something short and hard and questioning—Antonio. She recognized his voice. He must have been asking if the ladies' room was empty. Then she heard his footsteps as he entered, uncertain, hesitant footsteps.

Oh, God. She stood there, trembling, sweating, praying. *Don't look in the toilet, To-nee—don't look!*

Another cautious step. He was probably embarrassed to be invading the Damas, the ladies' room, a young man like that. Would he dare look in the stall?

Melanie wanted to close her eyes but she couldn't. She kept staring at the door of the stall, waiting for him to rattle it, waiting, heart pounding, legs shaking from tension. Would she be able to run or scream or hit him? She took quick, shallow, silent breaths—she was beginning to feel weak and dizzy from lack of oxygen. She couldn't take a deep breath; he'd hear her. *Please,* she prayed, *please, let him leave!*

Then, abruptly, the outer door opened and she heard quick, firm footsteps. A man's voice, speaking Basque. Dear Lord, she knew that voice! It was Teo! He said something to Antonio in an urgent tone, commanding, loud. Tony answered submissively; he sounded a little scared. She wished, more than anything, that she could understand them.

Then Teo was talking again, talking angrily. After that, she heard footsteps pattering on the tile, the creak of the outer door, and a few seconds later, the bang of the door slamming shut.

Then utter silence.

Melanie took a deep breath. Her knees felt as though they were giving out. She wondered how long she had to stay there to make sure they were gone. What if she walked out of the ladies' room to find them lying in wait for her? And then, if she waited too long, they'd have time to check the other floors and descend to the lobby again to catch her. She was torn with indecision.

Finally she couldn't bear to procrastinate another second. She straightened painfully and slowly, still standing on the rim, and risked a peek over the top of the stall. Empty. Gingerly, she stepped down, pushed open the first door, then carefully eased the other open just a crack. She could see no one, certainly not Antonio or Teo. She pushed it open farther. They must have mounted the stairs to the third floor.

Her heart beating wildly, Melanie raced down the hall, down the two flights of stairs and into the crowded lobby.

Antonio was not there. Neither was Teo.

Sweat still beaded her brow and upper lip. Automatically she wiped at it with one hand, her other still clutching the Iberia airlines bag to her chest.

She stuck her head outside. There was no sign of them there, either, nor was the other young Basque in sight. He still had to be out back, then. Thank God...

There was no Ted in sight and droves of tourists crammed the plaza. She hurried down the steps and merged with them. She thought fleetingly of the danger Cecily was in. Her plan had to work!

She headed purposefully away from the plaza, the late-afternoon sun pressing on her shoulders like a hot hand, the heavy crush of dancers and drinkers swallowing her up until her auburn head was only one of a thousand anonymous bobbing heads that filled the ancient, twisted streets of Pamplona.

Chapter Fifteen

Tuesday, July 13

Her timing was perfect. It was the hour that the *corrida*, the bullfight, started. Everything was so easy. All she had to do was let herself be swept along with the crowd that surged like a gigantic tidal wave toward the bullring. It was almost the end of the *feria* and people were gathering for the second-last bullfight of this enchanted week, a week that was suspended in time. A week quite apart from the concerns of the real world.

She took a moment to duck into a shop and buy a gray patterned silk scarf and white blouse. Lucky that Sevé hadn't taken her traveler's checks. The blouse covered her clothes and the scarf hid her unusually colored hair, in case Teo was still searching for her.

A man next to her offered her his wine bottle while they waited at the entrance to the bullring. She shook her head but smiled her gratitude.

She had no ticket, of course. The doormen were yelling *"Billetes!"* on either side of the entrance and snatching the slips of paper people held out. Melanie just stayed in the middle of the crowd and was carried into the stadium on its tide. Even if she'd had a ticket, she would never have been able to hand it to anyone.

The bands were playing and the stadium was nearly full. The hot afternoon sun beat down. Melanie looked around and tried to get her bearings. It would be best, she thought, to reconnoiter while the place was full. Then, if anyone challenged her, she had an excuse: she was just another *turista*—a tourist—who was lost.

It didn't seem to matter that Melanie was laden with an airline bag and her purse and camera bag. Most of the young people had bags of some description over their shoulders; they had to tote their belongings around, as they slept in the open soccer field and had nowhere to leave their things. She fitted right in.

Making her way around the tiers of seats, she looked for the entrance to the interior of the bullring. Teo had pointed out the corrals where they kept the bulls and the stables for the picadors' horses. There must be rooms for the *toreros*. And corridors leading to the doors in the outside walls. She had to find out.

She had to smile a lot and act carefree and hang around the very bottom row of seats in the hope of figuring out how the amphitheater was designed. But there were barricades everywhere—not a chance of getting into the ring itself and that's where she needed to be. The doorways all opened out of the ring itself. But she studied them, just in case.

She had to sit through the whole bullfight, wishing she could have enjoyed its stark, formalized beauty. Time crept by in odd, jerky snatches. Her watch seemed to crawl and then suddenly a whole hour would be gone.

Each bull was loosed into the ring as the matador stood waiting. They circled each other warily, the massive beast pawing the sandy earth. Melanie could almost see the hot breath puffing from the bull's nostrils. The red capes flashed, the bulls charged, once, twice, three times. *Olé!*

It was brave and beautiful and hypnotic.

The fallen beasts were dragged from the ring. Once, it was the matador who was carried out on a stretcher, and the cheers of the crowd caught Melanie totally by surprise. They

were cheering and saluting the bull. Of course. The beast
had fought valiantly and won.

The afternoon waned, becoming a blur of richly clad
matadors in black-and-gold jackets and of great-humped
beasts with murderous horns and massively muscled bodies
glistening under the sun.

Melanie was hot and tired and hungry. A vendor came by
yelling *"Naranja! Naranja fresca!"* Orange drink. She
bought a bottle and drank the excessively sweet stuff. She
got some peanuts from another vendor.

She didn't dare drink any of the wine offered her by the
laughing, inebriated people who packed the stands around
her. She was afraid she'd fall asleep or burst into tears or do
something ridiculous.

The last bull was dragged out of the ring through the
cavernous, double-doored opening. The *torero* bowed and
accepted the cheers and whistles, the flowers and hats and
even T-shirts thrown at his feet as accolades. Then the people began to leave, filing out slowly, body pressing against
body. Melanie went with them, dragging her heavy bags,
mingling, her scarf pulled over her hair. She was swept with
the others around the curve of the bullring. But instead of
following the crowd back into town, she fought her way out
of the traffic and walked around the bullring to the far side.

Yes, there was the truck that had come to collect the bull
carcasses. Several men were lifting a bull onto the truck,
unharnessing the donkeys. They talked and laughed in a
familiar routine. The big week was almost over for them.
She saw immediately that there was a wide door gaping
open, a door that led into the bullring.

"Perdóname," Melanie said, stepping up to one of the
men—an official-looking sort. *"Por favor, yo soy*...
photographer. I am photographer. *Time* magazine."
As she spoke, she busily pulled her camera out of the bag

and made a show of checking the light meter and the lens. Then she smiled and held up the empty camera. "Please, can I take pictures for the magazine?"

"*Periódico,*" translated one of the men.

"*Sí,*" she said, nodding, "*periódico. Fotografías.* Okay?"

They grinned hugely. She focused, then pretended to take several pictures of them and the dead bulls and the donkeys. They acted like small children at a birthday party.

"Can I go inside? More *fotografías*?"

The official-looking one nodded, pointing to himself. He strutted proudly.

Oh, lord, she thought, he wanted to go with her.

"*No, no, por favor.* You are working. I can go alone." She gave them each some of the last remaining pesetas in her purse, thinking of the half million in ransom money.

They finally let her go. She walked in through the broad tunnel that opened out into the ring. The white sand had already been smoothed over; it glistened dully in the twilight. She stood in the empty ring, and the wall encircling the arena was blood-red in the fading light. The rows and rows of seats climbed in a circle around her and she heard in her head the echo of cheering, the noise, the music. Right here the bull had thundered toward a tiny magenta scrap of material and the *torero* had spun away, his gold-encrusted suit flashing sparks in the gilded light.

And here Sevé would come to collect his money. Did he plan for her and Cecily to die in the ring like the huge, powerful, hump-necked bulls? Or was that to happen later? And Teo—would he be there to watch?

She looked toward the corral that housed the heifers that were loosed into the ring after the running of the bulls. They had not yet been brought back to the bullring. What time was that going to happen? It had better happen soon, she thought.

She pretended to take pictures in case anyone was watching. Click, click. Too bad she had no film. There were interesting angles where the dusk's long shadows reached across the circular tiers of seats. A hushed feeling of expectancy hovered in the ring. Or was that merely the reflection of her own tension?

The empty heifer corral lay right behind one of the barricades. Past it a long narrow corridor reached blackly toward the outside wall of the bullring. Looking around to see if anyone noticed, Melanie opened the corral gate and slipped through. There was another gate, then the corridor. It smelled damp, of cow dung and mold. But at the end she found a smooth, heavy metal door. She felt around in the dimness for the latch; it was open. Thank God—she'd been afraid that it might lock from the other side. But what lay beyond? She pushed the massive door; a crack of light showed, and she saw that it did indeed open to the outside. Good. She had their escape route. Still, she wondered when they would return the heifers to that empty corral.

Regardless, Melanie needed a place to hide until Sevé arrived with Cecily. She knew he'd come armed and with his five youthful bodyguards. And she suspected he'd come early, hoping to surprise her as she walked into the ring—alone—with the Iberia airlines bag full of money.

She passed an old man with a broom. Nodding and smiling and holding up her camera, she got by him. Somewhere there had to be a room, a closet, something. Yes, there, down another corridor. Several doors. She tried one after another. Locked. Finally one was open. She peeked inside, ready with an excuse if anyone was there.

It was empty. Obviously a dressing room, with capes and shoes flung on the benches, a dirty shirt and some rags. It smelled of blood, male sweat and grimy clothes. It was perfect. Locking the door, Melanie sank down on the bench and closed her eyes in relief.

Now, if only the cheerful fellows working outside the back door didn't notice her disappearance and start looking for her...

She must have dozed. She was jerked awake by a muffled explosion. A heavy thud, then another, then a whole volley, like gunshots. Sevé! She looked around frantically. The unfamiliar walls of the room stared blankly back at her and it took a moment to reorient herself.

She glanced at her watch: 9:37. Her heart thumped wildly. Sevé would come soon—or perhaps he was already there, waiting. Those explosions... she must be very careful. He had guns and men and strength. She had nothing but the Iberia airlines bag and her wits.

She crept out of the changing room. It was fully dark now in the corridor. The bullring seemed deserted but she stayed in the shadows, stopping every few feet to listen. There was only silent velvety darkness and the palest glimmer of sand in the ring.

Suddenly the sky lit up in an explosion of color. Boom! Boom!

Fireworks! Of course! That was what she'd heard—part of the *feria* celebrations. The sky split with another resounding crack, and Melanie could see the red and white and gold sparks blossom above her.

Beautiful. The flower spread, popping, into appendages that sagged downward, exploding into more blossoms at their extremities. She shuddered at the violent beauty of it and the frightening similarity of its sound to gunfire. Sevé...

Hugging the wall, Melanie hid behind a barricade in the inky shadows. She could see all the entrances and the tiers rising around her, row upon row. Empty, hushed. Or were they hiding Sevé and Teo and the five boys? The Cax Carot. A dance, she had been told. A dance of violence and terror and madness. A shadow dance.

A sound intruded upon her thoughts. A stamping, a shuffling, the low whoof of an animal's breath. Her eyes shifted instantly, searching for the source of the noise. There, in the corral. It was filled now with dark forms. Her eyes had grown accustomed to the darkness and she could make out the milling shapes. Then a deep lowing sound confirmed it.

The heifers were there in their pen, awaiting the next morning when the men in white and red would stream into the ring, followed by the bulls. It would be the last morning, the last running of the bulls, the last day of the Fiesta de San Fermín.

She could hear cheers and screams and music coming from the city outside the circular walls that contained her. The penultimate eve of mad celebration.

Was Sevé already in the bullring somewhere, waiting for her?

The heifers stamped nervously in their pen and snorted as another brilliant blossom exploded in the black sky. She'd seen these cows bowl over a lot of strong men in the bullring that first morning. But then there had been noise and chaotic excitement and men running everywhere. Would the heifers be as edgy at this time of night? Melanie could have filled a book with what she didn't know about cows.

She thought fleetingly about the door at the end of the tunnel. The latch. She'd checked it. What she hadn't checked, though, was whether there was a lock on the other side. She'd assumed—

A noise, something, a movement, snatched her attention. It was coming from across the arena. Yes! There was a shadow, moving along the wall. And another. Her heart lurched in apprehension.

She stood perfectly still, watching and listening.

Another explosion of fireworks lit the night sky, briefly illuminating the arena. Then there was darkness again.

A minute passed. Then another. Finally she heard a voice.

"Where are you, *señorita*? Are you here yet?" Sevé. His tone was taunting, sarcastic, too loud in the echoing, empty stands. "Where is my money?"

Melanie crouched by the cattle pen, afraid he would shoot when she spoke up. She tried to make herself as small a target as possible. "Where is my sister?"

"I'm here!" Cecily cried, sounding terrified.

Melanie swallowed hard. This was the time, her only chance. It had to work. "I'm here! Over here! I have the money."

She could see the dark forms moving again, rounding the curved side of the arena. Closer, closer. They were there, in front of her, dim shadows against the pale sand of the ring. Would they shoot? But if they did the noise would attract attention and the police would come. Or would the shots merely sound like fireworks? Her heart thudded like a drum in her chest.

Sevé was there and three other boys. She thought Carlos was one. Cecily. And Teo. He stood there, tall and slim, his features blots of darkness, his expression impenetrable, slightly diabolical in the night.

Slowly Melanie held out the airline bag toward Sevé. He must come to her. "Bring my sister here."

Cecily was pushed forward, stumbling to her side. "Oh, Mel! Boy, was I—"

"Shh!" Melanie hissed. Quickly now, only a few moments. If they were going to shoot—

Now, now was the time... She felt for the latch on the gate, praying her movements went unnoticed in the dark. "I'm going to throw it, Sevé, out into the ring, then we are going."

"*Sí, señorita,*" came Sevé's rough voice. "You have your sister. The money, *por favor.*"

Then, all at once, Melanie threw the bag as far as she could, swung open the corral gate, grabbed Cecily's hand and ran into the midst of the heifers. She shouted, slapped the nearest bony, dusty rump, kicked at them, swung her heavy purse at their heads. There were startled snorts and moos and the clatter of hooves and horns on wooden walls. She dodged, dragging Cecily with her. Then the heifers began to stream out into the ring, snuffling and pawing and shoving at one another.

A man cried out in surprise, then fear. The shadowed forms moved faster, swinging their horns, panicking in the dark, unfamiliar place, unable to recognize their enemy.

Melanie was pulling Cecily into the back of the corral, feeling along the wooden walls for the other gate. Her breath came in tearing gasps. "What?" Cecily kept asking. "Where are we going? What's going on?" Melanie could hear the heifers stampeding among the men, careering around the ring in a nightmarish dance. There were thuds, curses, a gunshot, the terrified snorting of the creatures as they raced, bumping and crashing into the men.

She could hear Sevé shouting furiously in Basque. By now he must have seen the contents of the airline bag.

The gate. Fumbling, hurting her fingers, she unlatched it and pulled Cecily through, shoving the gate shut behind them. "This way!" she panted. "Come on!"

She tried to hurry through the pitch-black tunnel, the corridor to the outside, to freedom and safety. One hand felt against the dank wall, the other held on to Cecily for dear life. Cobwebs stuck to her face; she felt as if nameless, slimy things were crawling over her body. As if bullets would flame out of the blackness behind to mow them down.

Had anyone seen where they went? Or were Sevé and his cohorts too busy with the heifers?

Cecily was behind her, panting, too, and sobbing in fear.

"There's a door," Melanie gasped. "Right up here."

The corridor seemed endless. She stumbled on the uneven dirt floor, utterly blind in the unrelieved darkness. Cecily tripped once and cried out, falling to her knees. Melanie dragged her up, feeling for the door. It was there, nearby—she knew it was! It had been there a few hours before!

Behind her, the voices were cut off but she could hear muted gunshots from the bullring. Were they shooting at one another or at the heifers—poor, terrifed beasts? And what would happen when Sevé realized that his men were chasing shadows? She tried to imagine what he would do then, but her head was pounding with fright.

At last her outstretched hand bumped into the smooth cold metal of the door. She felt feverishly around for the latch. Which side had it been on? Yes, there it was. She tugged on it; it didn't give. She rattled it, pulled harder.

It was locked from the outside.

There was no time to think or regret or even cry out in frustration.

"What is it?" Cecily panted.

But Melanie didn't answer. She was frozen, paralyzed with horror.

Another shot echoed down the long corridor. Had it come from the arena or was someone shooting blindly into the tunnel's blackness? Maybe Sevé wouldn't find her and Cecily. Or maybe he would flee before people outside realized that there were shots coming from within the bullring.

"Oh, God," Cecily moaned, her sweat-damp body pressed to Melanie's.

Melanie pulled on the door, again and again. It merely rattled implacably. A sob welled in her breast.

A moment later they both heard it. A footstep. Another footstep. Someone was in the tunnel!

The hollow steps echoed in the musty corridor. Melanie's hands groped around her as if a door would appear by some miracle. Nothing . . .

There was no escape! Only the locked door, the solid walls, the hard-packed dirt floor...

The footfalls grew louder, louder. It was as if all the air had been sucked out of the narrow, claustrophobic passageway. Melanie tried to draw in a breath but couldn't. Her heartbeat pounded in her ears.

Then he was there, a presence in the inky blackness. Melanie heard her sister's sharp intake of breath and clutched Cecily's arm, as they tried to shrink into the cold wall.

Who was it? What would he do? She waited, tense, her muscles rigid and tight, as if that would protect her from the bullets she expected would smash into her at any second.

"Do not do anything foolish," came a deep voice and Melanie desperately searched her mind for knowledge of its owner.

She knew that voice! They were lost, then, trapped, condemned to death in a dark hole while crowds celebrated exuberantly a few feet away.

It was Esteban Sanlucar.

Chapter Sixteen

"So, after you lost Teo and Antonio in the hotel, you returned the money to the bank." Esteban chuckled. "What a trick."

The setting sun thrust long shadows onto the patio at Esteban's house. Melanie sat with her hands in her lap, feeling drained and relieved and a bit light-headed from the abrupt release of tension. "I was sure Sevé was planning to kill us, anyway. After all, we knew who he was and could identify him. I was determined that he wouldn't benefit from his crimes."

"Now tell me once more how you planned to get away from those two who followed you. And with Teo there, also."

Again she described hiding in the hotel's bathroom. Esteban laughed, throwing back his handsome dark head.

Melanie smiled a little self-consciously and sipped her brandy.

"I certainly wish I'd known that you were on my side," she finally said. "It would have made things a lot more comfortable for me."

"Ah, but I could not risk it. We could not," Esteban replied. "My nephew feared a slip. Knowledge on your part might have made you act suspiciously and Sevé might have caught on. So you had to hate and fear us."

She turned to study Teo, who sat silently in one of the patio chairs, hands clasped together in his habitual manner. His dark eyes returned her gaze without emotion. Quickly she snatched her glance away.

"Most clever of all was to walk away from Sevé, right in front of the bank, carrying the money."

"I had no choice," Melanie said quietly.

"And the *novillas*, the heifers," Esteban went on. "A stroke, a coup of great perfection."

"Yes," Teo put in dryly, "it almost ruined my own little surprise."

"The *policía*," Esteban said, nodding. "They were nearly as surprised as Sevé to enter into the ring and find a true *corrida* happening."

"Nobody was as surprised as I was," Melanie said. "I mean, to think I was going to be killed in a second and then . . . to find you had come to *save* us and the Guardia Civil had the Cax Carot surrounded in the ring."

"I apologize again for putting you through such an ordeal," Teo said quietly, "but I was afraid to call the police until the last moment. And then I was almost unable to reach a telephone to call Esteban. I think perhaps Sevé did not quite trust me."

"And in the hotel when Antonio was looking for me?" Melanie asked. "Did you know I was there?"

"I knew you were somewhere in the hotel. I assumed you planned to evade us somehow, so I told Antonio that I'd seen you running out of the kitchen door. I called him all sorts of rude names of stupidity." Teo shook his head ruefully. "I had no idea we were so close to you. I only wanted him out of the hotel."

"You'll never know what I was going through in there," she breathed.

"I am sorry. There was nothing else I could do. Sevé watched me like a hawk. He is not such a bad judge of men. He knew he could not trust me."

"I can't imagine why not. You certainly had *me* convinced," Melanie said.

"Well, he knew I disapproved of violence. We had already argued. You see, I had hoped to get Cecily away from them without involving the police."

"And without me complicating things," she put in.

A thin smile curved Teo's mouth. "Yes. But you were too much for me." The smile left his lips. "Those boys—Carlos and the rest—they are good boys. I've known them all since they were children. It was Sevé's influence. He was their idol. The man wanted his own little kingdom and he needed followers, slaves, if you will. I tried very hard to see that their kidnap plan did not succeed."

"So that was why you were at Torremolinos," Melanie mused.

"I was trying to prevent them from going through with the plan, hoping you would both fly home to Ohio as soon as possible. But unfortunately..." And he shrugged his shoulders.

"And then I found you in your office and accused you of...all those things. I'm sorry, Teo, terribly sorry."

"There is no need for apologies. You have suffered. I think perhaps I should have gone to the police immediately, as soon as you told me Cecily was gone. I knew what was going to happen then."

"But Sevé might have killed her."

Teo nodded gravely. "That was my fear."

"And the night we would have escaped—"

"Except for my most unpropitious appearance," he said wryly.

"How is our little Cecily?" interrupted Esteban.

"Asleep, I hope," Melanie replied. "Your doctor gave her some pills."

"The poor child," Esteban said, shaking his head.

"She's not too young to realize her own responsibility in all this," said Melanie.

"But all young ones make mistakes. Did you not?" Esteban went on and Melanie thought of her too-quick, futile marriage. "These boys were misguided. Truly, they are victims, too. Victims of Sevé."

"What will happen to them?" asked Melanie.

"They will go to trial," said Teo. "Our system can be very severe. I will do my best with the authorities."

"I hope they've learned something," she said quietly. "And Cecily, too."

"You are worried about your sister." Teo's eyes reached across the patio to hers. His features were sun-dark and handsome in the gilded Spanish evening.

She held his gaze. "Yes. She's going to need help to forget this. She feels so guilty and ashamed."

"And what will you do now?" he asked softly.

"Excuse me," Esteban broke in, "but I must discuss supper with Lucia." He rose and smiled benignly down at them, holding out a restraining hand. "You two stay here, relax and talk. It is over now."

To Melanie, his absence seemed a thing of heavy significance because it left her alone with Teo for the first time that evening. For the first time since their picnic on the magical, misted Roncesvalles Pass. She shifted nervously in her chair and played with her brandy snifter, turning it around and around in her hands, watching the sun's last rays glow on the amber liquid.

"Well?" Teo insisted gently.

"Well, what?"

"What are your plans?"

"Oh. As soon as the police are through questioning Cecily, I'll take her home. My parents are wrecks—you can imagine."

"But of course. So you go back to Cleveland, Ohio."

"For a while, anyway. Then I'll probably go somewhere on an assignment."

"Where?"

"Oh, who knows? I was thinking about Bangladesh to see how they're recovering from the flooding last year. Or China. I'd like to see the new China." She looked off into the distance, to the green mountains of the Basques. "Maybe some magazine will send me somewhere."

"So you keep traveling, Melanie. Running from whatever it is that bedevils you."

She looked up, startled, into his somber gaze. "I hadn't exactly thought I was running. I do my job."

"Ah, yes, but nevertheless you are running away."

"From what?" she asked coolly.

"From love, from commitment."

She stirred uneasily in her seat once again. "I thought you were a history professor, not a psychologist."

"What is history but the study of mankind's behavior?" he asked, smiling.

"I hardly think my behavior is worthy of anyone's study."

The sky was turning lavender and purple behind the mountains. Crickets chirped beyond the patio, and the first star hung low in the east. Mist began curling up from the hollows.

"There is much good in my people and my country," Teo said. "I would like you to see that side of us. I wish you would allow me to show it to you."

Melanie looked down at her hands. What was he asking her? Was he merely being the professor? The proud Basque? The perfect host? "I . . . I really have to go home. It's very nice of you but . . ."

"I see." He smiled and reached out to cover her hands, still held in her lap, with his own lean brown fingers. "You must keep running, then?"

"I'm only going home, Teo." Her skin burned under his touch. She could not meet his gaze, afraid that she'd say— or do—something stupid, something irrevocable. To stay with Teo, to let her heart fly free, to strike off its shackles. To learn about him and his beloved Basque country, to know him...

He withdrew his hand and left her feeling strangely forsaken. "Home? Melanie, somehow I cannot see you in your Ohio. Can you be happy there?"

"As happy as I can be anywhere," she replied, knowing it was a lie.

THE DRIVE BACK TO MADRID was a dismal one. Cecily was uncharacteristically listless and quiet, thinking, no doubt, of her guilt and her lost Carlos, of her kidnapping, of her loss of innocence. They wound down out of the green hills into the sere brown ones, then to the dry plateau of Madrid. The city teemed with traffic, but unlike Pamplona's masses, Madrid's were sober, intent Castilians.

Melanie and her sister went to the elegant private hotel that Melanie had stayed in before. Cecily had not even suggested that she return to her apartment, and Melanie had no intention of letting the girl out of her sight. If Cecily returned to school in Madrid, her things would be there. If not, someone could box them and send it all back to Ohio.

Esteban had phoned and arranged everything for them: the hotel room, the airplane tickets. He'd sent Lucia into Pamplona to pick up some clothes for Cecily, as her suitcase had not been located. The woman had returned with stockings and a slip and a print dress that somehow did not suit Cecily. She'd put it on, however, without a word and her apathy had Melanie worried.

Esteban had done everything he could to make things easy for them. He'd kissed them both goodbye and invited them back to stay with him. But Teo had not been there the morning of their departure. "He is gone back to his classes," Esteban had said offhandedly.

Was Teo in Madrid then? Was he in his featureless office, working, reading, wearing his horn-rimmed glasses? Or had that merely been a polite lie?

Neither Melanie nor Cecily had the heart to go out to dinner. They ate quietly in the hotel's small dining room. *Paella*, the saffron-flavored rice, chicken and seafood concoction, and fresh bread. No wine. Neither of them could bear the thought of wine.

Melanie phoned their parents late that night, knowing it was early evening in Ohio. "Yes, we're in Madrid. We'll be home tomorrow, Dad. You already have the flight number. We're fine, really."

"I'm flying to New York to meet you," her father said.

"Oh, for goodness' sake, you don't have to do that."

"I'm going to, anyway," replied Oscar adamantly. "Kennedy, tomorrow."

"Dad—"

"See you, Mel. Let me talk to your sister."

Reluctantly, Cecily took the phone from Melanie's hand. "Dad?" she ventured brokenly.

Melanie found it painful to hear her sister's side of the conversation, painful to see Cecily's misery and guilt.

"Yes, I'm fine," Cecily said. "Dad, I'm so sorry. I never thought this would happen. You must be furious. You must hate me." She broke into tears at something Oscar said. "Daddy," she wept, as she had when she was a child. Then wordlessly she handed the phone to Melanie and the tears were still making shiny paths down her face.

"Mel, try to calm her down. I'm not mad, just relieved. Tell her. I tried to."

"I will, Dad. See you tomorrow."

She hung up and turned to see Cecily huddled on the bed, crying hysterically. "Oh, look what I've done!" she wailed. "I can't stand it. Everyone will hate me and talk about me behind my back. I'm horrible, hateful!"

Melanie went to sit by her sister, awkwardly putting a hand on her shoulder. "No one will ever think that, Cecily. You had a big adventure. Thank heavens it turned out all right."

"But . . . but Carlos and the boys, in so much trouble!" She lifted her tear-streaked face. "I told the police they were good to us, I tried to help them, Mel—truly I did. Will it help, do you think?"

"I'm sure it will," Melanie soothed. "I said the same thing."

"And Esteban—oh, he must think I'm a terrible, ridiculous person. And Teo and you—"

"Everyone was worried about you, that's all. It was not your fault."

"You may say so, but I'll never forgive myself." Cecily sniffed miserably.

In the morning Cecily looked a bit puffy around the eyes but she obviously felt better. She put on the print dress and made a face at her reflection in the mirror. The stockings and slip went into the wastebasket.

They drove to the airport in the dense Madrid traffic and returned the gray Seat. Melanie felt a curious tightness in her throat and behind her eyes. They were leaving Spain, leaving the light-hearted Mediterranean beaches of Andalusia, the sober, cosmopolitan streets of Madrid, the isolated green hills of the Basques.

She was leaving Esteban and his serene retreat. Leaving the frenzied streets of Pamplona during the *feria*.

And Teo. His face would appear in her mind's eye at odd times, jolting her, sending her heart racing. His features would flash before her as if on a movie screen; sometimes he would be smiling, sometimes angry. Or serious, his hands folded under his chin, his dark eyes scrutinizing her. Or she would see the unruly, curling dark hair with its sprinkle of gray. His hands lean and tanned and capable, his strong neck as he turned his head, perhaps. Or the glint of the sun, golden on his cheek and jawline.

At times she would turn, hearing his voice in her ear, hearing him call her name, but he was never there. A man in a crowd would suddenly look familiar, but then she would glance at him a second time and see that he was a stranger, with only the remotest resemblance to Teo.

The Madrid airport was very crowded; this was a weekend during the busiest time of the year, the tourist season. There were more Americans than Spaniards, Melanie thought. She was sure some of the faces she saw looked familiar; they had been on the streets of Pamplona or in the bullring during a *corrida*.

Her luggage was checked through. Cecily had none, only her passport. The police in Pamplona had promised to send her luggage when and if they found it.

The sisters wandered over to the airport departure lounge, which was noisy but cool. They were settling down to wait for their flight, when Cecily asked, "Should I buy Dad a bottle of duty-free Scotch?"

"With what?" Melanie retorted, smiling.

"Oh, that's right. I don't have a cent. I could borrow some from you."

"Sure, I guess it's the least we can do. And some perfume for Mother. Something exotic. I'm just going to sit here."

"Okay, I'll be right back."

Good, Cecily was thinking of someone besides herself. It was a start, anyway.

Melanie tried to relax in the hard molded-plastic seat. The air conditioning was so cool that it was almost uncomfortable. Hard to believe it was about a hundred degrees outside. She closed her eyes, leaning back, one hand on her camera bag. Teo's face appeared in the dancing blackness, smiling at her. He was saying her name, "Melanie," in that way he had, British but with a touch of elegant, rolling Spanish, too. "Melanie." She heard it in her head, echoing, but if she opened her eyes he wouldn't be there.

"Melanie." So clear, so familiar.

A hand touched her arm, her eyes blinked open. "Cec..." she started to say, but the word faded on her lips. She gasped and felt her heart give a wild surge.

"Melanie?" he said softly again.

"Teo?" she breathed.

"I thought you were asleep," he said, smiling. "You wouldn't open your eyes."

"Teo?" Slowly she stood, facing him, the roar of the airport receding. She put out a hand to touch him, to see if he was real. He caught her hand, imprisoning it in both of his, turning it over and kissing it.

"Melanie, I couldn't let you go without seeing you once more. I was a coward at Esteban's. I couldn't bear—"

"Teo?"

"Is that all you can say?" His eyes met hers questioningly.

"Yes," she whispered.

"Well, then. I will say it for you. Come back with me. Stay here. I love you; you must know that."

"I...I can't...Cecily. My luggage..." She was stunned, unable to think; he still held her hand.

"Cecily can go home by herself. And as for your clothes—unimportant. You have your camera, don't you?"

"Yes," she murmured.

"Well?"

"But...but..." She was flooded with confusion and delight and an odd kind of release.

"The only reason for you not to come is if you do not love me, Melanie," he said gravely.

She stood there, buffeted by artificial coldness, by children crying and people speaking a dozen different languages, by the roar of a jet taking off outside, and she decided. Her face split into a smile, her heart burst open, her soul flew into her eyes. "Yes!" she said firmly, "I'll come."

"Hey, Teo, what are you doing here?" Cecily cried, returning with her plastic bag of presents.

"I'm going to marry your sister," he replied.

Cecily stared at Teo, then turned to Melanie, and finally stared at both of them, open-mouthed. "Is this for real?" she asked, astounded.

"You bet it is," Melanie said with a soft laugh.

"What'll I tell Mother and Dad?" Cecily cried.

"Tell them...tell them...I'll send them a picture!"

What the press says about Harlequin romance fiction…

"When it comes to romantic novels…
Harlequin is the indisputable king."
— *New York Times*

"…always with an upbeat, happy ending."
— *San Francisco Chronicle*

"Women have come to trust these
stories about contemporary people,
set in exciting foreign places."
— *Best Sellers*, New York

"The most popular reading matter of
American women today."
— *Detroit News*

"…a work of art."
— *Globe & Mail*, Toronto

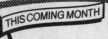

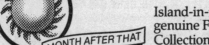

WHAT READERS SAY ABOUT
HARLEQUIN INTRIGUE . . .

Fantastic! I am looking forward to reading other Intrigue books.

*P.W.O., Anderson, SC

This is the first Harlequin Intrigue I have read . . . I'm hooked.

*C.M., Toledo, OH

I really like the suspense . . . the twists and turns of the plot.

*L.E.L., Minneapolis, MN

I'm really enjoying your Harlequin Intrigue line . . . mystery and suspense mixed with a good love story.

*B.M., Denton, TX